Want You Moore

Moore Family Series

Frankie Page

Frankie Page Books

Copyright © 2022 by Frankie Page

All rights reserved.

No portion of this book may be reproduced in any form without written permission from the publisher or author, except as permitted by U.S. copyright law.

The characters and events portrayed in this book are fictitious. Any similarity to real persons, living or dead, is coincidental and not intended by the author.

Editing by Pagan Proofreading

This book was designed and created with the use of a licensed stock images and fonts from:

https://fonts.adobe.com/

https://www.stock.adobe.com

Asset ID: 248945741

Asset ID: 564388335

For the ones we love to hate and hate to love, but we wouldn't have any other way...

Contents

1. Letty   1
2. Jake   12
3. Letty   19
4. Jake   26
5. Letty   32
6. Jake   41
7. Letty   49
8. Jake   58
9. Letty   68
10. Jake   78
11. Letty   84
12. Jake   91
13. Jake   100
14. Letty   109
15. Letty   115
16. Letty   121

17.	Jake	127
18.	Letty	133
19.	Jake	141
20.	Letty	148
21.	Jake	154
22.	Letty	162
23.	Letty	170
24.	Jake	179
25.	Letty	184
26.	Letty	189
27.	Jake	197
28.	Letty	207
29.	Letty	217
30.	Jake	230
31.	Jake	236
32.	Letty	242
33.	Letty	249
34.	Jake	254
35.	Letty	258
36.	Jake	270
Epilogue		276
Epilogue		283
Moore By Frankie Page		290

1

Letty

"Fuck," I grumble out loud to myself while wiping the sweat from my brow. *I really should get myself an AC unit.* Barely halfway into June and it's already hot as hell. Recently, we've been skipping spring and diving headfirst into summer. It's Minnesota. We shouldn't be forced to suffer ninety-degree heat, with oppressing humidity, until at least the end of July. Even then, it should only last a week or two.

Most sane people wish for the summer months and dread the winter. Not me. I'm always busting my ass behind the bar and don't have time for things like the beach or sunbathing. Plus, poor air flow and an ancient duct system, combined with the heat from the coolers and kitchen equipment, make it constantly warm downstairs. Then, on top of it all, running around like a chicken with my head cut off increases my internal body temp tenfold. At least during the winter months, it's tolerable. Summer can feel like a sauna. On the bright side, with all the exercise and sweating, I don't need a gym membership. Maybe when this place is officially mine and I have the extra income, I will add some functional windows and upgrade the HVAC.

My ass plops down on the unforgiving, dusty wooden floor. I reach inside my cooler, fish around the melted ice, and grab a bottle. Using the opener I affixed to the lid, I pop it open and watch the fizz. The ice-cold beer cools me from the inside out as I chug it down. *I really shouldn't drink this shit.* I know first-hand how this poison can ruin someone's life. Yet I push my luck. Daily. Desperate to prove that I am better—stronger—than *him.*

Looking around this place, you wouldn't know that just two months ago it was nothing but a clusterfuck, filled with boxes Ted never wanted to deal with. The old coot doesn't know how to throw shit away. Seriously, I found boxes and boxes of newspaper clippings from decades ago. And not the interesting ones you'd think someone would keep, like major events. No, these were local papers filled with random wedding and birth announcements, obituaries, and town events.

I'm sure the coupons that expired years ago were the real keepsakes.

Thankfully, Ted told me I could toss it all. I guess this collection of junk had more to do with laziness than true sentiment. Despite it being as hot as Hades up here, I smile. Because after almost thirteen years of blood, sweat, tears, and booze. Harper's is mine.

Okay, not technically.

But that is nothing but paperwork and formalities. We did the math. It will only take five years before this place is completely in my possession. Four, if I can sustain myself with a diet of ramen and tap water. Because Ted loves me like the granddaughter he never had, he made me the deal of the century: I pay off the rest of his mortgage, and he'll call it even. Sure, he could have gone through the process of selling it and making a profit that could help cushion his retirement. But with his debt paid off and no family, he told me that if he could eat and drink on the house, *that* was all he needed.

My pride really wanted to get a loan and do this the proper way, but my dad fucked all that up. And with no collateral, well, the assholes at the bank practically laughed at my application. So, instead, Ted and I worked with the county clerk's office to draw up some sort of "contract for deed." You know, for legal purposes. As it stands now, he is still officially the loan holder. But once everything is finished, it'll be my name on that dotted line.

I can't wait.

Since I will outright own the bar, there should be a good amount of extra income, after our operating costs. Even though Ted took out an equity loan about a decade ago (one of the things I'm paying off), the building could use some serious updating. That's the plan: own the bar, make it mine, spend the rest of my days keeping the locals' bellies and cups full. While it doesn't sound like much, to a girl who literally has nothing, the small victory means everything. Harper's will be mine, and no one short of God will take it from me.

A light knock forces me to peel my ass from the floor. My hands wet with condensation, I rub them on the back of my denim shorts before opening the door. I am pleasantly surprised at the sight of my petite best friend in front of me. Her golden-blonde hair is an organized mess piled on top of her head. Looking very mommy chic, she's strapped down with two of the most adorable babies I've ever seen. A smile spreads across my face. "What the hell is that?"

Tilly laughs, glancing down at herself. "A baby carrier."

I study the weird scarf contraption, which snakes around her body and holds Alexander and Gavin to each side. "Is that thing really going to keep them up there?" I'd be terrified that it would come untied and drop the babies.

"Yes." She sighs. "It's the biggest lifesaver. When Scar gave it to me, I had the same expression as you. But after five YouTube tutorials, Jax and I finally figured it out. Now I live in this thing."

Shaking my head, I open the door farther, guiding her in. "Please tell me you have photos of Jax wearing that torture device."

Tilly gives me a knowing smirk before glancing around at the now slightly-less-cluttered space. "It's really coming along."

I nod in agreement. "It is."

The upper level is fitted as a large studio apartment. The only closed-off areas are the bathroom and a small closet that is perfect for me. It's a lot like her brother Robbie's place above his garage. But larger. My favorite part is the set of giant floor-to-ceiling windows that overlooks Main Street.

"Do you want something to drink?" I ask. With the high temps and two mini space heaters fastened to her, she must be thirsty.

"Please." She lets out a sigh of gratitude. "I can't get over how much you've gotten done. The last time I was here, you could barely step foot inside—*Oh,* is that original hardwood?"

I shake my head, laughing as I get Tilly a bottle of water from the cooler and resume drinking my beer. Ever since she and Jax bought the new house and have been remodeling, they seem to speak this new language and notice the oddest things.

"I think so." I doubt Ted ever made any changes to the interior. "I would have been done months ago. But I hardly have the time. Also, it is so much easier taking loads of crap out of here when you don't have to walk through two feet of snow and slush."

"I'm sorry." Tilly frowns. "I wish I could have helped more."

I drape my arm over her shoulder, careful to not disturb the babies. "Don't beat yourself up. It isn't exactly like you've been lazy or out partying these past months. Until the other week, you had these two taking up residency in your body. I'm still not sure how it was scientifically possible that those things fit in there and you didn't topple over. Not to mention, you moved and have been doing your own remodeling. I'm proud of what I've accomplished." *On my own.*

And that's the truth.

Apart from my best friend, I am alone. Not physically. All day I'm surrounded by people at the bar. What little free time I have is spent sleeping or hanging out with Tilly. I learned the hard way that the only person you can rely on is yourself. No one can be trusted, and eventually, everyone will let you down. Tilly is the only exception to this rule. She's my soul mate, my other half. And that's all I need.

In all honesty, while I appreciate her offer to help me, this is the way things need to be. I love her. But as much as she's my person, I'm not hers. She has her brothers, Jax, and now these two little guys. Although I know she'd drop everything in a heartbeat to help me if I ever needed it, the knowledge of that fact is enough for me. I don't need concrete proof.

"Well, how about this weekend? Instead of doing the cookout at my house, Jax can be on baby duty for the day, and I can come here and help?"

"I don't want to mess with our routine." Despite having to deal with *him*, I really like our Sunday get-togethers. It reminds me of when we were younger, and I got to experience what it was like to have a proper family. Mrs. Moore would cook up a feast, and Mr. Moore would always have some sort of project or activity planned.

Shit... I take a deep breath, swallowing down the tears. They may not have been my parents, but they raised me as one of their own. They never made me feel as though I were an outsider—like the other assholes in this town. I was always welcome. No matter what, they included me in all their plans. Without the Moores, I worry how I would have turned out.

My mother died when I was eight, and though I have memories of her I cherish, she was gone before she could teach me anything about being a woman. My father, well, let's just say he had his own demons, and I was the least of them. I took care of him more than he ever cared for me. If it wasn't for me babysitting (until I could get a job busing tables at Harper's when I was sixteen), I doubt we would have been able to keep the lights on in our double-wide. When Mr. and Mrs. Moore died in that car crash, I was shattered. You'd think I'd be immune to loss by this point. Yet almost a year has passed, and I can't think about them without tearing up.

"Nah, it's fine. To be honest, it works out. While I love these two, I wouldn't mind a slight break and having some genuine grown-up time. It seems like it's been forever since I've been able to hang out with my bestie without feeling weighed down." Tilly flashes me a bright smile.

"You sure? The others won't be mad?" I think about the rest of the ever-growing Moore family. At the rate they're reproducing, they are bound to out-populate everyone in this town. The thought makes me snicker. Tilly raises her brow in question. I wave her off. "Sorry, I was just thinking about how your family is growing like weeds."

Tilly blushes. "*Oh my god*, did I tell you that Jax is already asking when we can get started on the next set?"

"You're joking, right?"

"No. He's dead serious. When I told him I'm terrified that the next time we may have triplets, he had the audacity to ask me if it would really be that bad." Tilly shakes her head. "Fortunately, the doctor already said I should give my body a year off to heal, so I bought myself some time."

"You don't want more?" I ask, surprised, given I know she's always dreamed of having a football team. When we were young and played MASH, she would pout when she only got three kids with Jax and not the ridiculous double digits we marked down in jest.

"No—I mean yes. Ugh," Tilly says in frustration. "I've always wanted a big family; you know that. It's just... having these two... It's more than I imagined. Even with Jax being *all hands on deck*, I'm always elbow-deep in poop or with someone sucking on my boob. And not in the fun, sexy way. In the *I'm not sure my breasts will ever recover* way. Who the hell convinced me that breastfeeding was a good idea?"

"I think it was Scar. I believe she mentioned how quickly you'd lose the baby weight. Which seems to be working, by the way. I don't know how it's possible. But I'm pretty sure you might be skinnier than before you were pregnant. On behalf of all women everywhere, let me say: *we hate you.*"

Tilly laughs, pushing my arm. "Yes, I remember her compelling arguments now. Seriously, how does she know so much about babies?"

"Maybe she used to work as one of those baby gurus when she lived out in California." I shrug.

"Perhaps. I love her to death and all. She's made book club so much more *interesting*. But seriously, she's so tight-lipped about her past." Tilly leans forward to whisper, "Do you think she's involved in the mob or something? Oh! What about witness protection?"

"Doubtful." I squash that overactive imagination my best friend is known to have (too much book reading, if you ask me). "To each their own. As long as she's not some axe-wielding murderer, it doesn't really matter to me."

"True. But aren't you curious?"

"No, not really. Unlike you, I never went through a Nancy Drew phase."

Tilly groans. "Are you ever going to let that go?"

"No." I cross my arms. "You robbed me of my innocence, Matilda Moore—*Harris?* Whatever it is now," I say in a teasing tone. "Because of you, I learned at way too young of an age why snooping in a boy's room was hazardous to our health."

Tilly shivers at the memory. The oldest Moore sibling—Robbie—was thirteen at the time. He got moody and started spending what Tilly thought was a suspicious amount of time behind closed doors. One day, while he was at football practice, she had the brilliant idea of sneaking into his room to uncover what he was hiding. I'm not sure what she was expecting to find. But (lucky us!) practice was rained out, and he came home early. Like the geniuses we were, we hid in the closet. And let's just say, at an age where I was much too innocent to comprehend what he was doing, I saw way *more* of *Robert Moore* than I ever wanted to.

"As traumatizing as that was, we still solved the mystery," Tilly says with her chest puffed.

I'm about to argue when Alexander or maybe Gavin (I honestly can't tell them apart yet) starts crying. Tilly sighs and goes to pull the inconsolable baby from the sling when the other twin wails. She tenses up. Her face betrays her and shows how much these two *bundles of joy* are wearing her down.

"Here, let me take him." I extend my arms and cradle the tiny human, attempting to settle him. Tilly seems equally unsuccessful. His little eyes are squeezed shut as he yells at the top of his lungs. Yeah, I'm good with never having one of these things. They might be adorable as all fuck, but I already deal with assholes who act like big-old babies all day long. I don't need to come home and have more to entertain. No, these two little guys and whatever Cassie spits out will be enough to curb whatever natural mothering instinct I have (if it even exists). I can get the snuggles, spoil them, then hand them over when it's all said and done.

"I should get going. A storm is rolling in. The change in pressure is making their ears hurt."

Lightly rocking the baby, I glance out the window. *Shit.* Ominous black clouds are approaching, sending a cool (not refreshing) shiver down my spine. Here, the sun is still high in the mid-day sky. To the southwest, though, it looks like nightfall.

"Sh—*dang*!" As best I can, I'm trying to mind my tongue while their little ears are around. Unfortunately, Aunt Letty swears like a goddamn sailor. The last thing I need to do is corrupt my godsons. "I hadn't even looked at the radar today. Hopefully, it will help break this heat wave."

"Hopefully." Tilly shoots off a text—presumably to Jax. "This Sunday. You and me, right? We can work up here or go get our nails done. I don't care. I just need a break from changing diapers. If we want, we could even make it a girls' day. I'm sure Cassie and Scar would love to join us."

"Let me see how much I have to do, and I'll let you know Friday morning. I usually end up finally crashing on Sundays, so a mani-pedi might be nice. How's Cassie doing, by the way? I haven't seen her since the wedding." Cassie is a recent addition to the extended family, even though Tilly and I have known her since they roomed together in college. Besides marrying Robbie Moore, she is pregnant with the next Moore baby.

Tilly gives a sad smile. "Good, all things considered. She's handling the news about her parents better than expected. Still, I can't believe she kicked them out of the wedding. I wish these guys could have waited one more day. I would have loved to have seen it."

"It was intense. Glad she did, though. I didn't get all the details, but from the little I heard, if she wouldn't have told them to pound sand, *I would have.*" Poor Cassie, as if she didn't have enough going on. My dad sucked, but he never pretended to be anything other than the asshole he was. She had the illusion of this perfect, loving family shattered on her wedding day.

Tilly laughs. "Robbie was pissed that Cian had him in the doghouse their first week married." Cian, Cassie's eldest brother, had been living in Tral Lake while spying on her without her knowledge like some special-op.

"Serves him right." I love seeing that big guy brought down to earth a bit more by his baby sister.

"Don't let him hear you say that." Tilly's phone chimes, and she glances down. "Jax is here. Text me later."

I lean over and kiss the baby. "Goodbye, Gavin."

"Alexander," Tilly corrects.

I pout. "No, I thought Gavin had the birthmark on his nose?"

"No, Alexander..." Tilly pauses, lost in her train of thought.

"You can't tell them apart, can you?"

She blushes. "I can tell my babies apart. You threw me off—that's all."

"Sure, keep telling yourself that," I say, returning the infant as she grumbles something about name tags.

"My mom had it so much easier. At least there was a sure-fire way to tell Jake and me apart."

I empathize with Tilly. This has been a tough year on all the Moores. It's been the hardest on her, though. I know she was terrified in that delivery room; all she wanted was her mother. Hell, I did too. I felt like a piss-poor substitute for what she needed.

Giving me a kiss on the cheek, Tilly smiles and waves goodbye prior to heading outside to meet her husband. I glance at the clock and note I have a couple of hours before the rush comes in for the evening. Plenty of time to do a little more cleaning and shower. While a packed house is always nice, with any luck, the storm will keep us from getting too busy tonight. I'm already exhausted for the day, and it's only two o'clock.

I rush to finish bringing down the boxes to the recycling bin. On my last trip, cool drops of rain hit my steamed skin. For a moment, I stand there, tilting my head back and embracing the slight chill. The crack of lightning has the hair on my neck standing up and cuts my reprieve short. Hurrying inside, I hop in the shower.

Ever since I was little, I've had this weird paranoia about being electrocuted in the shower by lightning. I'd skip it, except I'd prefer not to scare everyone away with my BO. On the other hand, most of the guys are farmers and smell way worse, especially in the early part of the year when they are working with fertilizer the most. Still, I pride myself on not smelling like a foot.

I pause mid-shampoo and listen carefully. *Is that a siren?* I bite my lip, unsure what to do. It might be—then again, they sound the damn thing off every time it rains. So you never know if it's a genuine alarm or someone just button happy. With this in mind, I resume shampooing.

Lights flicker and the ground shakes. I cover my ears at the rumble of a freight train's deafening roar. *Oh, fuck.* I panic and turn off the water. Half-blind, with soap in my eyes, I reach for a towel and come up empty. Damn it, they are still in the living room. I go to open the door, wanting to get downstairs to the basement as soon as possible, when I'm knocked back and everything goes black.

2

Jake

THE RIG ROLLS THROUGH the dark county roads of Tral Lake as we assess the damage of the neighboring farmlands. Nothing too major out in this region. Plenty of downed trees and branches. We've had to park the truck a few times in order to clear the street. The roof of a barn was blown clean off. Fortunately, the livestock were all unharmed, and Mr. Leuger had already worked to move them to a new structure. Ms. Locke's almost three-hundred-year-old oak tree is missing. And Eli's orchard sustained a lot of damage. The tornado ripped out the whole west side, while the remaining trees had a lot of hail damage.

Now that we've cleared the countryside, we are heading back into town to see what more we can do to help. Farms get hit the hardest during these sorts of storms. The wide-open fields and lines of forestry make it easy for a tornado to do damage to the nearby properties. Though the destruction has been minimal—given the circumstances—I have this sick feeling that *something* isn't right.

"What do you think? F3?" Stone estimates, pulling me from my thoughts.

I shake my head and grin. Swallowing down my unease, I get my head back in the game. Everyone expects me to be a happy-go-lucky guy. But since my parents' death, everything's felt... off-kilter. I hate it. At first, I thought it was a twin-link nervousness about my sister and the babies. But the boys are perfect and healthy. Theirs was one of the first houses we passed on our way out of town, and everyone was safely tucked away inside; it was the same when we drove by my older brother Robbie's place. So it's not that.

"Nah, F2."

"Wanna wager?" Stone gives me a cocky smile, which I return.

"Loser does dishes?" I offer, and he nods.

"Deal." We shake on the arrangement.

"You get many tornados around here?" he asks after a few moments of silence. Sometimes I forget he isn't originally from around these parts. He transferred in from an east coast station a couple of years ago.

"Not exactly. Usually, straight-line winds and hail. Not that they are completely unheard of, but not as common as you'd assume. Most of the time, we get jumpers."

"Jumpers?" Stone raises an eyebrow behind his black thick-rimmed glasses.

"Yeah. Weak tornados that can't maintain speed or enough momentum to stay on the ground. They do a bit of damage depending on what they hit. We had one about five years ago that relocated someone's garage down the block."

"That's fucking crazy. I've had to deal with my share of weather on the coast. But never been in a tornado before."

"How'd you like it?" I smile, knowing he's another adrenaline junkie. There is nothing quite like a tornado to get you going. Growing up, I'd try to chase storms with Mack. He used to think I was suicidal. I just always thought they were fascinating, and I wanted to watch them.

"It was insane—unlike anything I've seen before."

"Moore," Jenkins calls over the radio.

"What's up?" I ask.

"Got an update on the patrols done by the PD. So far, no calls for rescue assistance. Sounds like there was a bit of property damage we'll need to help clean up later. Captain is calling us back now before the next wave hits. He told us to detour through Main, to get some eyes at ground level." It makes sense: Main Street is in the middle of town and the buildings are old and sturdy. It is rare they take much, if any, damage. However, if they did, it would more than likely result in injury.

"There's another cell?" I glance out the window and sure enough, there is an angry, roaring black sky off in the distance. *Fuck.* At least we got the farms secured before another wave hit. I have a feeling this year will not be too kind to our farmers.

"Yup. Radar is showing the cell circling back around. It's gaining more momentum. Sounds like you might be doing dishes tonight."

I laugh. "My call was on the first twister. Care to bet on the second?" I ask Stone.

He shakes his head at me. "Sure. I bet the next one will be an F5."

I raise an eyebrow at him. "You don't know anything about tornados, do you?"

"Nope." He grins.

"An F5 would level the town in one pass." The east-coaster's eyes widen with understandable fear. "Let's hope you're wrong. I say second pass... F3." As we turn down Main, Jenkins slams on the brakes. Jostling forward, I brace myself. "What the fuck?" I call over my earpiece before glancing around to verify that Stone and Hopkins are good. They give me a thumbs up with equally confused expressions painted across their faces.

"Not my fault," Jenkins grumbles something about a crazy asshole. "Fucking Ted just ran out into the street. Almost hit the fucker. Wouldn't surprise me if he were drunk." I clench my jaw. Ted is eccentric and drinks a little too much, but he's good people.

There is a loud banging on the door, presumably the old man himself. I open it gently in an effort not to hit him. "Hey, Ted, you need to move on inside. Another storm is rolling in. Make sure everyone gets back to the basement."

Ted gasps, clearly out of breath. "Tree," he rasps.

At the same time, Jenkins comments, "I think we found Ms. Locke's old-ass tree."

I look over towards Harper's Pub. The upper level has a giant oak thrown across the roof. *What the hell is that doing up there?* Shit, that's going to be a pain in the ass to remove. The rain starts up again, and as much as he's concerned about his establishment, it's not an emergency and will have to wait until the storm passes. Then we can help him secure the building until we get a removal service out here.

"It's fine, Ted. We'll work on it later. The bar's sturdy. You'll be safe in the basement."

Ted shakes his head. "Letty," he struggles to say between breaths.

I frown. He's not making any sense. What does Letty have to do with any of this? Then it clicks. *Oh, fuck.* I'm moving before my brain even has a second to register what's happening. Letty moved into the loft a couple of months ago. Upstairs... right where that tree landed... I point with my axe. "Upstairs?" I verify out loud, even though Ted's frantic mumbling is enough confirmation.

He nods. "We can't... get into the apartment." He wipes the rain from his face. "The tree is blocking the door. We... tried to call... but..." The lines are down, and the cell tower was hit. We only have an emergency radio at the present time.

I'm already out of the rig with the old bar owner hot on my heels. "You're certain she's upstairs?" I repeat again. Letty might be a lot of things, but I never imagined she'd be stupid enough to remain on an upper level during a storm like this—not after the alarms sounded all across town.

Ted, still heaving, nods. "Last I saw, she was heading there to get cleaned up before her shift."

"Get down in the basement, sir. Join the others. We got this," Stone directs Ted to safety, while Hopkins follows to make sure no additional aid is needed. "What's the protocol here?"

I run up the stairs, taking two at a time. When we get on the second floor, sure enough, there are a couple of guys trying to pry the front door open. Stone instructs them to the cellar while I attempt to shoulder my way through, but the wood paneling won't budge. Feeling the change in pressure, I know I don't have time. If she's not already injured, with the roof open and exposed, she's going to be in trouble.

"Step back," I warn before raising my axe and demolishing the goddamn door. Stone helps me pull it off the hinges, and we are immediately hit in the face with branches. "Letty," I call out. There's no reply. "Come on, Letty, this isn't the time for one of your games." My heart rate picks up. It's not that I think she'd ever willingly stay up here. I was just hoping if I pissed her off with the insult, she would reveal herself.

Fuck, fuck, fuck. She can't be up here.

Ted must be confused. Maybe she took off and went to go check on the bookstore or some other perfectly reasonable excuse for her to be anywhere but here. Because the alternative for why she hasn't called out once the entire time twists my stomach in knots.

"Stay here," I instruct Stone before ignoring his protest and crawling over the branches. I power on my flashlight and take in the damage. The place is a mess, but the subfloor still seems strong. It's an open area. My anxiety intensifies when I still don't see her. If Ted is right and she's up here, this is the worst-case scenario and she's trapped under the tree. That's when I notice the bathroom door.

Of course. I'd slap myself if I didn't have so much gear on. If she couldn't make it down fast enough, the bathroom would be the safest place to hide. I struggle to maneuver around the branches, which keep getting caught in my equipment. Once I make it to the interior door, I note that it's blocked off by tangled tree limbs. The wind picks up. I know I'm running out of time. I quickly chop away, attempting to remove the obstruction. By the time I've made enough headway that I can pry the paneling back, I can't see past the darkness of the enclosed space. When the clouds shift and sunlight trickles in from the caved-in roof, I am finally able to spot a leg protruding from the rubble.

Fuck no.

I toss away the debris and reveal a very naked, unconscious pain in my ass. "Letty," I prompt gently. She doesn't respond.

I rip off my glove with my teeth and press a finger to her neck. Her pulse beats slowly. Carefully, I turn her to her back. I wouldn't typically do this without someone else to assist, but I'm worried about her lying face down on the wet floor. There is a gash on her forehead, likely what knocked her out cold. I need to get her out of here, but with the tree blocking the path, it will be difficult to carry her and navigate my way through.

Seeing her like this makes me sick to my stomach. Letty is always so bright and obnoxious, like bubblegum. There is no blending in where she is concerned. She sticks out like a sore thumb, with her pink highlights and loud-mouth remarks. Now, she's quiet and pale, and her lips are tinted blue. I remove my jacket and lay it over her, hoping it will help warm her up and protect her from the elements.

"Found her," I call over the radio.

"What's the status?" Jenkins replies.

"Twenty-nine-year-old female, unconscious but breathing. There appears to be a head injury, possible exposure. I'm going to need assistance removing her."

"Secure her as best you can, and I'll call for the ambulance. Stone, clear a path."

"Copy that," Stone verifies the order before the distinct sounds of him chopping away echo back through the mic.

While we wait, I take her shower curtain and tie it to one of the extended drawers. It isn't perfect, but at least it is keeping the rain from falling directly on her face. Then I rummage through her cupboards... unsuccessfully. I don't find any towels or other items to assist. The ground shakes, followed by the roaring of the winds, letting me know I'm too late. The last wave must have knocked out the sirens.

"Stone, what's your status?" I hold my breath, praying he's cleared enough to extract her quickly.

"Not clear," he replies, and I can note his regret.

Damn it, there is no way I can make it out in time... not with her. *Shit.* "Stone, go to the basement now."

"Moore," he protests.

"Now, Stone." I give the order firmly, so there are no further questions. "Sorry, Letty." Scooping her into my arms, I press a soft kiss to her forehead before laying her down in the bathtub. I cover her head with my helmet and position myself on top of her, careful to not add any unnecessary weight while using my body as a shield. It's not ideal, but it will have to do, given the situation.

On any normal day, she'd kick me in the nuts if she woke up with me over her like this. *But desperate times call for desperate measures.* My eyes squeezed shut, I rest my head against the cool helmet and pray we make it out of here, while hoping like fuck that Stone was wrong about the intensity of the next tornado.

3

Letty

THE UNBEARABLE STENCH OF alcohol assaults my senses. I groan. This isn't the type I'm used to slinging all day. No, this is the stuff used to sanitize and clean. It's an awful scent you can taste on the back of your tongue. My head is heavy, like it weighs a hundred pounds and is the size of a billboard. I crack one of my eyes open and immediately shut it again. The light is overwhelming.

"Shit," a deep male voice grumbles.

Is that a nurse or the doctor? I don't recall any of the docs I've met sounding that gruff before. Then again, except for routine maintenance, I avoid clinics like the plague. Not that I'm afraid of hospitals or anything—well, the staff and procedures anyway. No, it's the bill that terrifies me. *Oh, fuck.* If I was admitted, the bill for this is going to be astronomical.

I need to get out of here before they bankrupt me.

No longer concerned with the blinding light, I force my eyes open; thankfully, the room seems dimmer. There's an IV in my arm and some contraption on my finger. Where's that nurse? I need him to unhook me. I glance down at the gown I'm wearing—it's one of those hideous ones. White with that light-blue floral pattern. Some designer thought this made the experience cheerier. News flash, *it doesn't*.

Sitting up, I look around the room for someone to unhook me and get my clothes. I barely get myself to an incline when I'm startled by a hand firmly pressed against my chest, pushing me back down.

"Don't get up," the masculine baritone demands. My head turns. I'm fully prepared to give whoever decided it was okay to order me around—and sneakily cop a feel—a piece of my mind. *That's right, asshole. You just signed my ticket out of here, debt free.* I'm sure HR would love to hear about their gropy staff.

The threats die on my tongue. My jaw drops as I look up at him. That heavy feeling in my head intensifies tenfold. Confusion casts a new fog over my mind. *What is he doing here?* Out of all the people in the fucking world, he's the last person I'd ever expect to see at my bedside.

"Jake?" I ask with a frown. My throat is raspy, and the words slice like razor blades, but I continue forward. "Why are you here?" Maybe I'm hallucinating from all the drugs they gave me while I was out? It wouldn't surprise me if my subconscious tormented me with images of him.

It's nothing new.

He doesn't respond; instead, he grabs a cup of water and brings the straw to my lips. "Take small sips."

Drinking the ice-cold liquid triggers my memory. *Cracking open a beer. Cleaning out the apartment.* I attempt to remember what happened after that, but everything is hazy and only exacerbates the throbbing in my temples. Jake snatches the cup from me sooner than I'd like. My mouth opens to protest, but there are more *important things* to discuss.

"What happened?" I force the words out.

He sighs as he sets the water down and turns to look at me. The green in his hazel eyes grows more vibrant as his gaze fills with sympathy. "A tree crashed through the roof during the storm. You were knocked unconscious."

And like a tidal wave, it all comes rushing back: Taking out the recycling, the storm, needing a shower... The sirens and the roaring sound of the winds... No towel.

Oh my god, the tornado hit when I was in the shower. *Naked*. Great, how many people saw my bare ass passed out on the bathroom floor?

Sinking into the pillow, hoping it will swallow me whole, I close my eyes. I can't look at him. "Let me guess: the entire Tral Lake FD got an eyeful of my lady bits?"

"Like they haven't already?"

My lips turn up slightly. Hopefully, he doesn't notice. This is more like the Jake I know. It's comforting. The one having me sip water and giving me puppy-dog eyes? Yeah, that was just too weird. I didn't like it. Everything feels like it's spiraling. I need my obnoxious jerk.

"You know damn well I don't go for nozzle jockeys."

He cracks his neck before clearing his throat, whatever hint of amusement he had about our banter long gone. "Anyway, I found you before the second wave hit." He shivers as he recalls the event. "I covered you up with my jacket." Jake lifts his hands in defense. "I was nothing but professional. It isn't like you've got anything I haven't seen before."

His words sting. I'm not sure why. We've both said and done way worse over the years. All of this is ridiculous. I was injured. There was a fucking tornado. And yet, somehow, Jake not seeming even a tiny bit impressed by me pisses me off. I might not go to the gym or have giant tits like Madison Sinclair (one of Tral Lake's resident North Shore rich bitches)—tits that I'd be willing to bet my left ovary are all thanks to Daddy's checkbook. But carrying heavy crates of booze while running around on my feet ten to fifteen hours per day leaves me in amazing shape. If I could stop eating the shit we fry in the back and quit the beer, I'd be solid lean muscle. Besides, I enjoy having a bit of softness. I'm hot as fuck. Screw him if he doesn't appreciate it. Not that I'd ever want him to. Not really, at least. But the idea of him wanting me—knowing he'd never have me—yeah, that would make my day.

"...I couldn't get you out safely. We wouldn't have made it in time, and the bathroom ceiling was compromised. I did the best I could to shield you from the flying debris."

Somehow, I missed a part of the conversation while lost in my own thoughts. His words bring me back to what actually matters. As though some veil's been lifted, I see that his arms and face have minor cuts all over them. Glancing at my hands, I note that mine do too. But my injuries seem minor in comparison. Then realization hits me. If he hadn't found me, I would probably be dead or seriously hurt. As much as I hate to admit it, if anyone was going to find me in that state, I'm glad it was Jake. All joking and pettiness aside, deep down, I know he would do whatever he could to protect me—even risk his own well-being. Despite how much he hates me, he loves his sister. And that results in my protection by proxy.

"Thank you," I choke out, unable to make eye contact with him.

"I'm just glad you're okay." Jake surprises me as he brushes loose strands of my messy hair back. Risking a glance, I watch as a flash of sadness passes over his unnaturally handsome face. These drugs must be fantastic. For a second, you'd think he's genuinely relieved. Not because of some brotherly obligation, but for himself. Then, as if a switch has been flipped, the expression is gone. That caring stranger is replaced by the asshat I've been forced to interact with for practically my whole life. Straightening his spine, he gives me his signature grin. "Tilly would've killed me if anything happened to you." *Yeah, that's what I thought.*

Oh no, Tilly! I sit up in a panic and feel the blood drain from my head. "Tilly? The babies?"

"They're fine. She made it home before the tornado. It barely hit the north side of town. Everyone is okay. You just need to rest." He takes a deep breath. "Tilly sends her love. She wanted to come herself, but it wasn't safe for her to leave. Storms are still popping up in the area."

Thank God she's safe, I think to myself and lie back down. I already almost lost her in that accident that took her parents. If anything ever happened to Tilly or those babies, I couldn't stand it. They are the only family I have left. Another sudden thought has me jolting upright for a second time. Jake is quick, already pinning me down. "You said a tree crashed into my bar and my roof is missing?"

Jake gives me a solemn nod. Even though it worsens the ache in my head, I can't hold back the tears. Everything I've worked so hard to get... is gone. "Don't worry, Letty. We'll check out the damage later. I couldn't get a good look, but it seemed like most of the damage was upstairs. The building has strong bones. I'm sure everything will be fine."

The crooked, wind-beaten sign that reads "Harper's Pub" looms over me. I stand there, looking up while holding back a strangled sob. The sunken-in roof is visible from the sidewalk. And the large windows that overlook Main Street are *shattered*. Just like my soul.

"We're clear to enter," Jake announces, walking out the front door. He went in first—to talk to a member of the crew who was verifying that the structure was sound. "Just stay behind me, okay?"

I nod and trail his footsteps. Jake is typically the last person I can stand to be around. At this moment, though, I'm thankful. No one would let me enter on my own. He's pulling favors, and I know it.

The damage downstairs in the bar area doesn't appear too terrible. Broken glass and bottles strewn about. A few fallen photos and hanging lights. The floor took on a good amount of water. But otherwise, she seems intact, as Jake predicted—the rare occasion where I'm glad he's right.

Slowly, we walk up the stairs to my apartment. My heart squeezes tight as we approach the door that's hanging off the hinges. While I was forced to stay overnight at the hospital for observation, Jake made a couple of calls and had the tree removed. They came out a few hours ago and secured everything for me.

As I glance around the small space, my heart shatters. For a second time. All that hard work down the drain...

"It's okay, Letty." Jake drapes a sympathetic arm over my shoulder. "We'll get things secured to prevent any further damage. Ted assured me he already has a claim started with the insurance company. I'm sure this place will be fixed in no time."

"You don't get it, Jake." He frowns at me as I step out of his embrace. I don't need his secondhand comfort right now. "Everything I have... it's all gone." I wipe at the tear rolling down my cheek. Apart from the TLFD spare gear on my back, which Jake loaned me when we left the hospital this morning, everything I owned was in there. I take a tentative step into the apartment, and Jake thrusts out an arm to stop me from entering.

"It should be fine, but let me walk ahead and make sure." He cautiously approaches the disaster zone and tests the floor in several spots. Once he's convinced that it's safe, he waves me in.

All my possessions are tossed around and mixed with Ted's remaining junk. Even the stuff that was safely tucked away in totes is scattered everywhere. Most of my clothes are shredded or missing. I hold my breath as I see the broken music box on the floor. Dropping to my knees, without concern for the shards of my life inflicting additional damage, I pick up and inspect the simple token from my childhood. It's busted beyond repair. The ballerina and gears are missing. While the box holds sentimental value, it's the contents that have me praying to whoever might be out there to not take this last piece from me. I breathe a sigh of relief as I open the small compartment and locate my mother's locket. I hug it tight before I clasp it around my neck.

A warm hand on my shoulder makes me jump. "Let's get out of here."

"And go where, Jake? This was all I had. I gave up my apartment at the beginning of the month. I have nothing and nowhere to go."

He gives me a small smile before lifting me by the elbow. "We'll figure it out. For tonight, how about you crash at the house? I have plenty of space now that Cassie's moved out."

My usual will to fight with him is gone. His house is the last place I want to be, especially if he's there. But given my current situation, beggars can't really be choosers.

4

Jake

LIFTING MY SHIRT AND turning to my side, I look in the mirror; an angry black and blue bruise glares back at me from my ribs. I—no, *we* got fucking lucky. That branch could have come in at a different angle and we would have been impaled. I'm glad Letty was passed out. She would've freaked if she knew how bad it got in there. These few marks are nothing compared to the headache she'd give me if she knew what went down.

Bags under my eyes loom like a billboard advertising I've been plagued by nightmares. The horrible reenactments where I didn't make it to Letty in time. That when I found her body, it was a tangled mess covered by debris. The thought sends me back to the toilet heaving. Despite being a part of the Tral Lake Fire Department for over a decade now and seeing my share of worst-case scenarios, it was the first time I had to rescue someone close to me.

Okay, close might be stretching it. *Familiar.*

Letty and I have always butted heads. Over the last decade, it's been worse. Especially as of late. To say things are complicated is an understatement. Regardless, I've known her practically my whole life. Even if we aren't remotely resembling anything close to friends, it doesn't make seeing her like that any better. Not to mention, Tilly would be devastated if anything ever happened to Letty. My sister finally seems happy after the accident, Jax and the twins being a huge part of that. Within a single year, I'm uncertain she could handle losing not only our parents but her best friend as well.

It took me hours to calm down and reassure Tilly that Letty was okay. I had to promise to stay by her side, to not let her wake up alone in that hospital. When my sister is frantic, it puts me on edge. I know for a fact Tilly would have dragged the boys with her to the hospital, and if I hadn't been there, no one else would have been able to. Ted was busy trying to salvage what he could of the bar and assess the damage. Jax reluctantly agreed to leave Tilly and help our brother, Scott, secure the coffee shop. Robbie had his hands full with Cassie and the garage. Besides, I had to come here anyway, to get stitched up and make sure nothing was broken. I kept that tidbit of information to myself.

Getting dressed, I make my way downstairs to grab the morning newspaper from the porch before heading to the kitchen. I roll my eyes as I look at the front page. Of course, they had to take a picture of me emerging from Harper's carrying Letty in my arms like some big action hero. At least the jerkface didn't get her at a compromising angle.

I make a mental note to follow up with the photographer and inform him that if he has any money shots, he better delete them—unless he wants his camera shoved up his ass. This is the biggest disaster in our area since the fire at the feed mill about six years ago. All the aspiring journalists from the Tral Lake Times are salivating like the dogs they are, trying to make the story larger than it actually is.

Reading through the article, I note that it's laced with an undertone of disappointment over the fact there were no fatalities. There were a few other minor injuries, and some lost livestock. Letty was, unfortunately, the most injured in the storm, which means these vultures are going to be circling her. And not just for her firsthand account, but because of the damage done to everyone's favorite bar. Out of all the shops on Main, Harper's got hit the hardest.

Fuck, I sound like Robbie.

I shake the negative thoughts from my mind. Life's too short to be grumpy and brooding all the time. I'm not sure how my big brother manages it. Hopefully, now that he has Cassie—and soon a baby—in his life, a little of their sunshine and happiness will rub off on him.

Although, I caught him smiling the other day, and it sent a shiver down my spine. It reminded me of the second Addams Family movie. The one where Wednesday Addams was brainwashed at summer camp and they got her to smile. The fucking creepiest thing I've ever seen. So maybe not too much sunshine.

Footsteps descending the stairs have me tucking away the paper. It's probably best for everyone if Letty doesn't see it. At least not yet. She has enough on her mind as it is. The last thing she needs is to wake up to her name printed on the front page in black and white. I'm surprised she's up this early. Letty and mornings go together as well as orange juice and toothpaste.

"Oh." She skids to a stop at the threshold.

I glance at the woman herself, now standing in the kitchen's entryway. Overall, she looks good (she always does). Most of the minor cuts she had are healed and barely visible. The swelling from the gash on her head has reduced significantly. My eyes roam over her toned legs and up towards the hem of the t-shirt she's wearing—*my t-shirt*—which settles at the middle of her thighs.

All my self-restraint fights my sudden urge to tilt my head and determine if she's wearing anything underneath. I gave her a pair of my boxers when we got in last night. But for the life of me, I can't tell if she's wearing them.

Bad Jake. I need to stop checking her out. Besides, it isn't like I didn't just see her naked the other day. Granted, I didn't take the time to appreciate it. I was in work mode. Now? *Nope.* Not now, not ever. Letty is one hundred and fifty percent off-limits. I'm only checking her out for medical purposes. Yeah, that's right—*medical purposes.*

Fortunately, the girls are supposed to be stopping by today with some essentials for her. I'm not sure how long she's going to need to stay here. But for my fucking sanity, she can't keep walking around half-naked. In my clothes. The mental reaction I have to her wearing them, smelling like me, it's engrained. It's my natural instincts: to flirt, fuck her silly, mark her as mine. That thought is really confusing because the last thing she will ever be is *mine*. Letty is a no-fly zone for my cock. I might do a lot of stupid things, but she will never be one of them.

Yeah, I might be my family's designated *manwhore*. I still despise whoever came up with that damn term by the way. Man or woman, no one should be given a derogatory label because they enjoy having sex. Regardless, I might be the more promiscuous one in this family. But so far, I'm also the smartest of us all.

Tilly (who is supposed to be the smarter twin) and the almighty and responsible Robbie both ended up in hormone-fueled dazes, which resulted in accidental pregnancies. I still get a good laugh at that. I've probably had more sex than all my siblings combined, yet we don't see any Jake Juniors running around. That's why you can't keep shit pent up. It makes you stupid. They're just lucky they got into these situations with the people they were meant to be with. I shiver at the thought of what would have happened if Robbie had ever gotten his ex-wife Bianca knocked up. Granted, that bitch is so cold I wouldn't be surprised if her eggs were frozen.

Nope, I have no doubt that this is the typical guy reaction to seeing an attractive chick half-naked in his kitchen. It's embedded in our DNA, and has absolutely nothing to do with *her*. It could be anyone else standing there and I'd react the same. And when it comes to where I stick my dick, I'm the wisest Moore. Still, it doesn't make me hate my natural response any less—mostly the way I don't hate it at all.

"Morning." I give Letty my brightest grin. She's trying to hide it. But I can sense she's on the edge of the cliff that people leap off before making bad choices. "If you're hungry, I have some overnight oats in the fridge. There is a ton of fruit. I can whip up some bacon as well."

Her lips stretch into a sad smile. "Thanks. I think I will just stick to coffee and toast." She hesitates before entering the kitchen, gathering her breakfast, and taking a seat at the opposite end of the counter, farthest from me.

Whatever, sweetheart. It isn't like I'm thrilled to be stuck around you either.

"The girls should be over soon. Tilly mentioned bringing you some essentials," I say between bites.

Letty adjusts her ratted hair that's piled on top of her head and scrunches her nose in the most adorable way. Nope, not adorable. Most *annoying* way. "Good, I really need a shower."

I bite my lip and suppress some suggestive comment about us showering together. Fuck, I need one as well. Some cold water to wash away the unwanted erection I have. Casually, I adjust myself. "That'd be a start," I tease. I'm rewarded with Letty's signature eye roll. Good, this is what she needs—what we both need—right now. Some normalcy. This is what we do. *Provoke each other.*

"Yeah, I can't wait to get the stench of Jake off me." Letty leans down and sniffs her shirt. "Don't tell me you still use BOD?"

Crossing my arms, I let out a huff. "No, Dukes. Besides, you're one to talk. You've been wearing Love Spell since junior high."

She shakes her head. "Whatever it is, I can't wait to wash it off me. If I wanted to smell like a tree, I'd roll around in the woods." The mention of the woods causes us both to blush, followed by a moment of awkward silence. This is why we can't spend time together. Without trying, we always end up poking at old wounds. Rekindling memories I, for one, wish to forget.

Clearing my throat, I glance at the time on my phone. Thank God, it's six in the morning. "Well, as much as I enjoy your company," I say as sarcastically as possible, "I need to go to the station." Getting up, I wince, and Letty studies me carefully as I grab my side.

"Are you okay?" she asks, frowning.

"It's fine." When I walk past her, she reaches out and grabs my arm, then lightly presses into my rib. Against my will, I groan. *Fucking Letty.* She lifts my shirt and inspects the large bruise.

Heat from her hovering fingertips makes my skin prickle. "Is that because of me?" Her voice is riddled with guilt, none of which I want or deserve. Injury is a risk of my job.

My hand grips her wrist, pulling her away from me. Being this close to Letty, her scent mixed with mine, short circuits my senses. If I don't walk away, I'll do something we'll both regret.

"I was doing my job. It has nothing to do with you," I growl, before letting go of her to lower my shirt. "Don't read too much into it."

She holds her wrist to her chest. Unshed tears pool in her eyes as she looks away from me and stares down at her coffee. *Damn it.* I didn't mean to come off like such a dick. I fucking despise the knowledge that she is the only one who can bring out this side of me.

Not wanting to risk making this worse, I walk away without another word. It was stupid of me to invite her to stay here. It's exhausting wearing this mask in her presence. But I'll never give her the satisfaction of knowing the pain she's caused.

The only girl I've ever given my heart to... tore it to shreds and threw it back in my face.

5

Letty

"I'M SO GLAD YOU'RE okay." Tilly squeezes me so tight I think she might crack a rib. "I'm so sorry. I wanted to come to the hospital, but with the babies—"

"It's okay, Tilly. I understand," I assure her, and hopefully cut off any additional unnecessary apology she had in mind.

It's true. It might have sucked that the first thing I saw when I woke up in the hospital was Jake's stupid face. No doubt Tilly twisted his arm to be there, and he caved. But my best friend has responsibilities. She's a wife and mother. I can't *and don't* expect her to drop everything to come to my beck and call. I would have kicked her butt if she risked the twins by coming to see my sorry ass. Despite wishing that anyone other than Jake had been there, I won't deny that it was nice not waking up alone, but I'll never admit that. Not to anyone.

"Well, we brought you some supplies," Scarlett singsongs, waving a few bags around.

"Fortunately, we're about the same size. Well, before this thing." Cassie rubs her belly. I swear the other week at the wedding I could hardly see the bump under her flowing white summer dress. But now, it's there plain as day. Noticing my line of sight, Cassie laughs. "Yeah, I know. Seriously, right?

No joke! I woke up the other morning and was like: *whoa, where did that come from?* I found a hack with hair ties to help hold my jeans together." Cassie lifts her shirt to show me her pants, which are open at the zipper and clasped with a few elastic bands.

"I still hate you." Tilly huffs playfully. "I was already a whale at eighteen weeks, waddling around like I belonged in a zoo exhibit. And here you are, with this picture-perfect baby bump. From behind, you wouldn't know you're pregnant."

Cassie looks like one of the pregnant models in a magazine. The first time I met her, I *actually did hate* her. Okay, not really. It was more akin to a little bit of female jealousy. She had one of *those* bodies. Tall, not ridiculously so, but basically every outfit sold in store was made specifically for her frame.

My best friend may have a great figure herself, but Tilly still has her share of problems in the clothing department. Being petite is not a blessing. The cut of clothes is always weird.

And while I'm a respectable five-foot-seven, those two inches Cassie has on me make a world of difference when it comes to women's fashion. I may also be a little salty about those couple of inches because they are what kept me from a really stupid idea I had.

As a teen, a guilty pleasure of mine was watching *America's Next Top Model.* I wanted to compete in the show, even went to an audition they had at the Mall of America. They told me I had the right look, but the cut off height was five-nine.

So, yeah, I might have held a teeny-weeny grudge against her for that. Not that my dream was to become some hotshot model. But it looked fun, and it wasn't as if I had much going on in the education department, not like Tilly. It seemed like an easy way to make a living for myself. Of course, now they've lowered the limit and welcome a wider variety of body types, but that ship has sailed for me. And I found a new dream—one I'm hoping can be salvaged.

"Shut up, Tilly. You had two of these things growing in there. Not to mention, look at you. You're like freaking Kate Middleton, walking out moments after giving birth while looking photoshoot ready. I doubt I'll be back in any of these jeans after this baby is out in the world. So don't worry about returning them. I envision a new wardrobe in my future."

"Yeah, I'm never wearing a bikini again. I bet you don't even have a stretch mark yet." Tilly attempts to pull up the hem of Cassie's shirt. Cassie laughs and tries to turn away. "Aha, I'm right. I bathed in cocoa butter and still look like a zebra that lost its color. You..."

"Anyway." Scarlett smiles, laughing as she shakes her head at their antics. "We brought you some clothes, toiletries, a temporary cell—you should be able to just add your sim card."

"Books," Tilly adds excitedly. "We're reading this hilarious one right now. The characters are currently in New York, but they're from Minnesota. It has these two super-hot twin hockey players."

"I can't wait to read their books. Especially the quiet one." Cassie claps her hands.

I wish I had their enthusiasm when it comes to books, not that I don't enjoy them. But true crime or murder mysteries are what I prefer. I never got into romance like Tilly. I always told her those fantasies rotted her brain and gave her unrealistic expectations.

"Thanks. I really appreciate it." Though I have no intention of reading them, I do appreciate the fact they are going out of their way for me. "Now I just need to figure out how soon I can get the bar up and running, then find a place to live while I wait for the repairs upstairs."

Tilly frowns as though she's confused. "Why not stay here?"

"What?" I hiss. "No, there is no way I can stay here with Jake and his rotating door of women."

Cassie snickers, apparently finding something amusing. I narrow my glare at her. She holds up her hands defensively. "Don't look at me like that. Besides, Jake doesn't bring anyone home. He enjoys his fortress of solitude."

That's right. How did I forget Cassie roomed with him until just recently? My arms are crossed defensively. I'm still pissed at the insinuation she made at the wedding. Obviously, she is clueless about these sorts of things. Her own insecurities made her blind to the fact that Robbie was head over heels for her.

"Still," I whine. "Tilly, you know Jake and I will end up killing each other if I stay here. After five minutes, we were already pressing each other's buttons. It could be months before the apartment is livable. I know he's your brother, and I tolerate him for that reason, but this? It's too much."

Tilly bites her lip and nods in understanding, likely recalling all the instances Jake and I were at each other's throat when I would spend the night. "You can come stay with me, but I'm not sure you'd like it. Alex and Gavin are colicky. No one in our house gets any sleep, and the spare bedroom is where Jax has all his extra equipment. I could have him move it to the garage and set up the room though, if you really want."

I cringe and contemplate how important sleeping is. Also, I really hate the idea of putting them out and having to rearrange their house on my account. This is again one of those scenarios where I appreciate her offer and that she will go to such lengths for me. But I could never ask her to do any of that.

"Robbie and I have space, but we're only equipped for us right now. There is one working bathroom, which really sucks with me pregnant and in there every five minutes. And we have a ton of remodeling to do, besides getting the roof replaced, thanks to that storm."

"The Inn is booked." Scarlett taps her chin. "I have a couch in my master suite. You are more than welcome to use it," she offers.

I forgot she lives in what used to be the groundkeeper's cabin. It's a cool space. But like my apartment, it has a small studio-style layout. Being crammed in there with her might be better than here. I haven't gotten to know Scar very well yet. We are both workaholics with little free time. But I'm sure we could become fast friends. Despite her obsession with romance novels, I feel we are kindred spirits when it comes to having children and getting married: it's not on either of our radars. Since she's been here, I haven't seen her go out or flirt with anyone—I am all for the single life, but I really hope she is getting laid.

"Look, I know you and Jake have never gotten along. But you know this is the best place to stay. It's free. Less than a ten-minute walk to the bar. He has the extra room." Tilly counts her very valid points on her fingers.

Tilly and Cassie live too far out of town for me to walk, and I got rid of my car. It broke down earlier this winter and needed a new engine. Robbie told me the junker wasn't worth it and that I was better off buying a new one due to the cost of parts alone (because he'd never charge me labor). He offered to help me find something affordable, but I rarely used it unless I needed to go up to the cities.

"Besides, he'll be at the station most days and you'll be at the bar getting things up and going," she continues. "You'll hardly ever see each other. And on those rare occasions where you are both stuck in the house together, well, it's big enough for the two of you. Or maybe you guys could, I don't know, try to get along. I know it's a crazy concept and all, but I really hoped whatever childhood grudge you both had would be dropped by now. We're adults."

"He's not," I grumble under my breath. I know she's right. But Tilly doesn't understand how difficult it is to be near him. And that's my fault... "Fine," I huff out. "Doesn't seem like I have much of a choice. Hopefully, Ted will get the roof repaired and I won't be here for too long."

"There you go." Tilly pats me on the back. "Hey, how about we get out of here for a bit? We could go to the mall and buy you some more body spray. There are some options in the bag, but obviously we don't have your favorite. And we could grab some lunch. Take Cassie to the maternity store. It'll be fun."

"I should really go check the damage at Harper's." I gnaw on my lip. Maybe it won't look as bad. New day and all that.

Tilly places her hands on my shoulders, forcing me to meet her eyes. "Letty, you almost died. Take the day off, get out of town. I promise you the mess will still be there tomorrow. Besides, didn't you notice? No babies. Jax and Robbie are on baby detail today."

"I thought Robbie could use the practice." Cassie laughs.

As I look into Tilly's glistening amber eyes, a thought occurs to me. I feel like an ass for not asking sooner. "How's the shop?"

She winces. "Not as bad as Harper's," she says sadly. "But water and books don't exactly mix."

"Oh no," I gasp.

"Jax assures me it's not that bad. One window was broken by a tree limb, and we got a little rain damage. Everything is already boarded up, the dehumidifiers are going, and the books are lying out to dry. Like I said, the mess will be there tomorrow. Today, I think we could all use a break."

I nod in agreement. Tilly deserves it. A day without work or needing to care for the twins. As much as I would love to get started on the bar, I'll do this for her.

"Not me." Scarlett shakes her head. "We didn't take any damage. But like I said, I'm swamped with guests. We were already at half capacity with summer tourism starting, and a handful of rooms are out of commission with the construction. Now, we are booked solid, accommodating those who were displaced after the storm." Scarlett hides her smile.

While everyone else was negatively impacted by the tornado, she's prospering. Although I'm jealous, I don't blame her. If Harper's hadn't been hit, I know we'd be overflowing with customers. Historically speaking, natural disasters filled my booths and lined my bar top.

"Fine, Scarlett is a party pooper, like always. We'll go and have some much-needed fun." Tilly bounces on her heels.

"Yeah, we could always stop at K.O.'s. I'm sure Killian would love to see you." I give Cassie a death glare. She returns a sweet-as-sin smile, one that begs me to challenge her.

"Killian?" Tilly asks, shocked and a little giddy.

"You two looked pretty cozy when you left the wedding together," Cassie taunts, aware she's pressing my buttons.

I give the girl my bitchiest grin. Two can play that game. "I'd love to visit your brother."

Scarlett and Tilly look back and forth between the stare down Cassie and I are having. Cassie's honeyed smile burns my insides. I hate that she's so confident in her assumption. I may not be able to phase her, but she couldn't be more wrong if she tried.

"Good," she says as though she just won the gauntlet. "I'll text and let him know we're on our way."

"Good," I sneer. "I better go get showered and dressed."

"Yup, wouldn't want him to get the wrong idea when it comes to you wearing another man's shirt and underwear."

"Is there a problem here?" Tilly asks cautiously, sensing the tension we're hiding behind our smiles. My dear sweet friend assumes it's over the idea of Killian and me together, and not the fact that Cassie believes I have feelings for someone I can't stand.

"Nope." Cassie pops her P. "I think Letty and Kill are perfect for each other."

Tilly processes her words and smiles. "Oh my god. You're right. They *are* perfect for each other. I'd been so caught up pushing two watermelons out of my hoo-ha that it didn't even occur to me. Come on, we need to get you dressed and ready," Tilly squeals. "Maybe this storm is a blessing in disguise."

I stop and frown. "What do you mean?"

She sighs. "Letty, you're a workaholic. You don't make time for yourself. Do you really want to end up like Ted? Wake up one day, only to realize you're old and alone, with no one to pass your legacy on to?"

I wince—her observation stings. "Yeah. You weren't much better until your parents' accident."

Everyone freezes. I can't believe I'm being such a bitch right now, especially to the only person I have left in my life. But the reality of her words struck a nerve. With everything going on, my stress is causing me to lash out. Still, she's the last person who deserves even an ounce of my frustration.

"Tilly, I'm—"

She holds up a hand. "It's fine, Letty. You're right. After Jax left, I shut down. Buried myself in schoolwork, then the shop. Anything to keep me distracted from the pain he caused. And it only got worse after I tried and failed miserably at dating those few times. I regret that it took my parents' deaths to bring us together. Sometimes, I even wonder how different things could have been if one of us would have just picked up the phone." Tilly wipes a tear from her face and smiles. "It took one of the worst experiences of my life to make me realize there is more to it than just the bookstore. Maybe this will be your wake-up call, Letty." She looks down and groans when she notices two wet spots on the front of her shirt. "Damn it, I'm leaking. I'm going to pump and change my top while you get dressed."

Feeling like the world's biggest jerk, I quickly wrap my arms around my best friend, not caring that she is getting breast milk on the t-shirt I'm wearing. It's Jakes anyway.

"I'm so sorry. It's just everything that's happened... it hasn't brought the best out of me. I didn't mean to take it out on you."

Tilly squeezes me tighter. "I know. Come on, let's get ready and get away for a bit. I think we could all use a break."

6

Jake

I SIT IN THE office. Slack-jawed. This is not at all what I was expecting when I came in today. Pleading with my eyes, I look between the two men in front of me. "You can't be serious?"

"I'm sorry, Jake. Unfortunately, I agree with Chief on this one." Captain combs his fingers through his salt and pepper hair.

"Moore, this isn't a punishment," Chief Hawkins reminds me again.

I wince and cross my arms. "I'm fit for light duty. It's not like I'm the first guy to have a bruised rib." This doesn't make any sense. When I broke my leg a few years back, they kept me on. It was mostly bitch work around the station. Even so, it was better than sitting at home.

Captain Rollings sighs. "Look, this isn't just about your injuries. I agree; they are minor. This is about your mental well-being."

"What are you talking about?" I ask, confused. Did someone file a complaint? No, no way. The guys love me. If there was an issue, they'd talk to me first.

"Jake, you've been spiraling for some time now."

"Spiraling!" I shout. *Who the fuck is spiraling?*

"Since your parents' deaths, you've been taking too many risks." Captain runs a frustrated hand over his face. "This is my fault. I should have insisted that you took more time for bereavement. But I thought that the extra week you used to help your sister would have been enough—obviously it wasn't."

"I haven't been spiraling. I've been doing my job." My fist slams on the desk.

"No, you haven't, son," Chief scolds me. "In the past seven months, you've gotten burned twice, suffered from hypothermia when you got cocky on the thin ice, almost died on the bluff because you failed to check your gear, and now this."

"How many times do I have to tell you? *I thought it was tied off*. The car was slipping. I knew it was a now-or-never situation. I rescued her," I justify.

Given the same scenario, I'd do it again.

"You got lucky that Dunn was quick to notice and grab the line," Chief retorts. "I know this year hasn't been the easiest on you. And since your father isn't here to beat some sense into you, I feel like I owe it to him, to do it in his place. Jacob, I am requesting that you take the time off. Clear your head. Work out your demons in a healthy, constructive manner. You've got an overabundance of vacation hours that need to be used. Take a couple of weeks off. Get out of town. Come back refreshed and level-headed."

"I don't want to take time off." I cross my arms again and whine like a child being told to eat his vegetables.

"Fine," Chief growls. "The choice is yours. Take a two-week vacation, or refuse and it will turn into a four-week suspension." His eyes narrow in challenge.

A suspension would mean a black mark on my record, union hearings... I could get demoted, or worse. Though I don't think there have been any issues with my performance as of late, is it worth the gamble?

"Come on, Jake, don't make this more difficult than it has to be. Take the vacation. Go fuck your way through some resort," Captain offers.

Is that all people think of me? Not that I don't love sex, and his idea isn't half-bad. But is that it? I love fishing. Why not suggest renting a charter boat? Go deep-sea fishing somewhere?

"After your vacation, we can discuss if this is still the best fit for you," Chief comments.

"Wait, hold the fuck on. *If?* You mean there's a chance there might not be a place here for me?"

What in fuck's sake is happening? How did we go from a two-week vacation to destress, to potentially being suspended? And now the implication they might not let me return?

"No one is saying that." Captain eyes Chief. "It's just... *sometimes* after major life-changing events and taking time off, people discover there is something out there they want more. This job and lifestyle have a time limit for everyone. Perhaps you've hit yours?"

"This is all I have." The words taste like ash as soon as I say them.

Captain sighs. "That's the problem, Jake. If you think this is all you have, you're always going to be a risk. Each person in this station has something outside of the job, something that reminds them they need to go home at the end of the day."

"That's not what I meant. Obviously, I have my family. It's just... this is what I'm meant to do. I don't need a vacation, or sitting at home with my thumb up my ass, to tell me that."

"Good, then I'm sure we'll welcome you back in two weeks," Chief says with finality. "In the interim, enjoy the time off. Instead of sitting around pouting, if you don't want to go anywhere, how about working on that video store you've been teasing us with? This doesn't have to be a bad thing."

Groaning, I rub the scruff on my face. I guess a few weeks off won't be the end of the world. Tilly could use some help fixing the damage at the shop. I've also been wanting to work on the video rental addition. I just haven't had the extra time. Feeling as though I have no choice but to agree, my shoulders drop and I look down at the floor.

"Okay, I'll take the vacation."

"Are you serious?" Robbie asks, taking a swig of his beer.

"Yup," I say, popping the P as I tear off the label from the bottle in front of me. "Two whole fucking weeks, stuck on my ass."

"That doesn't make any sense," Scott says with Gavin cradled in his arms before passing him to Robbie. "You've gotten injured before. Don't they typically put you on desk and cleaning duty while you heal? Why would they want you to take a vacation? If you're that hurt, isn't it a workman's comp issue?"

"I guess I have too much vacation built up and need to use some before HR freaks out. They thought this would be better than having to go through some sort of medical leave." I give them the half truth.

I still can't believe they accused me of being reckless. I might have gotten more injuries recently than I have during my previous years. But I saved those people. That's my job. Alexander cries in Jax's arms.

Setting my beer down, I reach out. "Hand him over. AJ wants his awesome Uncle Jake."

Jax rolls his eyes before passing me the baby. "He will not be called AJ. It makes me think of when your sister was obsessed with the Backstreet Boys."

"I'm sure she still has their CD somewhere," I tease.

"Where?" Jax frantically opens cupboards in search of the disc that used to drive us all mad. "I'm going to burn the damn thing."

"Go ahead. I'm sure she will just get a new one at some yard sale this summer." I laugh as his face pales.

"I think you are just jealous of the fact that, for a brief moment in time, she thought someone was sexier than you." Scott joins in on the teasing.

"Not true." Jax crosses his arms. "It's because she and Letty played that garbage nonstop."

My eye twitches at the mention of *her* name.

"Speaking of Letty, have you two killed each other yet?" Like a shark smelling blood in the water, Robbie chimes in.

"Oh, yeah, I forgot. Tilly mentioned she was staying with you." Jax no longer cares about finding the CD; he's more interested in Robbie's ambush.

"No casualties." I take a swig of my beer to hide my grimace. "Not yet, at least. But I'm sure you'll be planning one of our funerals by the end of the week."

"Letty's scrappy. I'm betting it will be yours." Robbie flashes me that obnoxiously smug older brother grin.

"I'll see that action." Jax joins in on what I'm guessing is the new wager.

"I never understood why you guys butted heads so much," Scott ponders. "I mean, it was funny when you were kids—being jealous that Tilly made a friend other than you. Now, though? Figured you would've dropped your petty bickering."

"I don't know," Robbie says in a baby voice as he rocks Gavin. "I think Uncle Jake is a glutton for punishment. Or maybe he's pissed that she's the only girl in town who doesn't fall for his bullshit."

"Language," Jax warns. "Is that it? Letty too much for your ego to handle?"

"Believe me," I say, getting up and handing Alexander back to Jax. "Me and my ego have no interest in Letty. We have more common sense than that."

"Really?" Robbie grins at me. "So then, why'd you throw a fit when she left my wedding with Killian?"

"Look at you. You're making Daddy miss all the fun stuff," Jax says playfully to Alexander.

"How'd I miss that?" Scott asks, looking between me and Robbie.

"Probably because you had your tongue down some redhead's throat," Robbie adds.

"It had nothing to do with Letty making out with that washed-up fighter. I lost the bet. I never lose." At least that is what I keep telling myself...

"That's right. I forgot about the bet. What was on the line?" Robbie laughs.

"I'd rather not discuss that right now." *Fucking Killian.*

"That good, huh?" Scott teases.

"Shut up." I toss my peeled-off label at him. "You know what? Fuck you guys. I'm having a shitty-ass day. Thought I'd come here and have my brothers cheer me up. Not be dickheads." Jax hits me upside the back of my head. I wince. "What the fuck was that for?"

He hits me again. "What did I say about language?"

"Are you serious? They're barely two weeks old. None of this will stick."

"Don't care, Jake. Everyone swears way too darn much in this family. Put four dollars in the swear jar."

"You're kidding, right? We aren't seriously doing that." I can't believe what I'm hearing. I know getting married and having children changes people. But I never expected this.

Robbie pulls a dollar out of his pocket and places it in the jar. "It was Cassie's idea. She's right; we swear too fucking much." He cringes and throws another dollar in the jar.

"This is why I'm never getting married," I grumble. "Do they chop your balls off during the ceremony? Or did she wait until the wedding night?"

Robbie pins me with a disapproving stare that reminds me of the one Dad used to give me when my ass was in deep shit, and I gulp.

"What's your issue, dude? You're never like this. A week ago, you would have made some joke or wagered on who could develop the most non-swear-word alternatives. What's going on?" Robbie's tone is stern. He's worried. Maybe Chief was right.

Or is it because your sanctuary has been infiltrated by the enemy?

"Sorry," I offer sincerely. "It's just the storm, the forced vacation, and the pain from the bruised ribs, then add Letty as the cherry on top of my turd sundae." Smiling, I show I can play along with their no-swearing rule. "I've been in a foul mood. I think I'm going to head home and get some rest. Tomorrow's a new day, right?"

"Are you sure?" Scott asks, concerned. "You've seemed off recently."

"Nah, I'm good. Still salty at you, though." I point to Robbie.

"What did I do?"

"You stole my awesome roommate. Now I'm stuck with the ice queen from H-E-double hockey sticks."

Everyone laughs.

"Well, at least Letty's not home." I raise a brow in question at Robbie's comment. "Cassie texted a few moments ago. I guess they went to the cities."

"Good, then I'm definitely going to go home and enjoy some peace and quiet."

Hopefully, a nice shower and rubbing one out will center me. I should have taken care of myself this morning before leaving, but I was in a rush to get to the station and as far away from her as possible. Wait, better yet: go home, shower, and find someone else to rub me out.

Robbie's evil grin chills me to my core. "You might have the house to yourself tonight. Cassie says they're stopping by K.O.'s. Since Harper's is closed, who knows? Maybe Letty will spend the night up there."

I bite the inside of my cheek and copper floods my taste buds. Forcing a smile, I grind out, "Good, he can deal with the headache."

Robbie chuckles at me.

Not feeling like dealing with their bullshit, I grab the rest of my six-pack and head out. When I walk into the dark house, I glance around and see that it is indeed empty. "Welcome home," I say to no one before cracking open a beer and flopping down on the couch.

7

Letty

PULLING UP OUTSIDE OF K.O.'s, I groan internally. Cassie hasn't backed down yet, like I assumed she would. For the life of me, I don't even know why I'm playing this game with her. I should just tell her to shove it. Except now she's pulled Tilly into it. And my best friend is over the moon at the prospect of Killian and me becoming an item. Whatever. I can just play along for tonight. Even if I had the slightest interest in Killian beyond potentially being a fantastic fuck, which I don't, he lives almost two hours from me. And even if there was something going on, which there isn't, I don't see either of us uprooting our lives to move for the other.

"This is so exciting." Tilly beams before looking me over. "Don't worry, you'll do great."

"Calm down, Tilly. We're just grabbing some dinner with Moira," I remind her. Again. Cassie hasn't had much time with her best friend since the move, and this seemed like the perfect opportunity for them to catch up, while the Twin Cities native tortured me with her brother's presence—or so I assumed.

"Yes, but you haven't seen him since the wedding. Oh!" she squeals. "I can see it now. We enter. There is this cosmic shift in the atmosphere. He looks up and sees you from across the smokey bar. He's felt this loss since the wedding, but he wasn't sure why. Then like a punch to the gut, he figures out *you're* what's missing. As you lock eyes, you both realize you're madly in love with each other and can't live another moment apart. He tosses down whatever rag he was using to wipe the bar, storms across the room, scoops you up, and throws you onto the bar."

"*Oh my god,* Tilly!" I yell, interrupting her. "Take a break from the romance section, okay?"

"Sorry." She blushes. "You don't know how hard it was to be so horny for the last month of my pregnancy and too fat to do anything about it. Now I've got to wait two more months before I can get any relief."

"Seriously? None?" Cassie asks nervously.

"Well, not the satisfaction I want." Tilly gives a mischievous grin.

"That doesn't happen to everyone, right?" Cassie looks petrified by the concept of not being able to take dick for a while.

"As fun as it is to listen to the difficulties of sex and pregnancy, I'm starving. So, can we talk about your unusable vaginas on the way home?" *After I've had a few cocktails*, I grumble internally.

"Oh, I forgot. How dare we keep you from your *boyfriend*?" Tilly mocks.

I roll my eyes before getting out of the back seat, not even dignifying her with a response. Entering the bar, with Cassie and Tilly not far behind, I take in the atmosphere. I won't lie. It's impressive. Nothing like the places I've been to in the cities before. Most of them are trendy joints with music so loud you leave with a pounding headache. The drinks are overpriced and watered down. Surprisingly, this is one of those bars where you can sit down and relax after a long day. He even worked in space for a small dance floor and a karaoke machine.

"Impressive, aye?" A deep voice whispers in my ear. The hairs on the back of my neck stand up with his sudden proximity.

"Color me surprised." I shrug. "Granted, all the fighting memorabilia is a bit tacky for my taste." I turn, giving Killian a teasing grin.

Taking a step closer, he smiles down at me. "Miss me?" His tone is laced with seductive qualities that I'm sure melt the panties off several women in our vicinity.

"No, we were up here shopping." I glance over my shoulder to Cassie. She's talking to a girl with big curly hair and a blonde, both of whom are going nuts over her baby bump. "Your sister wanted to stop in and say hi."

Killian's smile brightens as he looks past me. "Cassie," he yells before interrupting her conversation and giving her a big hug. Holding her shoulders, he looks down at her larger belly. "This is new."

"Hi, Kill." She blushes.

"Cassie!" Moira calls out, running across the bar, and wedges herself in front of Killian to get a hug. "You look amazing."

"Hi, Moira." Cassie squeezes her extra tight. "I miss you." Cassie sniffles and wipes away a tear. "Sorry, hormones. I cry at everything now."

"Aw, it's okay, hun. Come on, I got us one of the comfy booth tables. I'm dying to hear all the details about your stay-cation honeymoon." Moira waggles her eyebrows.

"Well, that's my cue to leave." Killian leans back on his heels.

"No, Kill, stay. Have dinner with us," Tilly pleads. "No offense, Cassie. I really don't want to hear about you and my brother having sex. Obviously, I know you two are doing it." She gestures towards her sister-in-law's stomach. "But I really don't want the details. I did enough vomiting during my pregnancy, thank you very much."

Cassie and Moira both roll their eyes. "Fine, we'll talk about that later." Cassie motions to Moira. As we get to the table, Tilly makes a big fuss about the seating arrangement, ensuring I sit next to Killian. And when we place our orders, Tilly can't stop giving us a big dopey smile.

"Is it just me, or is there something wrong with your friend?" Killian leans over, whispering so only I can hear.

He brings his glass to his lips. I suppress my giggle before I whisper back, "Cassie might have given her the impression there is something going on between us. Now Tilly is on a mission to have me hitched and pregnant by the end of the month. Congratulations, Daddy."

Killian spits out his drink and wipes his mouth. I laugh at him, gaining the attention of a few nearby tables. I hand him a napkin. He plays it cool, but the panic is written all over his face.

"Anything you'd like to share with the class?" Tilly leans forward on her elbows, her face in her hands. She gives us both a dreamy smile. Moira looks at Tilly, then back at Cassie.

"Would you excuse us a moment, ladies?" I say suggestively before pushing Killian out of the booth. "Perhaps we can talk somewhere a little more *private.*" I run my finger down his chest.

He quickly regains his composure and gives them a smile before leading me to his office by the small of my back. Once the door is closed behind us, I let out a relieved breath and collapse into the chair.

"What the hell was that?" Killian gestures towards the dining area.

"*That* was your sister's fault." I throw Cassie under the bus in a heartbeat.

"I don't get it. Why is Cassie trying to hook us up?" He rubs his forehead, likely confused by the situation.

"She's not," I inform him.

"Okay, I really need some context here." Killian sits on the edge of the desk with his arms and ankles crossed, studying me intently. "Because despite my best efforts at the wedding, nothing happened."

I roll my eyes. He definitely brought his A-game that night, and as tempting as he is, I couldn't seem to go through with it. It most certainly wasn't because Jake's look of betrayal kept flashing in my mind. Nope, it was because a one-night stand with your friend's brother, even if he's as much of a player as you are, is a bad idea.

"I might not have clarified that to Cassie."

"Details please. Not that I have a problem with saying we hooked up, because, well, look at you." Killian gestures down the length of my body. "But if I'm getting pulled into some ploy without the implied satisfaction, I'd at least like to know why."

"This stays between us." I eye Killian carefully, and he nods in agreement. "Cassie is under the ridiculous and completely unfounded impression that I have a thing for Jake. So, for whatever reason, she is punishing me by having Tilly think wedding bells are in *our* future. I don't understand what she's trying to prove. Apparently, when your friends get married and start spitting out babies, they feel the need to bring you down with them." I sigh. "Sorry, Killian, I should have clarified that nothing happened. I didn't mean to drag you into this mess. It's seriously been a shitty week: I was almost killed by a tornado, found naked in my shower, and rescued by the one person I can't stand. My apartment and all my possessions are gone. Even the bar is shut down. To top it off, I'm stuck living with the same asshole who rescued me because I have nowhere else to go." I press my lips tightly closed as I realize I just unloaded on him—with way more information than he probably cares to know.

Killian whistles before taking a seat next to me. "That definitely sounds like a fucked-up week." He straightens his posture abruptly. "Wait, your bar was destroyed?"

"I don't know the full extent of the damage. Most of it seemed to be upstairs. Tomorrow, I'm supposed to meet with the owner and inspectors to see what we need to do to reopen. But from the little I saw yesterday, it won't be simple."

"That sucks. I'm sorry," he replies genuinely.

"Thanks." I pick fake lint off my shirt as we sit in awkward silence.

"So," Killian says with a long pause. "What's your plan, exactly?"

I shrug. "Not sure. I guess... take it one day at a time."

He laughs and leans toward me. "I'm talking about us. Since we are madly in love and so hot for each other that we had to run off to my office to have wild sex during the middle of dinner with our friends and family. Should we announce our engagement? Are you already with child? I'd like to know the plan before I accidentally make a fool of myself."

I punch Killian in his chest. Hard. "*We* are not madly in love or having wild sex."

"*We* could be," he whispers in my ear.

"But we won't be." I have to shut this down before it gets out of control. Letting Tilly believe something is one thing. I'm not about to start flat-out lying to her. So far, I just haven't clarified what happened and allowed her to believe Cassie's speculation. It's a thin line I'm walking, but I'm still on the side of honesty. And as much fun as I'm sure Killian and I could have, that's not a headache I'm interested in dealing with. If he wasn't Cassie's brother and forever entwined in my life, and instead just some random guy who lives far from town (my usual MO), I'd probably let him scratch that itch.

"Back to my original question. What's the plan? I don't really get how or why you are even pretending something happened."

Neither do I. "It's complicated," I huff out.

"Uncomplicate it for me then."

"Like I said, Cassie thinks I have a thing for Jake."

"Ah, I see." Killian leans back and drapes an arm over my shoulder.

"See what?"

His eyes darken. "This is all about making the firefighter jealous."

"This has nothing to do with Jake," I spit at the ridiculous notion. Seriously, what's with the Murphy clan and their gross misreading of people's feelings towards others?

"No?" Killian raises an eyebrow, the one with the scar running through it. "Other than giving your friend false hope that we're about to join her in wedded bliss, the only thing this petty act is going to do is get Jake's tighty-whities in a bunch. Which, based on your little performance at the wedding, shouldn't be much of an issue. He's probably sulking in a dark corner at home right now, at just the thought of you and me together."

Insulted, I stand up and cross my arms. "I'm not attempting to make Jake *jealous*. He'd have to give a flying fuck first. And, news flash, he doesn't." *Not that I blame him.*

"Really? Because what I saw at the wedding was one pissed-off looking bloke. And not just because he lost some stupid bet. But because the prize he truly wanted walked away with someone else."

"Really?" I ask, stunned, then shake my head. Nope, not falling back down that rabbit hole. "Doesn't matter. Once again, I'm sorry for dragging you into this mess. I'll get everything cleared up, and you can continue banging your jolly way through the Twin Cities."

I walk towards the door. Killian grabs my arm, stopping me. "Wait."

I look down at his large hand wrapped around my bicep. His inked knuckles read: *KILL.* "What?"

"This could be fun?" He gives me an evil grin.

"What's in it for you?" I ask him skeptically.

"Besides an excuse to be close to you?" He presses me against the door. "I like the idea of knocking the little firefighter down a peg or two."

"What did he ever do to you?" I ask breathlessly, suddenly feeling as though the thermostat was turned up a thousand degrees.

"Why does their need to be an ulterior motive? I'm competitive by nature, and so is he. There are many ways we could attempt to outdo each other. This just happens to be the most fun so far."

"Quit the bullshit," I demand.

"No BS. We're just a couple of roosters duking it out in the ring."

"You realize that, essentially, you just admitted to being fighting cocks?"

He shrugs. Either the man is *that* simple, or he really doesn't care. Neither of which would surprise me. "So, what do you say we seal the deal with a kiss?" Killian suggests, his eyes trained on my lips.

I consider the proposition for a moment. For whatever reason, when he and Jake are in a room together, they seem to need to hold some sort of dick-measuring contest. I glance down at Killian's groin.

Great job, Letty. Now you're wondering how big he is, and who the winner would be.

I bite my lip as I look up into his bright-blue eyes. He's hot, unfairly so. This could solve two birds with one stone. It's been a while, and Killian seems like the kind of guy who could fuck me stupid and not catch feelings afterwards. They always talk about females and their inability to separate sex and emotions. Clearly, *they* haven't met the men of Tral Lake. Every blowjob comes with a marriage proposal. It makes it impossible to have no-strings-attached fun, especially when I would risk losing business.

I let out a sigh as I shake my head. "Sorry, Killian. As appealing as your offer might be, it's unnecessary. Jake is nothing but a pain in my side, has been and always will be. I'm not attempting to make him jealous, because he doesn't care about me. This little charade would result in nothing but getting Tilly's hopes up before crushing them."

"Sleep on it." He studies me for a moment, then leans in and whispers in my ear, "Whether you're looking to make the firefighter jealous or not is irrelevant. I can sense your need. It's written all over your beautifully bruised face and tense shoulders. You need a release, and I'm more than obliged to give it to you—multiple times." Killian pauses a moment, letting his implication sink in. "I promise you this: when I finally get the chance to mount you, the last thing you'll be thinking about is tapping out."

With that, he pushes back, giving me enough space to exit the office.

8

Jake

THE THUD OF THE front door opening and closing startles me. It takes a minute for me to get my bearings and my eyes to adjust to the darkness. But based on my stiff neck and aching lower back, I must've fallen asleep on the couch. Looking up, I see Letty sneaking in like a teenager out past curfew, trying not to wake Mommy and Daddy. A wise man would continue to lie here and pretend to be asleep. There is no reason we should interact. It always ends badly. It's late and I'm already in a mood—worsened by being woken up.

"Late night?" Of course, I couldn't keep my stupid mouth shut. Whatever. The damage is done. Let's hope we can finish it without one of us ending up in a body bag.

Letty gasps and places a hand on her chest, her eyes wide like a deer caught in a set of headlights. "What the fuck, Jake? You scared the piss out of me." She crosses her arms, pushing up her already amazing cleavage. I wonder why she even bothered to wear a shirt. It's so tight and low-cut I can see the top half of her breasts, and it's one of those shirts that stops right above her belly button, revealing her flat stomach. "What are you doing sitting alone in the dark?"

I shift upright and stretch my neck. "What? I'm not allowed to sleep on my couch?"

"No," Letty exhales. "That's not what I meant." She pauses and shakes her head after a moment of consideration. The defiance burning in her eyes extinguishes as she drops her shoulders. "You know what? Never mind. I've had a long day—no, *week*—and I just want to get to bed." Without another word, Letty storms into the kitchen. Bottles rattle in the fridge before the door slams shut. I stand quickly and make my way to the staircase but, somehow, end up running smack-dab into the exact person I was trying to avoid. "Excuse you," she sneers with one of *my* beers in her delicate hand.

"You're the one not paying attention to where you're going," I retort. Letty's eyes narrow at me. I snatch the bottle from her hand and take a swig, despite her protests. "Enjoy the visit with your *boyfriend*?" I hiss. I can smell the distinct odor of Irish Spring and douche all over her. My eyes roam over her bare neck, inspecting for love bites. Any marks showing me he's had her.

"What do you care, Jakey?" Letty's flared nostrils are the only sign I've struck a nerve. Interesting. "Look, I wouldn't be here if I had any other choice. So how about I don't ask where you stick your dick, and you don't ask about what dick is sticking me? Deal?"

Something about Letty's implication has my blood boiling. Before I can comprehend what's happened, I pin her to the wall. Her brown pools stare up at me, wide, as her chest presses against mine. "I don't like that arrangement," I whisper, and her body shivers beneath me.

"What? I'm not allowed to *fuck* anyone while I live under your roof? That seems a bit hypocritical." Letty's chest rises and falls quickly.

"I didn't say that." Some demon must have possessed my body. Because the next thing I know, I smell the curve of her neck. I smile at the familiar scent of cherry blossoms. She must have purchased new body spray at the mall. I wonder what else she purchased from Victoria's Secret...

"Then what do you want, Jake?" she retorts. This close, I feel her squeeze her thighs together. *Well, if she got some, she didn't get enough.* I knew that over-the-hill leprechaun was all talk.

I move so that I'm nose to nose with her, Letty's breath tickling my lips. She closes her eyes, preparing herself. I stop to think for a moment.

What do I want? What the hell am I doing?

Shaking my head, I let go of her wrist and take a step back. When she looks at me, I don't miss the hint of disappointment. "Sorry, I'm half-asleep and had a shit day. Clearly, I'm not thinking straight. I'm going to bed." I hand Letty back her beer.

"Do you want to talk about it?" She surprises me with the question.

With a hand on the railing, I stop and take a deep breath. "No, it's nothing for you to worry about. Goodnight, Tee." I quicken my pace up the stairs and escape to my room. To avoid another mistake, I lock the door, lie on my bed, and close my eyes.

How is it after everything she's done, she still gets under my skin?

I should want nothing to do with her. But whenever she's around, my mind always drifts back to that night.

"Letty, wait up," I yell at her retreating form, out of breath. This stupid monkey suit doesn't make running easy. I'm still trying to figure out how she's moving so fast in those death contraptions she calls heels.

"What, Jake?" Letty stops. Turning around, she cocks her hip to the side and gives me a pointed stare. "As if this night hasn't been crap-tastic enough, I'm now stuck with

you," she sneers. *"I'd just like to go home, crawl under my covers, and pretend none of this ever happened."*

"It hasn't been that bad, has it?"

She rolls her eyes. "Are you blind? Did you not witness the train wreck that just happened? My date to senior prom was using me to get to my best friend. This isn't how my night was supposed to go."

I approach Letty cautiously; I've never seen her so dejected before. "Were you really into that douche? I never pictured him as your type."

"I can't talk about this with you." She turns to walk away. I quickly grab her arm, pulling her back to me. As she looks up at me with those rich brown eyes, I wonder if those golden flecks had always been there. How have I never noticed them before?

"You can talk to me," I protest. Typically, she's the last person I'd ever want to interact with. But I can't seem to let her leave.

She shrugs from my grasp and takes a step back. "How long have we known each other, Jakey? We can hardly stand to be in the same room together. The only reason we tolerate one another is for Tilly's sake. But other than that, we aren't friends. We have nothing in common. I think this is probably the longest conversation you and I have ever had. I'm not about to open up to you. Standing on the sidewalk. In the middle of the night. Wearing this ridiculous dress I couldn't afford in the first place. In front of the high school where I no doubt am going to be the talk of the halls come Monday. I'm tired, drunk, and just want to go home. Wake up tomorrow and pretend like none of this happened."

"At least let me walk you home?" Tral Lake is a safe town. But her house is a couple of miles away. If she falls and hurts herself, it'll be my fault and Tilly won't let me hear the end of it.

"I'm a big girl, Jake. I can handle myself. Goodnight."

"Come on, I need help finishing the champagne." I hold up the bottle Jax left for us before he and Tilly drove away in the limo Letty's dipshit date rented. They offered to drop us off back at home, but I could tell they were eager to get going. Besides, I didn't feel like ending my evening just yet. A benefit of small-town living: it isn't too far to walk anywhere.

"Fine." Letty snatches the bottle from me. "Just walking, no talking." She turns on her heel and stalks away, taking a big swig from the bottle as her hips sway. "I wish Jax snagged the hard stuff."

"Like these?" I pull two tiny bottles from my pocket. "I took them from the mini-fridge in the limo as one more fuck you to Keith."

"Genius." Letty reaches for one, and I pull my hand back and shake my head.

"Nope," I tease. "Not until you tell me what's really bothering you."

She frowns. "You wouldn't understand, Jake."

"Come on. Try me. What do you have to lose?"

"My dignity," she retorts.

I place my hand over my heart. "You pain me. I promise no judgement."

"Fine," she sighs.

"Let's take the trail. I'd prefer not to get busted by Lafferty tonight." Once on the wooded path behind the school, I trade Letty the champagne for a couple of small bottles of vodka. "Now, spill. What's got poor Letty so down and blue?"

Her eyes narrow into slits. "Good one. Why not call me trailer trash while you're at it? Come on, don't hold back."

"What the fuck are you talking about?" I'm not sure if she makes zero sense because I'm drunk or she is. Maybe both. One second, we've come to an agreement. And the next, she's got her claws out.

She downs one of the shots and wipes the remnants from her lips. "Never mind, forget about it."

I grip her arm before she can take off. "Seriously, what's going on? Don't tell me your panties are in that much of a bunch over a douche like McCalester."

"What makes you think I'm wearing panties?" She gives me an evil smile before drinking the second bottle. The thought of Letty not wearing underwear, to my surprise, has me adjusting myself. Unfortunately, she notices and rolls her eyes. "Really? Does my misery turn you on?"

"No." I let out a sad chuckle. "But now I can't seem to get the visual out of my mind."

"You're the worst." She playfully hits my chest before taking a seat on a downed tree in the little clearing us kids sometimes hang out at after school, mostly to smoke pot. "You really want to know what's bothering me? Ugh... I must be pretty drunk if I'm about to talk to you." Letty rubs a frustrated hand over her face, smearing a bit of the heavy eyeliner she's wearing. "I just really don't think you understand what it's like to be me..."

As if almost seeing her for the first time, I look at Letty—really look at her. Unlike the other girls all wearing formal gowns tonight, while attempting to look like small-town royalty, Letty appears ready for the nightclub in a tight, hot-pink, glittery, strapless dress that shows off the amazing flare of her hips and tiny waist. The fabric rides high enough that if I tilted my head just right, I could probably verify the validity of her panties comment.

"You don't look bad from where I'm sitting."

"Come on, Jake. I'm trying to be serious here," she huffs out. "That's what I mean by not understanding. Your life is perfect."

Her comment pulls me out of the daze her breasts have me under. Have they always been that perky? "My life isn't perfect."

"Please." She rolls her eyes again. "You're fucking Jacob Moore. Tral Lake's hottest senior. You have a million friends. People lining up to be close to you—however they can. I'm just Leticia Ruiz Frost, the girl from the wrong side of the tracks, in a town without a train."

"That's not true." My stomach feels uneasy with the knowledge of how little she thinks of herself.

"It is. The only reason anyone even talks to me is because of Tilly. If we weren't friends, no one would even associate with me. I thought tonight was finally my night to be in the spotlight. Step out from my best friend's shadow. For Christ's sake, Keith McCalester, the popular rich boy, asked ME to prom. Not Tilly, or one of the cheerleaders. Me. I've never been asked out before."

"Really?"

Her admission shocks me. She's stunning. Based on all the locker room chatter, I assumed she had a line around the block waiting to take her out. Hell, the other month I beat some guy's ass for the things he said he wanted to do to her. Why? I'm not exactly sure. But at the time, whatever he said was really pissing me off.

"Yeah, people look at me and all they see is the daughter of the town's drunken fool. I've had more conversations with the guys at Harper's than I've ever had with anyone at school." Letty lets out a sad chuckle. "Now, instead of being in some swanky hotel in the cities—losing my virginity like Tilly and half the other girls in this town—I'm stuck here. In the woods. Getting drunk. With you."

"Sorry." Though I'm not sure what for. Honestly, I'm glad she is here with me and not getting poked by that needle dick. Or some other asshat from our class. Letty might be the bane of my existence, but no girl, including her, deserves some two-pump chump.

She sighs. "There is nothing for you to be sorry about. It's just how things are. And what's worse? In a few months, Tilly is going to go off to college and leave me behind. I'm sure she and Jax will get some apartment near campus, so he can be with her while she's in school. By the time they return, she will have a ring on her finger and a bun in the oven—living their fucking picture-perfect life. All the while, I'll be stuck here. Alone."

"I'll be here."

"Yeah, exactly. I'll be alone," Letty scoffs.

I get up, a fire burning in my gut, and look down at her. "You know, my life isn't as perfect as you think it is."

She stands in her heels. But I still have a good five inches on her. "Jake, I've known you practically our whole lives. Your life is one step short of a fucking Hallmark movie. I'm certain when they need inspiration for their next heartfelt family series, they just follow the Moores around."

"No, Letty, you're the one who doesn't understand what it's like for me. Yeah, sure, you're right. I have a pretty fucking awesome family, with loving parents and close siblings. But it sucks when everyone is as damn near perfect as people like you seem to think, and you're the odd man out."

Letty pinches her brows. "What are you talking about?"

"Yeah. That's right. I'm not super athletic or a master mechanic, like Robbie. I can't cook like Scott. I'm not obsessed with books or running the shop. I have no plans for the future. No colleges lined up. I have no idea what I'm going to do in a few weeks when they hand me the diploma I earned by the skin of my teeth. You don't know what it's like to be the stupid twin, with a valedictorian sister."

"You're not stupid," Letty whispers. Her voice causes this weird fluttering in my chest. I feel exposed. As though she can see me down to my core.

"I've got nothing, Letty. My good looks and charm will only take me so far in life. Just like you, in a few months, I'm going to be left behind by all my so-called friends. Maybe I'm the hottest senior right now. But I've peaked. This is the best my life is ever going to get, and I've been enjoying every second of it before it's all over."

Letty pulls my face to hers and presses her mouth to mine. Her lips are soft and taste of champagne. Without hesitation, I deepen our connection. Holy shit, I'm kissing Letty. And I don't hate it. I actually kind of like it. Painfully so. Letty's hands work to remove my pants. With the restraint of a saint, I pull back, my hard-on screaming at me to come out and play.

"Wait." Tears well up in her eyes—she thinks I'm rejecting her. I guess I am, but not for the reason she thinks. "This isn't right."

"Fuck you, Jake." She turns around and stomps away. I grab her before she can make it two steps, pull her close to me, and press a light kiss to her mouth.

"Shit, I'm saying this all wrong," I confess, tucking her under my chin as I hold her close. "It's not that I don't want to. Because I really do." I press my erection into her stomach, showing her just how much that's true. "But you're upset, and you've been drinking. The last thing I want is for you to wake up tomorrow and regret it."

She sighs, hugging me tighter. "You're right."

I stiffen at her comment—and I don't mean my dick this time.

Of course, she doesn't want this, not with me. Why would she? Letty might not see it, but the girls in this town don't hold a fucking candle to her. They all run around looking like carbon copies of each other. Dressing and talking the same. Letty walks to the beat *of her own unapologetic drum. I hate that I've spent all this time hating her for something as stupid as being best friends with my sister and taking her attention away from me. If I didn't have my head so far up my ass, I would have seen this amazing woman before me. But now there is too much bad blood... She'll only ever see me as Tilly's asshole twin, who has taken pleasure in making her miserable since the day we met.*

I take a step back, immediately feeling cold without her body pressed to mine. "Come on, let's get you home."

"Jake." Letty glows in the moonlight as she looks up at me, her eyes wide. "I meant you're right. I'd regret losing my virginity fumbling and drunk in the woods. I'd probably end up with a tick in my vag and mosquito bites on my ass." She steps forward, taking my hand in hers. "But I wouldn't regret it being with you, which is insane, considering our history. For some unexplained reason, you and I sound right."

I kiss her again, hard, showing her how much I agree. With my tongue. Letty deserves something special. The fancy hotel, candles, flowers, and chocolate. And I'm going to be the one to give her that. Just not tonight.

"Come on, Tee." I drape my arm over her shoulder and escort her home, while planning the most amazing night—something she'll never forget.

9

Letty

"WHAT ARE YOU DOING here?" Scott asks as he opens the doors to the café. "I don't think I've ever known you to be awake this early. Unless you stayed up all night?" He taps his chin in contemplation. "That would make more sense."

"Something like that." I'm not about to admit that I stayed up all night, beating my head against the wall because (like an idiot) I was going to let Jake kiss me. Worse? I wanted him to. My heart was racing as I sat there, stupidly waiting and hoping he'd change his mind. Storm into the room and apologize for being a moron. After a couple of hours, it was clear *that* wasn't going to happen. Shame settled in, and I spent the rest of the night chastising myself for even fantasizing about his lips on mine. Over a decade has passed, and even now—if I think about it—I can still feel a phantom tingle from back then.

"I understand."

I look at Scott with a quizzical brow. My pulse quickens at the fear he somehow knows. It makes no sense. But illogically, I panic.

"I get my best ideas for the expansion or a new recipe whenever I lay my head down. So instead of sleeping, I end up sketching out plans and getting everything on paper before it's gone."

Oh, thank God! He thinks I'm talking about the bar. "Yeah, exactly. I'm eager to begin work on Harper's. Make it operational as soon as possible. Figured I should get an early start on the day."

"Technically, we don't even open for another hour." Scott rubs the scruff on his jaw. "But, fortunately for you, I have an in with the owner." He winks at me.

"Thanks, Scott. I appreciate it." I considered taking Tilly up on her offer. Even with the screaming babies, I think I'd get more sleep than I would staying in that house with *him*. But then I would have that whole transportation issue again. No, my best option is to get the bar up and running. I will sleep in the office if necessary until the apartment is livable.

"The usual?" he asks, then verifies, "Nitro Death cold brew and a banana nut muffin?"

"Thanks." I smile, taking a seat at the counter.

"So, living with Jake's that bad?" Scott says absentmindedly while gathering my order.

"Nope, everything is peachy. I think we're going to make bracelets this afternoon that say *BFFs.*" I smirk before taking a sip of the iced goodness he hands me.

"Hopefully, this time off does him some good." Scott begins setting up for the morning rush.

"Time off?" I query.

"Oh, I figured he would have already told you. I guess they used his injuries as an excuse to twist his arm into finally taking some of that vacation time he's built up."

That explains why he was so pissy with me. Of course, the asshole would have to hurt himself while rescuing *me*. "That sucks. I'd assumed he would do desk duty or something. But, hey, a couple of weeks off isn't the end of the world."

"Try telling him that." Scott rolls his eyes. "Honestly, I'm glad they made him. I only wish it was for longer."

"Really?" Even though I'm curious, I attempt to act disinterested while I pick at my muffin.

"Yeah, he didn't really take any time off after the accident and what he did was spent here."

"Did any of you?" I counter.

"Touché." Scott sighs and flips the towel he was using to wipe down the counter over his shoulder. He crosses his arms over his chest. "It's probably why I didn't press him. Working through grief seems to be an inherited Moore trait. But Jake overworking himself at the firehouse differs from me putting in too many hours at the café. He's going to get himself seriously injured, or worse. I know you guys aren't exactly friendly, but come on, Letty. Don't tell me you haven't noticed?"

"Not really," I lie. At first, it felt like Jake was in the bar almost every night if he wasn't on duty. He's never been shy about picking up girls before, except it seemed different. Usually, he was all carefree and fun. But then, his game seemed more desperate—like a distraction. That all changed when Cassie moved in. It was why I'd assumed they were hooking up. My jaw about hit the floor when she said she was pregnant, with Robbie's baby no less. After everything was clarified, I figured he must have tapped Harper's dry and moved on to one of the surrounding bars, in search of new prey.

"Sure." Scott draws the word out sarcastically.

"What's that supposed to mean?"

"Nothing." He gives me a suspicious look. "So, you and Killian?" He quirks a brow at me.

I groan. Tilly and her big mouth—no doubt with Cassie's help. I plaster on my best smile. "You and Courtney?"

Scott shrugs. "Eh, not really my type."

"No?" I tease. "She seemed like your type when you guys were mauling each other at the wedding."

"It didn't go much farther than that." Scott shrugs again.

"What? Did she have garlic breath or something? That seems a little shallow for you."

Scott laughs before he grabs the rag from his shoulder and throws it at me. "No, she started calling me *Daddy*." He visibly shivers at the thought. "It really weirded me out. It was an immediate boner killer."

"That's cringy." I scrunch my nose at the idea. "Never got the whole daddy kink thing. But, hey, to each their own." Any thought of my father in association with sex would dry me up like the Sahara. I'm certain if someone wanted to psychoanalyze me, they'd say I have "daddy issues." And they'd probably be right. But my *issues* have never manifested in that way. Instead, I do things despite him. To prove to myself (and others) that his DNA doesn't determine my destiny. I'm stronger than him.

"Yeah. Dating's hard." Scott sighs.

"Then why do it?"

I study him for a moment. It's surprising no one has snatched him up. If I had any interest in the white-picket fantasy, I'd probably be first in line. He makes a killer cup of coffee and knows how to cook. Obviously, he is ridiculously handsome—all the Moores are unnaturally attractive. Except, much like Tilly, I don't think Scott even realizes it. Or he just doesn't care. His hair is always disheveled like he just got out of bed, and he has that constant five-o'clock shadow. Not to mention, those super sexy forearm tattoos.

Stop it, Letty. Ugh, maybe I should take Killian up on his offer. Clearly, I'm horny and at risk of making bad choices. Sleeping with Scott would be a terrible idea. He is definitely the type who'd expect the total package. The only thing worse than sleeping with him would be to jump in Jake's bed. While Jake is definitely Mr. No-Strings-Attached, I'd have zero self-respect afterwards.

Scott considers my question for a moment. "I just think I'm ready to settle down. I see how happy Tilly and Jax are.

Now Robbie and Cassie too. I never imagined him getting remarried after Bianca. This chapter has been enjoyable. But I'm ready for the next one."

Told you! Scott is the kind of guy with happily ever after written in those emerald eyes.

"Nice analogy." I point to the sign for Moore Books and Coffee.

"What about you? Is Killian the one?" Scott smirks, knowing very well there will never be *the one*.

"Killian is nothing. That whole situation has gotten blown way out of proportion. All I did was give him my number and a peck on the lips, without enough pressure to be an actual kiss."

"Ahh, that explains it."

"Explains what?" I ask, tilting my head.

"Why Jake flipped when he heard you were seeing Killian last night. Robbie made it sound like wedding bells were around the corner. But I see it's just your normal song and dance. You get under his skin and remind my brother that there is at least one girl in this town who will never sleep with him." The statement catches me off-guard, and I choke on my coffee. Clearing my throat, I hit my chest. "Interesting," Scott says, studying me. "When did *that* happen? Not recently."

"Drop it, Scott." I stand, pulling my bag over my shoulder.

"So, it's not that you're the girl he can't have. It's because you're the one who got away?"

"The coffee tastes burnt. You should really clean your pots." I'm lying. His coffee is always delicious. I don't know what he does that is so special.

Scott shakes his head. "Don't attack my brew because I figured out your dirty little secret. Besides, it's cold brew—no heat."

"Well, Ted should be here soon. It was nice chatting with you." I turn and walk out.

"Letty," Scott hollers while my hands are on the door. I glance over my shoulder and give him my best smile. "You're secret's safe with me."

"I have no idea what you're talking about."

After waiting three hours out front of Harper's, I sigh when Ted and the health inspector finally show up. Together, we walk around and I take in the damage downstairs. It's bad. Not as disastrous as upstairs, but this will take a lot more than an afternoon of elbow grease to fix.

As the inspector gives us the laundry list of things we need to clean or repair before we can reopen, my eyes glaze over. There is so much to do. The biggest concerns are the water damage and food safety. We're going to need to replace the cooler and get new deep fryers—probably a new oven too. It wasn't damaged, but as the inspector looked it over, he noted a bunch more concerns about grease buildup and poor wiring. We don't have the funds to do anything on our own, and we will need the insurance check. *Shit,* it might be weeks or months before we can reopen. Without the revenue, there is no way I'm going to make the payments.

"If we cleaned up out here and could wash dishes, would we be allowed to open for limited service?" I ask, getting an idea. We draw in a large percent of the income from food, but making a portion off booze is better than nothing.

The inspector looks over his paperwork and makes a few notes. "I think that could work. I would need to do a follow-up inspection and verify that the proper measures were taken. But if you limit your employees to the bar area and kitchen to wash dishes, that should be fine."

"Thank you," I say, smiling and shaking his hand. I'm grateful for the small win. "Hey, so people can still eat in here. We just can't cook anything, right?"

"Essentially, once the debris is cleaned out, the bar area is safe to consume food and beverages. You wouldn't be clear for any perishable food storage or food preparation."

"So, we could have chips and things like that? Or a food truck out front?"

"Yes, as long as they are licensed, and your establishment is okay with individuals consuming food purchased outside the premises, there is nothing preventing you from doing that. It's what a lot of the wineries and distilleries do. You'll need nothing more than a hand-washing station, and everything must be disposable."

"That's good to know." I immediately start planning in my head. I have worked my ass off at this place. It's almost one-hundred percent mine. There's no way I'm losing her now. "If I haul ass, do you think we could be reopened by the Fourth? It's one of our biggest days, between here and running the beer garden."

The inspector types some information into his tablet before mumbling to himself. After a moment, he runs out to his state vehicle, then returns with papers in his hand. "Here's my report. I highlighted the items that need to be addressed in order to open the bar area. The best I can do is come back on Tuesday the second, at one—for the walkthrough. Sound good?"

It's gonna have to be. That gives me less than two weeks to get the bar ready for inspection, resupply our alcohol (we lost a lot in the storm), and negotiate a contract with a food truck.

"Yes," I say, shaking his hand and taking the report. I go over the list as Ted escorts the man outside.

"How're you holding up, kid?" Ted asks, leaning on the bar next to me.

"Good. Nothing I can't handle."

"Smart thinking on your part. I was doing the math and felt like I was being crushed by dollar signs. Unless you got a hidden piggy bank, you know we won't be able to repair the kitchen until the insurance claim goes through, right? It could be months."

Ted eyes me, and I shoot him a reassuring smile. "I know. Tilly will need to take a second glance. But I'm certain the booze sales will sustain us enough. Probably won't make a profit, but we'll be able to keep things going while waiting on the insurance."

He pauses. "Are you sure, kid? Maybe this is a sign."

"A sign of what?" I ask, baffled.

"That it's time to move on." Ted sighs, looking around at the broken-down establishment. This place has always been his pride and joy. I can't imagine how much it hurts him to see it like this.

"No," I plead. "I know this is a setback, but don't sell it on me."

"Are you sure, Letty? I could give you back the down payment—hell, I'd give you a cut of the profits from the sale if you wanted."

"This is my home," I assure him. "It's my dream to own this place. I can't imagine doing anything else."

"I never understood why you wanted to work here. If I were you, I'd hate this place with a passion..." Ted shakes his head. "I'd probably purchase it just to burn it down and piss on the ashes."

I swallow the bile his words raise in my throat. He's right. In a way, I hate this place. But it's also my home. "These drunk assholes are my family. Someone needs to look after them."

Ted runs a frustrated hand over his face. "I knew giving you a job here to pay off your daddy's tab was a bad idea."

"No, Ted, it was the kindest thing anyone has ever done for me." My hand rests on his arm. "I mean it. Without you and this bar, I'd be lost. Please don't sell it on me." My pride would usually prevent me from such a blatant plea. However, I refuse to be embarrassed. "It isn't about the money. If you need to, use what I gave you for the repairs. I will just pay the mortgage longer or work on getting a loan."

There is nothing else for me to do in this town. Sure, I could get some minimum-wage job at one of the other shops. But it would be nothing like running this place. I'm in charge here. In control. Despite having several shitty memories of scraping my dad off the dirty floor and dragging him out of here kicking and screaming, I have three times as many happy ones to replace them.

Like my twenty-first birthday when I could officially drink (not that I hadn't been already). Ted and the guys threw me a huge bash. Decorated the place with hot-pink and black streamers and got me a three-tiered cake to match. *With sparklers.* He even coordinated with Tilly while she was away at school. He surprised me, having her show up at the last minute. Tilly said she couldn't make it because of winter finals. I had been so bummed I hadn't even planned on celebrating.

Or the time my appendix had to be taken out. Everyone chipped in and flooded my hospital room with flowers and get-well cards. This place made me more than just the daughter of the town's belligerent drunk. It made me a valued member of this community. I don't serve them. I allow them to drink in my establishment, and they know it. If they don't want to follow my rules, they can get their uptight asses out of my bar and go to the bowling alley, the VFW, or the next town over. That being said, I know *for a fact* we have the best drinks in the county. That's right. On my days off, I visit local bars and verify that we aren't slacking.

Shit, maybe Tilly was right and I do work too much.

"All right, kid, the claims adjuster should be out early next week. Before we do any clean up, take pictures of everything to show them."

"Thank you," I say, placing a kiss on Ted's cheek before running off to get started.

"Letty," he calls out. I turn to look at him. "Promise me one thing."

"What's that?"

"Don't make the same mistakes I did. I get what you mean about this place being like your family. It's why I'm happy to hand it down to you. But, please, don't let this be your *only* family."

"I have Tilly and those two new adorable babies." I smile.

"That's fine and all, but you deserve more than that. You deserve someone who will love you and be here to grow old with you. It'd break your mom's heart if she knew your whole life revolved around slinging drinks in this dump."

I choke back my tears at the thought of my mom and put on my brightest smile. "It's not a dump. It's home."

10

Jake

SHIFTING MY TRUCK INTO park, I groan as I gaze out at The Mill Tavern in the next town over. Not my first choice in establishments, but with Harper's out of commission, I needed somewhere to go. I haven't been out this way in a while. Hopefully, there will be something new and unfamiliar here.

It might make me sound like a pig. But my usual rotation was getting a little too attached. I make it clear upfront. It's nothing more than sex and a good time. But, unfortunately, all good things must come to an end. Either they blur the lines, or they just genuinely want something I can't give them. Yes, that's right. Jake Moore has been dumped on more than one occasion. Although my extracurricular activities might not be traditional, they are relationships nonetheless, and many have ended because the other party wanted a connection deeper than I could offer.

Not that I'm some cold-hearted dick who hits it and quits it. I go on dates, even ones that don't result in anything but heavy petting—not everything is about sex. While that part is amazing, it's also about having fun. And do you know what committed relationships aren't? *Fun.* One way or another, it eventually ends in heartache. I think that's why I love Cassie. Not that I'm *in love* with her, but I certainly admire her.

That girl has had nothing but a string of heartache attached to the belt weighing her down, yet she kept trying—looking for that happily ever after. I took one stab to the chest, and I was done. Game over. I believe in trying anything at least once, because you can't knock it until you've tried it. That, however, is one experience I have no intention of repeating.

Adjusting my hair in the mirror, I get out and lock up the truck before entering the bar. I take a glance around and see a few suitable candidates for this evening. This should be easy. I probably won't even need to do any work.

But is easy what you really want?

Tonight? Yes. As much as I love Cassie, she's a bit of a cockblock. I didn't lie to her. I don't bring girls back home. It was clear she needed a friend, which was a role I was more than happy to fill while Robbie got his shit together. Even though that happily-ever-after bullshit isn't for me, I respect her beliefs. So, on my nights off, instead of going out, I was usually with her, watching movies and what not. I was having fun, so no skin off my nose. Because at the end of the day, having fun is all I really care about. But now realizing how long it's been since I've come with something other than my hand, I worry I'm losing my touch.

I planned on picking someone up at the wedding. Cassie had been hinting at Moira needing a fun-filled night, except she had to run off with Derek *fucking* Lafferty. I can't believe he snagged my sure thing. Not that I need one, but sometimes it's nice. I mean, come on! She's a fiery hot redhead. There was no way I was going to turn her down. Then Killian had to flap his ignorant fucking mouth, which not only distracted me from my original mission of scoring, but also resulted in me losing a stupid bet.

Sure, keep telling yourself that.

Yup, it was a combination of losing the bet *and* my guaranteed hookup that has me salty. It has zero to do with Letty tipping the scales in his favor, then the fucker walking out with the grand prize.

So, she's the grand prize now?

I remind myself to shut up. The whole point of getting out tonight is releasing this built-up tension, so I don't make the stupid mistake of pinning Letty to the wall and almost kissing her again.

Do you think she still tastes sweet like bubblegum?

No, I don't. After years of frigid bitchiness, she'll taste bitter.

The bartender slides me the drink I ordered. My watch shows its 9:15. *Wonder how long this will take?* Coat off, beer in hand, I wait.

"Hi, handsome," I turn to see a blonde woman purring at me. I peek at my watch: ten minutes.

Huh, I really must be losing my touch. I flash her my trademark cocky smile, guaranteed to incinerate the most resilient of panties. "Hello, gorgeous."

She playfully pats my arm. Showing off, I flex my bicep as she squeezes it. Her eyes focus on my shirt logo. "Are you a fireman?" She looks up, batting her thick eyelashes.

"Why yes, ma'am, I'm a lieutenant with the Tral Lake Fire Department." *At least I still think I am.*

"Oh my." She fans herself. "Do you have any scars?" Leaning forward, she purposely displays her impressive cleavage. Not bad. I'm guessing D cups—real too.

"Maybe," I tease.

"Can I see them?" Her legs open slightly, the angle allowing me to see up her micro miniskirt.

"Hmm, I rarely take my clothes off for strangers." Eyebrow arched, I cock my head to the side. I'm rewarded with a glimpse of the tiny pink triangle covering her crotch. Pink has always been one of my favorite colors. Most guys fantasize about black underwear. Give me hot pink or red any day of the week.

"Harmony." She extends her manicured hand to me.

"Jake," I reply, kissing her knuckles. Lastly, I double-check for a ring. Like I said, I'm not some animal. I have no interest in poaching someone else's girl.

"Well, Jake, now that we're not strangers anymore, how about we get out of here and you can show me some of those scars?" She draws circles on my thigh with her pink-painted fingernail as she leans forward to whisper in my ear, "I got a room at the motel next door." She gives my lobe a little bite before pulling back to gage my interest.

She's a kinky one—I have a sixth sense for this sort of thing. I don't even need to have the whole "no strings" talk with her. She's a kindred spirit; she just wants a good time and a few mind-blowing orgasms.

All of my boxes are checked: sexy, confident, not looking for anything more than Mr. Right-Now, presumably single, and ready to go. She's also my favorite type of woman. Mature. Yes, she might wear an outfit meant for a twenty-year-old going to the club (not that she doesn't have the body for it) and way too much makeup, which makes her look like she's in her lower thirties rather than her forties, but I also have a knack for pinpointing a woman's age—an essential skillset for avoiding those underage hose chasers. I hate that she feels she needs to "age down" in order to attract someone. Personally, I prefer an older woman. There's none of that coy stuff. They know what they want and aren't afraid to vocalize it. Too much of their youth was already spent shy and silent. All they want is to be fucked and fucked good.

If she's so perfect, then why the hell isn't he rising to the occasion?

I give her puppy-dog eyes. "I was recently injured while rescuing someone and could really use a little tender loving care."

"Well, aren't you in luck? I happen to be a nurse and extremely qualified to kiss all your owies and make them better."

Seriously? A sexy, mature nurse and still nothing? He isn't even entertaining the idea, the traitor.

"Good thing the doctor recommended bed rest." With a smile, I stand and grab my coat. A twenty is tossed on the bar as I let her escort me outside.

We're barely around the corner before her mouth is on mine. Harmony is an absolute dream. Zero hesitation, her tongue strikes with exact precision as her lips brush against mine. It feels fantastic, but it's doing nothing for me. The only time my body responds is when I close my eyes and see giant brown pools with sparkling gold flecks looking back at me.

Why is God punishing me?

Gently, I grab Harmony by the shoulders and distance myself from her.

"Did I do something wrong?" she falters. *Damn it.* I hate making this sexy, confident woman question herself.

"No, Harmony. You are absolutely perfect. It's me."

"Seriously." She crosses her arms. "You're going to give me that lame *it's not you, it's me* line?"

"Yeah, it's probably the lamest thing I've ever fucking said. Unfortunately, it's also the truth. I'd love nothing more than to take you back to that motel room right now and fuck you so hard you won't know if you should beg me to stop or continue." Sighing, I run my fingers through my hair. "But my mind is somewhere else tonight."

She studies me for a moment before she nods in understanding. "Sounds like a lucky girl."

I laugh at the ridiculous notion. While she's technically correct—another girl is on my mind—it isn't in the way she thinks. "No, she's a fucking curse."

She looks me over once more and shrugs. "I don't mind if you think about her." She runs her nail up and down my chest. "I'm not looking for anything beyond what happens behind that door."

My gaze wanders to the motel. I consider her proposal. Desperation squeezes my insides with the need to fuck this tension out of me before I combust. But, instead of getting excited at the prospect of all the dirty things this woman will no doubt let me do to her, images of Letty flood my mind. It's like a punch in the gut. One moment, she's laughing and smiling with my family. The next, her lips are brushing against that geriatric has-been fighter's mouth. And finally, she's lying helplessly on the ground.

Why, after all this time, is she still fucking with my head?

I thought every bit of her was purged from my system. Even now, when I'm off being my best self far away from her, she ruins it. One look at Harmony—sophisticated sex wrapped in a bow—and I know I can't give her what she needs. With a groan, I shake my head. "As tempting as the offer is, I'm going to have to decline."

"Well, that's a shame." She pouts. Then, pulling a card out of her purse, she writes her number down and hands it to me. "Here. If you change your mind, call me. I live in Wisconsin. But I visit my sister in town a lot."

"Believe me, Harmony, the second I get my minor problem fixed, you'll be the first call I make." I press a light kiss on her cheek before going back home, more frustrated and worked up than I was when I started the evening.

Great. I just hope Letty isn't around. The last thing we need to do tonight is cross paths.

11

Letty

I GO OVER THE documents that Cassie told me to gather. Initially, I called Tilly to help me put together a few sets of figures. But she reminded me that numbers were Cassie's area of expertise. While I'm still a little pissed at her antics, I'm willing to put that aside for the greater good. Besides, it's really all my own doing anyway. I could have spoken up immediately and clarified that nothing happened with Killian. Instead, I clammed up, and now my best friend is on a mission to get me settled down.

Come on, Letty, pull up your big girl panties and tell Tilly the truth. She's your best friend, and will be hurt when she finds out you lied.

I've never lied to Tilly before—well, except when it comes to her brother. It makes me sick just thinking about it.

11 Years Ago
My skin slick with sweat, I collapse back on the bed, panting. I can't move a muscle. Jake leaves a trail of kisses up my stomach until he reaches my lips. His tongue

plunges into my mouth, allowing me to savor myself on him. Although my limbs are still tingling from my release and practically useless, his hard cock rubbing against my inner thigh is rekindling that desire he seems to always make burn in my core.

I've masturbated before and brought myself to what I thought was an orgasm. But a few weeks ago, when he finger-fucked me for the first time and I came so hard that the heels of my feet burned, I realized I'd been doing it all wrong. Whenever he's within a ten-foot radius, my body joneses for his touch, kiss, lick—whatever we can have. Regardless of the instrument he uses, the result is the same: earth-shattering.

That being said, and as great as this has been, each time I reach for him, ready to go to the next step, he pulls back. Just like now. My hand sneaks behind the band of his elastic shorts, and Jake looks down at me. Despite the fire burning in his gaze, the second my fingertip grazes the bulge hidden behind his briefs, he shifts away from me. "Ready to go again?"

"Always." *I pout.*

"I can never get enough of you."

"Well, maybe it's time for you to have all of me." *I broach the subject of him finally popping my cherry again. As usual, instead of saying anything, he distracts me. This time by leaning down and sucking hard on my neck. I playfully hit his chest.* "Hey, I said no hickeys."

"How will anyone know you belong to me if I don't leave my mark?"

My thighs clench as he leaves a small love bite. "Jake," *I grumble.* "We've talked about this."

He lets out a frustrated breath before turning to lie next to me. "I don't get why we have to keep this a secret. Tilly won't care. If she did, she'd be a hypocrite."

"I know." *I sigh. This can't be why he won't take things further, can it? Because I want to keep us on the down* low? "It's just... this is all still so confusing. I mean, we've known each other forever. You've always been like my annoying brother, and now we're doing... this." I gesture between us.

"Annoying brother, huh?" Jake turns back on his side and resumes placing light kisses on my throat while his finger traces a trail up and down my abdomen, teasing and getting me wetter for him.

"Yes, obnoxious." My breath hitches as he skillfully rubs my clit. Already overly sensitive, my body quickly coils tight, ready to burst.

"Tell me you're mine," Jake demands, withholding the pressure that would push me over the edge. He has me desperate—teetering on the precipice of ecstasy—just like he intended.

"I'm yours," I whisper. Jake smiles against my neck as he hooks his finger inside me, hitting my G-spot. Harder, faster, he reminds me how intimately in tune with my body he is. In absolute bliss, I cry out my release. Never before in my life have I been so happy to have my dad passed out drunk on the barroom floor, not until recently. Because there is no way I could ever remain silent.

"I belong to you, Tee. All of me," Jake says before kissing me deeply.

The slamming of the front door pulls me from those memories that would best be forgotten. That damn tornado took all I had left. Why couldn't it have taken those too? The old living room clock ticking on the mantle reads 10:30. He's home earlier than expected on a Friday night. Honestly, I didn't expect him home at all. I quickly gather my piles of paperwork. Looking up, I see Jake staring at me from the entryway.

"What are you doing?" His foul mood is clear based on the way he grumbles.

"Strike out?" Against my better judgement, I taunt the bear.

"No, just wanted to make sure you didn't destroy this house too."

As intended, the retort hits me where it hurts the most. *Fuck him.* I refuse to let him know how much he can hurt me. I turn away and resume picking up my mess. Why didn't I just review these in my bed, like any sane person would have?

"Sorry," Jake offers, rubbing a frustrated hand over his face while mumbling something to himself. "What are you working on?" His neutral tone catches me off-guard.

What is he up to? Setting me up for another punch line?

"I'm gathering some numbers for Cassie. She's going to help me come up with a few projections for the bar," I reply hesitantly.

"I'm getting a beer. Do you want one?"

What game is he playing?

I look at the two empty bottles next to me. "Sure." Confused by his sudden friendly demeanor, I set my stack of papers on the coffee table and sit back down. A moment later, Jake plops on the couch next to me, handing me a drink.

"Are you looking at remodeling?" he asks while flipping through the pages haphazardly.

"No, the damage is too extensive. The inspector came today. He agreed to a partial reopening if I can get his list of tasks completed by next week. So now I'm trying to get an idea of how well—if at all—we can sustain ourselves by selling booze only. We won't be able to reopen the kitchen until we do major repairs or flat-out replace most of the equipment."

Jake lets out a whistle. "That sucks. What are these?" He holds up one of the food truck menus I printed out.

"Oh, we may not be able to cook and serve anything, but I was thinking we could have a food truck stationed out front. That way, people can still get a meal while stopping in for a drink. These are a few local ones I found. Hopefully, someone calls me back."

Being around Jake gives me whiplash. One second, he's an asshole and knows what nerve to strike. The next, he's like this familiar old friend I can confide in. Though that period in time was very short-lived, I hate that despite everything between us, it's easy to find our way back here. Hating him is sometimes the hardest thing to do, but it's also a more painless option.

"You should talk to Scott," he suggests.

"Scott doesn't have a food truck." *At least I don't think he does...*

"No," he huffs out. Obviously, I'm missing the point. "But he has that newly licensed kitchen he's not using. He'd probably be willing to have menus created, then your staff could take food orders and run them over."

"That's a fantastic idea." My mind is already reeling with the possibilities.

"Don't act so shocked. I'm known to have a good idea now and then," Jake grunts out before taking a swig of his beer.

"It's not that..." I stop. I told myself to keep away from him, to not feed into this bullshit anymore. No matter what I say next, I know it will be an argument. So, I stop.

"What is it then?" He seems determined to fight. *Great.*

"Nothing." I quickly finish my beer. "Thank you for the idea. I'll talk to Scott tomorrow. There's a ton of shit I need to do. I'm going to bed. Goodnight." Papers in hand, I walk away.

Less than two steps later, Jake mumbles something under his breath. He's baiting me. I know it. Why? Who the hell knows? An intelligent woman would keep hauling her ass up the stairs. But, apparently, I inherited my daddy's smarts as well as his hot temper.

Arms crossed, I turn on my heel with the papers still clutched tight to my chest. "Do you have something you want to say?"

"Nope." He pops his P.

The documents scatter across the wood surface as I toss them down on the coffee table. "If you have something to say, Jakey-poo, then be a big boy and say it to my face."

With a hard thud, he sets his drink down. Beer sloshes onto my paperwork. He towers above me as he rises to his feet. Matching my pose, he leers at me. "I said go ahead... walk away. It's what you're good at."

My blood boils and my cheeks burn. And not from embarrassment. No, it's pure fucking rage that's heating my face. "It's not walking away, Jake. It's called picking your battles. We can hardly speak three sentences to each other without starting a fight. I'm exhausted—*stressed*—which makes my tolerance for your bullshit almost nonexistent. If we are going to cohabitate here, it's best if I just stay out of your way."

"What does that mean?"

Is he mad that I don't want to be around him? I seriously don't know what's going through his head half the time. "It means just that. You'll hardly know I'm here. Hopefully, I'll have the bar up and running soon, and then I'll be out of your hair."

"Good," he huffs out.

"Good," I parrot petulantly. We stand off, glaring at each other in the living room. I hate how, even when he's pissed off with his nostrils flared, he's hot. With his chiseled jaw and furrowed brow, he reminds me of a statuesque brooding god.

"FYI: storming off usually works better when you actually, you know, *storm off*. Instead of standing here ogling me." He grins, clearly pleased with himself. I open my mouth, but a witty comeback fails me, so I focus on the ticking muscle in his jaw. "If you're going to hang around down here with your mouth open, I could help you make good use of it." The innuendo is clear as day, as he takes a step closer to me.

Why does he always smell so good?

But the worst part? I consider dropping to my knees and giving him the best blow job of his life. Just to see his look of surprise, followed by utter bliss, and then finally devastation as he realizes he will never get sucked as good by any of those bimbos. I really need to stop drinking around him. Clearly, the booze is clouding my judgement.

Gathering what remains of my self-respect, I take a step back. "Go fuck yourself, Jake."

"I will," he yells at my retreating form. "And it'll be ten times better than any slob-job you'd give me."

I don't reply verbally, raising my middle finger and flashing it to him as I continue up the stairs.

12

Jake

I WOKE UP EARLY. Not that it's unusual for me. On my off days, I typically go for a long jog, stop by the café, grab breakfast for the crew, and drop it at the station. Today, though, I had an ulterior motive. I wanted to catch Letty leaving the house. My alarm went off at six. I rushed through my morning routine, headed downstairs, and grabbed some grub before perching myself at the counter. After an hour of waiting, I peeked in her room—to see if she was awake, not to catch her getting dressed.

To my surprise, she was gone. Unfortunately, I've known Letty practically my whole life. Not that I've paid particular attention to her schedule, but I know she's not one to be up before noon—on a good day. Yet, somehow, she was. All before my alarm even went off. Unless she snuck out during the night? I shake my head. No, the only place she'd go would be Tilly's. And if she called my sister in the middle of the night begging to come to her house, my twin would have given me an earful already. Besides, the chaos of her small wardrobe still litters the room. If she split, she would have taken her stuff. Nope, Letty woke up at the ass crack of dawn and snuck out of here to avoid yours truly.

Why does that make my stomach twist with guilt?

It shouldn't. For whatever reason, I'm reading into this way more than any sane human should. I only glanced at it, but I saw the laundry list of fucking things she needed to do. If she plans on getting it all done by the second, she needs to be there from sunup to sundown.

Well, it's only a little after eight in the morning. What the hell am I going to do with my day? I consider bringing drinks to the guys. But I have a feeling Captain Rollings wouldn't be too happy about that. I'm supposed to be on vacation, not loitering inside the firehouse. Not to mention, unless someone is there to stop me, if we do get a call, I'll suit up and land my ass in deeper boiling water. No, I need to do something else.

Fuck, I miss Cassie. She was the perfect fit here. Why'd my brother have to go and knock her up? Steal her away from me? Not that I'm really all that upset. It was just nice having someone around to chill with. Growing up, this house was always crowded and loud. The chaos of having all of us kids here, plus our friends, I thrived on it. Eyes closed, I can still hear them.

Pans clanking around while mom is in the kitchen with Scott. They are testing out new recipes for the café. The air is filled with aromas of yeast and sugar. Tilly and Dad sitting at the counter, tasting the new concoctions while discussing their latest reads.

It brings a smile to my face. For a moment, it feels like everyone is still here. Until I open my eyes, and it's quiet. Empty. And I'm alone. *I need to get the fuck out of this house.*

That's it. I can go visit Cassie at the garage today. They should open soon. Maybe if she's free, I can pick her brain about the video store. It will get me out of this tomb and keep me away from the station. With a renewed sense of resolve, I grab my keys and run out the door. I glance at my pickup but decide I need the exercise. I can't do my normal routine right now, but I'm not about to get lazy either. As I stroll into town, eyeing all the blooming flowers and green foliage, I see why Cassie enjoyed walking to work all the time. Rounding the corner, I notice the sign for Moore Books and Coffee. A smile spreads across my face, knowing Cassie would probably love a pick-me-up. Heck, I can grab something for the other guys at the shop too.

Scott grins at me as I enter the café. "What's going on, man? You look chipper this morning."

"Thanks, I'm feeling good. I'm about to head over to the garage and chat with Cassie about the video store. Would you mind hooking me up with everyone's favorites?"

"Sure thing. I'm glad you are finally getting a move on with your plan. Tilly has been hinting about making a new reading corner back there if you don't do something soon," he teases. My sister knows that space is mine and wouldn't do anything without talking to me first.

I roll my eyes. "Of course she has." I look next door and notice everything is still dark and boarded-up. "It looks gloomy over there."

"Ugh, don't remind me, or Tilly. Thankfully, they will be here tomorrow to put in a new window. Oh, by the way, thank you." I quirk an eyebrow, uncertain what he's talking about. "Letty," he clarifies. Then I realize she must have come in here earlier this morning.

"You guys figure something out?" I inquire. Not that it matters. It was a logical suggestion. She can take it or leave it for all I care.

"I'm looking into some options. One way or another, I will figure out a way to help her. It will be an awesome opportunity to showcase a new menu and get some excitement for the restaurant opening."

"Yeah, when are you doing that?"

Scott shrugs. "I don't know yet. There is still a lot to do, and I don't exactly have the time."

"I get it." *I don't*. Not exactly. He's been drawing up plans for the expansion for years. I have a feeling it's nerves holding him back. But that's just Scott and his process. He will get to it in his own time.

"Here you go." He hands me a drink carrier and a bag.

"Thanks, man. I'll see ya later." Leaving the coffee shop, I quickly make my way to the garage and smile when I see Cassie sitting at the main desk. "I've come baring gifts." I hold up the bag and drinks.

"Oh my god, Jake, do I smell chocolate?" Cassie's pupils dilate.

I laugh. "Probably. I asked Scott to pack everyone's favorites."

"*Gimmie, gimmie, gimmie.*" Cassie extends her arms in desperation.

"Is my brother keeping you satisfied? Because if not—"

"Don't even think about finishing that statement," Robbie booms.

I peer up and smile at my scowling big brother. "What? She's the one begging me to *give it to her?*"

Cassie stares at me, her eyes wide and chocolate smeared on her face. "Jake, that's not what I meant. And you know it," she grumbles, her mouth full.

"I don't know, Cassie. You were giving me that *hungry* look. I thought you might swallow me whole."

Her face goes red. "*Oh my god*. Jake. You dang well know that was actual hunger. And not what you're insinuating. You were holding a bag of delicious baked goods."

"Are you here for a reason?" Robbie wraps his arm possessively around Cassie's waist, placing a hand on her pregnant belly. "Or are you just here to torment my wife?" His eyes glimmer with satisfaction. Unlike his first marriage, my brother takes every opportunity to declare that she's his.

"Well, as much fun as I'm having, I came here hoping to get help from my best friend. If she isn't too busy."

Robbie rolls his eyes. "You realize she *is* working."

"Right now, it appears she's devouring that muffin." I point as Cassie takes a bite too large for her mouth, her cheeks puffed out. She looks up, guilt written across her face.

"Ugh, you two together are just a recipe for disaster." Robbie places a kiss on Cassie's head. "Cass, why don't you and Jake take your food back into the office?"

"Thank you," she says around another mouthful of muffin. She presses a kiss on Robbie's cheek, leaving a trace of chocolate. Cassie wipes the chocolate off his face, but before she can retract her hand, Robbie pulls her finger into his mouth. Yup, there's that hungry look again. Robbie leans forward and whispers something into her ear, causing Cassie to blush like crazy.

I want that. No. No, I don't. Damn it, I need to get laid.

I follow Cassie back to the office and smile when I see her new chair. Robbie used to have this god-awful shop stool he made from our grandpa's salvaged junk. It was a fucking hard metal tractor seat. I mean, it wasn't that bad when you only needed to sit for two seconds, but it's not meant to be sat on all day. Robbie finally upgraded and got her a large cushioned high-back chair with armrests. It also has a built-in back massager.

"Okay, spill," Cassie says, suddenly serious and no longer playful.

"Spill what?" I raise an eyebrow at her.

"We're friends, right?" she prompts, and I nod in agreement. "Best friends even?"

"Yeah..." I drag on, wondering what she's getting at.

"Well then, tell me what's bothering you." Cassie's steel-gray eyes pin me down.

"Nothing. I just wanted your help with the video store. I figured, with my time off, I could work on getting things going."

She sighs and rubs her temples, her mannerisms hilariously similar to Robbie's. "Jake, I'll help you with the video store. But that isn't it. You seem tense, on edge. I'm worried about you."

Am I really that bad? Suddenly, everyone is coming out of the woodwork to tell me they think I'm circling the drain.

Grabbing a muffin, I take a big bite and groan. Damn, Scott makes the best food. "It's nothing you can help me with, Cass. Not unless you and Robbie are interested in an open marriage, which I'm not exactly opposed to." I rub my chin in contemplation. "We would need to work out some logistics. I don't think he's exactly the sharing type, and given the whole *brothers* thing, a threesome might not be the best option. I'm not opposed to swapping though."

Cassie crinkles her nose. "You can't get laid?"

"It's been a while," I admit.

I'm sure if Tilly were here, she'd tell me it isn't kosher to discuss your sex life with your sister-in-law. But she's my best friend, and friends talk about these sorts of things. I will not make a perfectly healthy topic of discussion taboo, just because Cassie's a girl. She's never shied away from talking to me about Robbie. Knowing Tilly, she wouldn't want to hear about it and with Moira living a couple of hours away, I'm all Cassie has. Well, I guess there's Cian, Cassie's older brother, but I have a feeling he wants to hear about her sex life less than Tilly does, considering he could kill Robbie before the big guy knew what hit him and leave no evidence. So it's definitely a good thing she has me.

"At first, I used you as an excuse. That instead of going out, I was spending my free time with my friend. Then I blamed it on the fact that Moira hooked up with Derek at your wedding."

"Moira did what?" she exclaims. "That sneaky little..." She takes a deep breath and centers herself. "Sorry, not important. Please continue."

"Last night, I went out." I release a harsh breath. "The woman was perfect, exactly what I look for: mature, sexy, kinky, no expectations, just perfect."

"Okay, if she was so perfect, why are you crying about not getting laid? Did you get interrupted or something?" Cassie crosses her arms, resting them on her belly. For as big as she's gotten recently, I wonder if she's going to have twins also?

"Or something," I mumble.

"Jake," she says pointedly. "I can't help you if you don't tell me what's going on."

I hide my face behind my hands and groan. I'd never admit this to anyone else, but Cassie is different. She trusted me with her hard truths when she didn't want to. I owe her the same. "I couldn't get it up."

"What?" She coughs, spitting some of her muffin on the desk before wiping it up.

"You heard me. She said and did all the right things. Based on her kiss, I imagine the blow job would've been on point. But *he*..." I motion to my dick. "...refused to perk up. He would only stir to life when—" I stop myself from uttering the admission I was about to make.

"When you what?" Shit, Cassie is like a dog with a bone. There's no way she's going to drop this now.

"He only seems to get hard when I think of a specific individual." Yeah, I'm not sharing more than that.

"This *individual*, you like her?" Cassie's mischievous grin tells me she knows exactly *who* I'm talking about. But she's polite enough not to say it out loud.

"No, *we hates her*," I reply like Sméagol from *The Lord of the Rings*.

Cassie covers her snort. "If you both hate her, then you must be a glutton for punishment."

She has no idea. "Fix this for me," I beg.

"Jake, I think you already know my solution."

"I can't do it, Cassie. Nope. No way."

"Why, Jake? Obviously, you have strong feelings for her. So much so, you are having problems *performing*," she says carefully. Effort appreciated, but my ego has already taken a major blow.

Fuck, if only Killian could hear this conversation—that sick bastard sure would get a kick out of it. *Killian,* the reminder stokes the ambers of rage inside me. "No." I jump up. "It could never happen, Cassie. The only strong urge Letty gives me is to join the priesthood. I'd rather commit my dick to a life of celibacy, than let him anywhere near that icebox between her legs."

"Seriously?" She looks at me pointedly.

"Besides, let's pretend we live in this alternate reality where she isn't a pain in my ass and I could fuck away whatever confusion I have about her. She's already fucking your brother. I have a feeling KO Murphy wouldn't be happy about me touching his toy."

Cassie shakes her head. "I'm not even going to comment about how ridiculous you're being. Just a minute ago, you were planning on sharing me with *your* brother. But the idea of sharing Letty with mine is a no-go."

"It's different," I justify, in a world where it only makes sense to me.

"Not really," she counters. *No, it's not.*

To a normal person, the second scenario is better, considering sharing a woman in general might raise some eyebrows. But two brothers using one sheath is pretty taboo and walking a fine line. The actual difference here is that I know Robbie and I will never share Cassie. One, she is my best friend. And as hot as she is—I'm not blind—the thought of her getting rammed from behind while she chokes on my cock doesn't even make *him* (my cock) twitch. The hypothetical image of any chick in that position should get my dick to stir a little. Swap in Letty, and it gets my blood pumping all right. But not just to that one traitorous extremity that is at half-mass at the image of her pink lips stretched around my girth. The fire is also flowing to my fists—the ones I'd use to add another notch to that bastard's nose when I broke it.

"Whatever," Cassie says with disinterest, shrugging her shoulders. She's pissed. About what? I don't know. Best guess? She's insulted that I won't share someone with her brother... But who knows? Pregnancy hormones are making her hard to read. "Sorry. Do you have a plan or anything for me to go over?"

I smile. It's as though whatever little tiff we just had is long-forgotten. "How about we catch up on this later?" My mind isn't in any condition to think about business. "I've got to burn off some steam. Can I stop by tonight and talk about the video store?"

"Of course, anytime." Cassie smiles at me. I give her a quick hug and turn to leave. As my palm clutches the door handle, Cassie adds innocently, "She's not sleeping with Killian." I turn and see her victorious smile. "I thought you might want to know. Or maybe you don't. Since you don't care and all." She shrugs. "But what do I know anyhow?" Leaving me stunned, Cassie strolls past me and through the door, muffin and drink in hand.

Shit.

13

Jake

SHE'S NOT SLEEPING WITH Killian.

Cassie is cute, thinking I'd give a damn about whatever poor sap Letty has lured into her web. But for some reason, her words keep running through my mind. What I don't understand is why. We've been happy, my dick and me. Both of us powered on after she shit on us. Found sanctuary in a sea of pussy. Now, this traitor seems to perk up at the mere thought of her. Doesn't he remember what she did to us? I sure as fuck haven't forgotten.

11 years ago

This hotel might not be fancy like the swanky ones in the Twin Cities, but it's nice. The room even has a two-seater jacuzzi tub in the corner, not far from the bed. Perfect.

Sneaking around all summer has been incredible. It's crazy, but this dormant part of me she's awakened thinks this is it. I'm young, and so far, I've enjoyed sampling the fine cheerleaders our school has to offer. Maybe it's because school's out. But with Letty, instead of fucking her the instant the opportunity arose, I've been dating her. If you can call sneaking around and heavy petting in the shadows... dating. The concept of a girlfriend is foreign to me. But I know being seen together and not hiding it from your family is typically part of the deal. The closest thing to a date I've had with her is the occasional slow night at Harper's when she sits in my booth and steals my fries. She says she's mine, but she's not—not in the way I want her to be.

Letty's made her frustration over me not fucking her yet... known. Not that she's full-on complaining. I've kept her plenty satisfied. My plan was never to hold off this long. But with her being so adamant that we keep this a secret until we're sure about each other, it's made me less confident about us. I've been held back by the fear that once I pop her cherry, she'll be done with me. That once she realizes I have nothing more to offer her than a few life-altering orgasms, she'll find someone who can give her more. I mean, that is all I've given her so far—which isn't my fault exactly, since she wants to be sneaky.

But it's still all we've had. That is about to change, though. As soon as I share my news with her. A secret I haven't told anyone, including Tilly. Because, for once, Letty is the person I want to share this excitement with. Considering it affects us and our future, it seems fitting that she's the first person to know that I'm joining the fire department and will begin training in a couple of weeks.

Yep, tonight will change everything. Letty will see how good we can be together; she will hear how I can provide for her. We are far enough away from town that we can go out like a normal couple. Have a proper date and then come back to the hotel, where I can give her the night she deserves while we plan our forever.

Chocolate, champagne, and oriental lilies.

Like a good potential boyfriend, I've listened to her. I covertly started a conversation the other week about flowers. She doesn't hate roses, but she mentioned that oriental lilies are her favorite. So, I got her the largest bouquet I could. Robbie, without question, was cool enough to secure the champagne and room for me. In return, I've had to do oil changes for him for the past couple of weeks. I've even made dinner reservations at some fancy steakhouse.

Now, all that is left to do is wait for Letty. We should have driven together, but she had to work the lunch shift at Harper's, and I needed time to set up. The alarm clock on the nightstand reads 6:30. She should've been here by now; we agreed to meet over an hour ago. Grabbing my phone, I send her another text. More than likely, she got caught up at the bar and is running behind.

I turn on the TV and absentmindedly watch whatever infomercial channel comes on. Realizing it's getting dark, I glance at the clock again. It's almost nine. My heart races. Did something happen to her? My phone has no missed calls or texts. I attempt to call her this time, and it goes straight to voicemail. I quickly grab my key, prepared to drive along the route I know she'd take and make sure she didn't get in an accident and doesn't have signal, when my phone vibrates. I open it immediately and see a message.

Letty: I'm sorry. I can't do this anymore. We should end this before anyone gets hurt.

Defeated—maybe a little shellshocked—I plop on the bed and pop open the champagne. Not caring about it overflowing onto the mattress, I take a swig and read her text repeatedly. And like an idiot, I wait, hoping she'll elaborate or show up and laugh at me. Praying that it was some shitty prank. She's never been any good at them...

But she doesn't come. And she doesn't call. I disregard the now-empty bottle and turn off my phone. I toss the flowers in the waste basket—I can't stand to even look at them. Then I reach into my bag and grab my last surprise for her. Two tickets to Disney on Ice. No, it's not quite Disney World. But when she told me it was her dream to go there, all I could think about was making that dream come true. So I thought to myself, after I was done with my training and finally working full-time, I could take her to see the real deal in Florida. But this was all I could afford right now...

I stare at the tickets for a moment before tearing them up and throwing them away, along with everything else.

Fuck relationships. Fuck white-picket fences. But most of all, fuck Leticia Frost.

Present

Pink flashes in my peripheral. Letty's dark hair is pulled out of her face, leaving a hot-pink ponytail whipping back and forth. A string of curses explicit enough to make a sailor blush floats through her plump lips while she fights to drag a table out of the bar. Abandoning all good reason, I find myself walking across Main and over to her.

"Whatcha doin'?" I inquire. Hands tucked into my pockets, I rock back on my heels. It's mesmerizing, the way her perky breasts jiggle when she struggles with a table leg that's stuck in the doorway. My dick stirs as I imagine how great those tits would bounce while riding us.

Down, boy.

"Redecorating," she replies sarcastically. "What does it look like I'm doing?" She must know it's me asking, unless she is this much of a bitch to everyone—though I'd like to think the attitude is reserved especially for me.

Although this is highly amusing and (unfortunately) arousing, it's time to cut things short. God knows it will be my head if she hurts herself. Not that I care about her, but the sooner she gets her shit taken care of here, the quicker she'll be out of my hair at home. Alone in that ghost house is better than having the she-demon lurking in the shadows, waiting to suck my soul from my body. *Preferably through my cock.* I'm also not interested in hearing my sister's lecture if she found out I left Letty alone. Tilly would probably be here helping if she didn't have her hands full with the twins.

"Here, let me." I nudge her out of the way.

Letty drops the table, throwing her hands in the air. "Have at it. I've been doing this for about twenty minutes and there is no way—"

Her incessant ranting stops. Despite the slight twinge of pain, I lift the table overhead and walk it through the door. "Parking lot?" I verify. I remember seeing other items staged there on my way over.

She huffs out an agreement before following closely behind me. She plops down on one of the bar stools in the lot and reaches into her cooler to grab a bottle of water. I avert my eyes as she takes a drink; the trail of water droplets rolling down from her chin to the valley between her breasts is just cruel. It's this moment that has me deciding the devil must exist and that God's an asshole. Because that is the only explanation I can come up with to explain why the world's most perfect pair of tits have been granted to the bride of Lucifer herself. Those perky mounds are barely contained by the thin white scrap of cotton she calls a tank top. *Fuck, she's wearing a red lace bra.* Like a beast rearing to charge, I focus on her hard nipples as if they're my bullseye.

"So, where's the cleanup crew?" I ask, looking towards the blue sky. My mind conjures up images of dirty diapers, the station toilet after chili night, anything to lessen the painful hard-on I'm sporting. The sun is hot and glaring. It's only ten in the morning and it feels like it's about eighty degrees outside.

"You're looking at her."

I make the mistake of dropping my eyes as she fans out her top, giving me a glimpse of the jewel dangling from her belly button. *Is that a new tattoo?* I can't see it entirely as it extends from her thigh and angles over her lower stomach. But the speckled petals are unmistakable. It's a black and gray shaded oriental lily with some swirly designs that flow with the curves of her body.

"Seriously?" I ask. She shouldn't be doing this alone.

Letty sighs. "Yeah, Ted's too old and I can't afford to pay anyone."

"That's bullshit. Where is the rest of the staff?" Not that Harper's has a huge roster of employees, but Chet and Simon from the kitchen should be here helping.

Letty shrugs, standing from the stool as she wipes her hands on her too-short shorts. *Is she trying to give half the town a heart attack?* "Whatever. It is what it is. This isn't their mess; it's mine. They have their own lives and issues to deal with."

Still, I can't believe neither of them are here. Chet? I guess I'm not as surprised about him. He's almost as ancient as Ted. But Simon is in his mid-thirties and more than physically capable. Knowing Letty, I doubt she even asked them—or anyone—for help. Proud and headstrong, she probably came here amped up and prepared to take everything on by herself. I should just walk away and leave her to deal with this mess on her own.

"What do you need me to do?" The words are out of my mouth before I can stop them.

"Go home," she scoffs and reenters the bar.

I'm hot on her heels. Her stubbornness is going to send her to the hospital. Again. She's lifting all wrong. "Letty," I scold. "Are you trying to kill yourself?"

She lets go of yet another table and turns to glower at me. "No, I'm handling my shit."

"No," I seethe, taking a step into her space. She doesn't flinch a muscle. "You're determined to be a pain in my fucking ass."

She fists her hands on her hips, refusing to back down. "And you're the one *determined* to *ride mine*."

Great! And now I'm hard, thinking about stretching that tight ring of muscles. *I wonder if she's ever been fucked in the ass before...* "You'd love that, wouldn't you?" She lets out a little gasp as I push my erection into her stomach.

"I'd rather fuck myself with a broomstick wrapped in Brillo pads." Her words contradict the lust-heavy gaze staring back at me. *Fuck, this is turning her on too.*

"Probably the only way to get a reaction out of a frigid bitch like you."

Smoke radiates from her as she stares at me. Stewing. Trying to come up with a reply. It seems the hornier she gets, the weaker her comebacks are. "I hate you—"

My mouth crashes onto hers, cutting her off and saving her from what I'm sure was just another lame retort. At first, I worry I read the signals wrong. She remains still as I do all the work. This isn't the first time we've kissed. I know she's capable of more. I move to pull back when her fingers thread through my hair, her nails digging into my scalp.

Ah, there's my spitfire.

My tongue plunges into her mouth. *She still tastes like bubblegum.* My heart swells. It's like coming home after a long vacation. Her leg hooks over my thigh. The thin piece of denim and whatever underwear she's wearing does nothing to hide her scorching heat. I pull her up by her ass and set her down on the long-forgotten table. Like a heat-seeking missile, my cock wedges his way forward, pushing aside the crotch of her shorts. He weeps precum, realizing there's a ridiculous amount of fabric still separating us.

I don't know what I was hoping for when I came over here. But it wasn't this. Now, I can't imagine doing anything else.

A thick fog has been lifted from my mind, and everything is crystal clear. This is what I need. To fuck Letty. To get the lingering curiosity out of my system. Then I can finally be free of whatever spell the Wicked Witch of Tral Lake has cast over my dick. He and I can resume our routine. Her moans seem in agreement with my plan. I snake a hand between us to unbutton her shorts. The second the tips of my fingers graze the scrap of fabric keeping me from my salvation, the table vibrates, and a tune fills the air.

"Fuck," Letty hisses. Like a bucket of ice water has been poured over her, she's sobered up from whatever lust-induced daze she was under. "Get off me," she says harshly while pushing at my chest.

Hands raised, I take a step back. She stands from the table, quickly rebuttons her pants, and pulls the still-ringing cell phone from her pocket. She glances at the screen and lets out a string of curses. For a moment, she looks at me—really looks at me. It isn't quite the heavy-lidded gaze from earlier, but that spark is still there. However, she rapidly extinguishes it with a shake of her head.

What the fuck's wrong? She wanted this. Why the one-eighty?

I open my mouth to ask just that, when she raises her hand at me. Her index finger indicates to give her a minute. She redials the number she missed and puts the phone to her ear. "Hey, *Tilly*," she enunciates the name. "Sorry, I was dealing with a little pest problem."

Letty listens to the other end of the line. I raise an eyebrow. If she rolled her eyes any harder, I'd worry she might tip over.

"Nah, it's all good. I thought I saw a *cockroach*... Fortunately, it ended up being a June bug on steroids. Gross, but at least those can be easily squashed. The last thing I need to add to my list is an infestation—especially one that could survive a nuclear bomb." Letty rakes her eyes up and down the length of my body, before she turns and walks away to resume her conversation in private.

Message received.

She might think this is over, that she's won, but it's only just begun. I was looking for something to do with my vacation time, and I found it. I'm going to fuck Letty out of my system and finally be free of her.

Once and for all.

14

Letty

THIS IS WHY TILLY is my best friend. You see, best friends have this sixth sense that tells them their bestie is in danger of making a colossal mistake. For example: hate-fucking said best friend's twin brother in the remaining shambles of her bar. One, mind you, that has its door wide open, leaving us exposed to the occasional passersby.

Double stupid. Actually, if I had a pen and paper, I'm sure I could come up with at least ten reasons sleeping with Jake would have been the biggest mistake of my life.

One of them being that WMPD—Weapon of Mass Pussy Destruction—between his legs. And I'm not just referring to how deliciously large he is. No, the actual damage would be the decimation of whatever crumbs of dignity I have left. For over a decade, the guilt from that summer fling has eaten me alive. I've wanted to spill the beans, confess my sins and seek absolution. But I haven't been to church since my mom's funeral, and I doubt there're enough "Hail Marys" to save my damned soul.

While he was tongue-fucking my mouth, I was looking for a sign, any sign to tell me this was a mistake. If Tilly's ringtone wasn't it, I don't know what else to call her perfect timing... other than an act of divine intervention.

As much as I hate to admit that I could have used a hand, I was relieved when I came back in from my conversation with Tilly to see he was gone. If I wasn't already resolute to get this place back up and running so I could move out, I'm highly motivated now. Before, I just wanted to avoid fighting with him for sanity's sake. But, apparently, we're both psychotic and get turned on by that fact. The wettest I've ever been, and it was wasted on Jacob Moore.

Tequila settles my nerves as I throw back my third... I think? I haven't been paying attention.

"I know I suggested you drink a margarita or two for me. But I didn't think we were going full-on spring break," Tilly comments as she slides me the frozen beverage she just finished blending up.

Her offer to pick me up from Harper's and come over for dinner was exactly what I needed. Not only do I get to see my best friend, who I've hardly spent any time with this past year, but it gives me the perfect excuse not to go back to Jake's house. While there's a good chance he realizes what transpired earlier was potentially an apocalyptic mistake, in the event he's waiting for round two, this seemed like the safest option.

Unfortunately, since Tilly is breastfeeding, her own drinks are still virgin. Hence her request to have a drink or two for her. Not that she's ever been a huge drinker, definitely not one of my regulars or anything. She's the special occasion or customary glass of wine with dinner type. I think the pressure of her body not being her own is catching up with her. Even though the twins are out in the world, she still can't have sex, can't drink, and I'm sure there's more. The lack of control would be enough to make anyone go insane. It's one of the top three reasons I never want children. The other two are for genetic purposes. I could never risk cursing another human with my DNA. To damn someone else would be selfish.

I take a large gulp of the refreshing lime flavor. "The margaritas are for you." I lift my next shot of tequila. "*This* is for me." I polish it off and slam it on the table.

"Careful," Cassie says, entering the house. "A potential side effect of tequila is a parasite." Tilly snorts as Cassie points to her belly. I shiver at the idea, before remembering that I'm safe as long as I'm here.

"True." I smile while pouring another. "But it takes two for that tango." I nod to Robbie and toss back the tequila. *Fuck*, okay, I better slow down. I don't think I've eaten anything today. Add that to the fact that heat and booze don't mix well, and I'm in for a world of hurt. Like the bestie she is, Tilly seems to sense my train of thought and covertly takes the bottle and replaces it with a glass of ice water.

"You forget that it also requires sexual tension." Robbie presses a kiss to Cassie's cheek and drops a duffle bag by her feet.

"Trouble in paradise already?"

Cassie blushes and Tilly hits my arm. "No." Cassie chuckles. "Air conditioning."

I must be a little tipsy because I'm slow on the point there.

"The central air in the house was crap, and the new one won't be delivered until Monday," Robbie elaborates. "With the lows at night being in the eighties and matching humidity..."

"And the space heater attached to my midsection," Cassie adds.

"You're crashing out where there's cool air," I finish.

Cassie and Robbie get situated in the kitchen. Jax finally joins us after getting the twins down for the night. Moments later, both food and conversation begin to flow. The problem, however, is that I'm beginning to feel like a fifth wheel. Cassie and Tilly are engaged in a discussion about pregnancy and babies. Jax and Robbie ate quickly and are now walking around the house talking about remodeling and baby-proofing. Having nothing better to do, I break out the bottle of Jose Cuervo and go to town. Again.

I'm three sheets to the wind by the time anyone notices I'm still here. *Fuck,* I don't get drunk. I control alcohol; it doesn't control me. Yet, somehow, I slipped up. I must be really wasted because Jake is standing before me, as if he materialized out of nowhere. All three of him. *Them?*

"Come on, Letty." Jake guides me off the stool by the arm. "Let's get you home."

"I have no home," I slur and wobble on my feet.

Tilly comes over and gives me a hug. "Sorry... I'd let you stay here for the night. But with Cassie and Robbie in the guest room, I thought you'd be happier back in your own bed."

I frown at her. Is she really blowing me off for Cassie? I turn and point an accusatory finger at the woman in question. "She's *my* best friend."

Cassie shakes her head. "I know." She chuckles.

"Just because you're both stupid enough to push watermelons out of your uteruses... uteri? Whatever... it doesn't matter. Just because you both wanna do *that*, it doesn't mean you can take her from me. You have Moira and your brothers. I don't have anyone else." Jake's grip tightens on my arm. "Ouch, asshole."

"Come on, let's get going," Jake whispers in my ear. It might be the booze, but he sounds pissed.

"Are you sure you got her?" Tilly asks her twin, her tone laced with concern.

I roll my eyes and blow out a raspberry. *Like I need handling.*

"She'll be fine." Jake kisses the top of Tilly's head. "You guys get some rest, and we'll be back over tomorrow for lunch."

I open my mouth to call them out for talking about me like I'm not standing right here. But the next thing I know, my world flips upside down and all I see is the inverted logo of Jake's shirt. "Hey," I protest and slap his back. "Put me down."

"Goodnight, everyone." Jake ignores me as he marches us out of the house.

I struggle in his hold all the way to the pickup, where he opens the door and tosses me in the passenger seat. "I could have walked, you know," I huff out, blowing my long bangs from my face. Jake shrugs his shoulders before turning the key in the ignition. Like a child, I cross my arms over my chest and pout for the entire drive home.

I feel like shit. And not just because the tequila has turned on me and I have the sudden urge to expel it from my body. But because I feel empty. When Tilly went off to college, I dreaded it. I was convinced it would mean the end of our friendship. She'd be in the Twin Cities, stuck to Jax's side with all her new *city* friends. Tilly has always been the most sincere person in the world. I knew she'd make a million friends (just like in high school). And there would be no room for me in her new fancy life.

While we didn't hang out nearly as much as we used to, we remained close during those four years. A big part of that was likely due to her heartache over breaking up with Jax. But even long-distance, it felt like we were still two peas in a pod. When she graduated and came back home, it was like she was never gone.

Now I'm terrified there's nothing left for us. As time goes on, we will have less and less in common. Soon her focus will be on soccer games, PTA meetings, and making other mom friends so their heathens can grow up together. Meanwhile, I'll be slinging drinks at the bar with the same drunk bastards, night after night.

For the first time, the goal I've had my entire adult life seems fruitless. Ted's warning rings in my mind. Initially, I shrugged off his comment because I had Tilly and that was enough for me. But, apparently, I'm not enough for her. My stomach rolls with grief and worry.

Oh shit. "Pullover." I clasp a hand over my mouth.

"We're almost—"

"Pull... *oh my god—*"

The truck skids on the gravel as he slams the breaks. It barely comes to a full stop before I swing the door open and hop out. The tiny rocks slice at my knees as I fall to the shoulder of the street and sober up the hard way. I'm vaguely aware of Jake by my side. *Another sign I'm plastered.* Because I'm imagining him holding my hair out of my face and rubbing my back as I embarrass myself on the side of the road. I've officially hit my all-time low. Just like my father, I'm some drunk having to be carted around.

Eventually, I must run out of contents to expel along with the energy to keep my eyes open.

"Come on, Tee. I've got you." Jake's voice is distant. The last thing I remember as everything goes dark is floating in a cloud of citrus and pine.

15

Letty

11 Years Ago

Blowing my bangs from my face, I get a better read of the clock on the microwave. Shit, it's already a quarter after five. I'm late. I would have had plenty of time to finish work, come home, shower, shave, get dressed up, and make it to the hotel with minutes to spare. But fate had other plans.

With one leg smooth and the other lathered up, I listened as my phone started ringing off the hook. I tried to ignore it. I knew what that ringtone meant. But after the third interruption, I had to answer.

Two hundred and fifty pounds (give or take) of my father's five-foot-ten frame stumbles and goes limp as I try to wrestle him into the trailer. Using all my core strength, I hold him up. "Come on, Dad, we're almost there."

"Take me back to the bar." He tries to step down but fails, pulling me along with him. Great, I'm going to be exhausted and sore before we even make it to this evening's main event. I've been waiting all summer for this. I won't let anything, especially my father, ruin it.

"Dad," I say sternly, "Ted told you that you're cut off for the night."

The bar owner hated having to call me. He knows I'm off for the weekend. With plans. But when Dad throws fists, it's time to cut his day short. Because he's burned and pissed on the ashes of pretty much every bridge in this town, it was either me or the sheriff's office... And as much as I would love nothing more than to let Dad sit in the drunk-tank for the weekend, I can't risk him getting locked up. My income at the bar isn't enough to pay all the bills. While he's no better than ten pounds of shit in a nine-pound bag, his paycheck helps keep the lights on and the lot rent paid. No doubt, the guys at the metal shop are looking for any excuse to fire his ass.

I'm not stupid. Everyone in this town hates my dad and his toxic words. It's a small community, which affords my dirty laundry zero privacy. The only reason he has a job is because of me. It's their charity, giving him a chance to make money to help take care of his only daughter. But, now that I'm eighteen and I've graduated high school, his time is running out. Everyone expects me to take care of it all, including him. How I'm going to do that? I haven't the slightest clue. The only thing I seem to be any good at is waiting tables. But minimum wage and tips aren't enough to sustain us.

"Fuck Ted. And fuck Hank—bastard owes me twenty. I told him the Vikes would kill it in the preseason matchup," Dad continues to ramble on about pointless sports shit.

Finally, I make it to the living room and drop him into his favorite chair. He bitches the entire time I'm at the fridge getting a jug of water and a few tabs of Advil. I glance down at the medication in my open palm. After he chugs these and sleeps it off, he will wake up as good as new in the morning. Well, not new, but he'll be able to stand on his own two feet and get his ass to the shop.

"You know the drill," I state as I hand him the supplies. I rummage through the contents on the coffee table and locate the remote. "Here. Do you need anything else before I go?" Not really waiting for a reply, I turn and grab my duffle bag by the front door. While it may eat into our evening, I'm sure Jake will be fine if I finish getting ready at the hotel.

"Where you going?" Dad leans on his side as he works a pack of smokes out of his back pocket. His bloodshot eyes look up and down my body. "Dressed like a whore?"

I shake my head. Unless everything but my hands and feet are covered, he thinks I'm dressed like a whore. I'm in yoga pants, and though my tank top might be a little revealing, I wouldn't call it whorish by any means. "I already told you. I'm going away for a girls weekend." Not that it matters. I'm an adult. Nevertheless, the little girl in me finds the need to tell my dad I won't be home.

"Sure," he says sarcastically as he pulls out and lights a cigarette.

"What's that supposed to mean?" I ask with a hand on my cocked hip. I don't even know why I'm engaging in this conversation. My father is vile when he drinks. It's best to give him a wide berth.

"I may be a drunk, baby girl, but I'm not an idiot," he sneers at me. "Don't think I haven't noticed you whoring around with that Moore boy."

My blood runs cold. If he knows, who else knows? Does Tilly? I didn't want to say anything to her, not at first. The whole "Jake and me" situation is so new and confusing that I wanted to make sure there was even something to tell her. No way was I risking my best friend, my sister, over some minor fling.

But I've seen a new side of Jake this summer, one I didn't even think possible. We've spent many nights lying under the stars. Talking until sunup. About anything and everything. Okay, not everything. I haven't *really talked to him about my dad. He already knows the man's a worthless drunk. I haven't been ready to delve into the deeper aspects of my home life. But beyond my family situation, we talk about everything. Our hopes, dreams, ambitions. The only other person I've ever felt this comfortable with is Tilly, which I guess makes sense, given they're twins. He's like all the best parts of her, but wrapped up in this super-sexy man package.*

I'm not sure how. But I think I'm in love with Jacob Moore. A sentiment I never thought I'd have for the boy who used to pull my pigtails on the playground, or the teenager who ruined my seven minutes in heaven with Sam Larson (my first crush).

I remember that night like it was yesterday. I had been patiently waiting for the spinning bottle to land on Sam and almost jumped for joy and pumped my fist in the air when it finally did. The next thing I knew, we were in the closet, Sam's lips centimeters from mine. My first kiss, with the cutest boy in class. It was perfect. Well, until Jake and his rancid flatulence ruined it all. The asshole cracked open the door and gassed us out with a fart so vulgar we almost vomited.

But after I let that same asshole know how I feel about him tonight, and we have a whole weekend together like a genuine couple, I plan on telling his sister about us. It'll be weird at first (it's taken me a while to wrap my own head around it). However, if we're happy and in love, Tilly won't care. It'll just take some adjusting.

But if she finds out—from someone else no less—that we've been sneaking around, she's going to be hurt. Tilly doesn't deserve that. She's my best friend, my world. If she's going to find out about my relationship with Jake, it needs to come from me.

"You don't know what you're talking about, old man." *I shrug off his comment. At best, he might have seen Jake hanging out by my window or something. We've* been careful around town. My dad, if he knows anything, would never discuss it with anyone else. "I'll be home Sunday night."

"Don't turn your back on me, you little bitch." I swallow down the sting of his words and grab my purse. "Just like your whore of a mother." I stall with my hand on the screen door. "Too bad she died before she could fully teach you her whoring ways—guess you picked up on it genetically. But just so you know, if you're looking to fuck your way into security, you should have gone for one of the other brothers." He waves a hand dismissively. "The big one, he might have lost his football career, but that shop of his is doing well. Or the one who's always baking at the café. He might be a queer, but that would be better than picking the village idiot." My fist squeezes the handle of the door, the metal slicing into my palm. "Is that your plan? Get knocked up by the retard? Trap him and his family into caring for you."

My jaw clenches and my eyes burn from the tears. I should tell him to go fuck himself. Yet, somehow, my tongue has swelled in my mouth, leaving me speechless.

"It's what your mother did to me." His recliner clicks down. I hear his footsteps through the kitchen and the creak of the fridge opening and closing, before the distinct sound of a can of beer popping open. "She came rolling into town like some exotic beauty. You look just like her, you know? The spitting fucking image. I fell for it all. The sweet smiles and soft touches. Like a siren, she lured me into her trap. I didn't even care. At first, I was excited when she told me she was pregnant. I thought I was the one to catch her. That with this baby, she could never leave me."

He crunches the can with his palm and tosses it behind him. The crushed aluminum skids across the tile. He missed the trash bin.

FRANKIE PAGE

"I gave up on my college plans and learned the first trade I could, to put food on the table and a roof over her head. And I didn't even fucking mind. It all seemed worth it for her. The family dinners and dancing in the kitchen. I thought I was the fucking luckiest guy on earth. But that bitch had the last laugh, didn't she? She just had to die. Leaving behind her succubus daughter. Some useless mouth to feed. I won't let you fulfill your destiny. I'll make certain he knows exactly who you are. The kid might be a retard, but he doesn't deserve the damnation of whatever spawns from your womb."

"I'm not—" I turn around, prepared to continue, but he doesn't give me the chance.

"Don't try to fool yourself. It's genetics, sweetheart. You'll make that boy fall in love with you, and one day, you'll abandon him. Just like your mother did to me."

Flashes of coming home from school to find Mom lying on the kitchen floor—pale, her eyes wide and glazed over—assault my mind. My stomach churns and vomit rises. Not only at the memory, but at the truth in my father's vile words. He might be a cruel drunk. But he's not a liar.

I drop my bag on the floor and walk down the hall.

"I know you hate me, baby girl," Dad yells after me. "But you're doing the right thing."

I wave him off, not having anything more to say to him, and slam my bedroom door behind me. Then I pull my phone from my pocket and break my own heart, and no doubt Jake's, with a single text.

Me: I'm sorry. I can't do this anymore. We should end this before anyone gets hurt.

I turn off my phone and toss it aside. With my music cranked up, so I don't have to listen to my dad's drunk ranting, I pull a pillow over my head and cry myself to sleep.

16

Letty

MY HEAD WEIGHS A thousand pounds and must've been trampled by a stampede of goats. Why goats? No idea. They were the first livestock to come to mind. Reluctantly, I crack open one of my eyes and immediately shut it again.

Sun, bad. Eyes closed, good.

My throat burns, my lips are chapped, and my mouth tastes like I drank directly from Jose Cuervo's asshole with a hint of lime and shame. I need water and aspirin. Lots and lots of aspirin.

"Morning, sleepyhead."

I startle at the deep voice coming from behind me. I must still be drunk, because that sounded just like Jake. Though my muscles scream at me to stop moving, I turn towards the speaker. When I open my eyes again, my blood runs cold at the sight of him. Not only is he in my room. Lying in *my* bed. Under *my* blanket. But from what I can tell, he's not wearing a shirt. Lifting the sheet, I inspect my own state of undress. And as I feared, I'm naked.

No, no, no. Please don't tell me I've slept with him. Sacrificed my dignity and labeled myself just another notch on Jake Moore's bedpost. And I don't even have the pleasurable memories to ease the blow.

"Please tell me we didn't—" I ask regrettably, embarrassed by having to do so. I can count the instances I've been truly drunk on one hand. And this is the first time I can't remember the night before.

"Sleep together," he finishes with a smile and a wink.

"Oh no," I groan as I whisper to myself about how stupid I am.

"Oh yes." He chuckles. "Don't you remember?"

No. But I don't want to admit that out loud. This isn't like me. I'm not like *him*. I don't need to get drunk. I can have a drink—singular. I don't lose control. I'm in charge of my body and mind. Not the alcohol.

Then why are you waking up naked—next to Jake, of all people—with zero idea as to how it happened?

"In that case, allow me to refresh your memory." The glee with which he says that statement makes me hate him more. He's enjoying this. He won, got what he wanted, and I'm left with the shame of it all. "Tilly called me to bring you home. It was late. I had to drag you out of there kicking and screaming."

I cringe, because it sounds vaguely familiar.

"On the way home, we had to pull over so you could give your best Linda Blair impersonation."

I'm not sure what's worse: That I had sex with Jake. Or the fact that at almost thirty, I vomited from drinking. For the first time.

"When you were finished, I got you home. Needed to strip you down because, well, I'm sure you get the visual. As soon as your clothes came off, you slid your hands down my pants, telling me how you wanted to finish what we started earlier." He gives me a suggestive smile.

"Get to the point, Jake," I snip at him. I can't stomach this anymore.

"Ah, there's the spitfire we all know and love."

Lying on my back, I close my eyes and drape an arm over my shoulder. My blood runs cold as a flash of Cassie's warning about tequila causing babies pops in my mind. "Tell me we at least used a condom. I might be on birth control, but I don't trust that even that's enough to stop the Moore super sperm." I'm seriously not interested in pulling a Cassie. Or a Tilly for that matter.

"Nope, no condom."

"Great, now I need to add stopping by the pharmacy to my list of shit to do today," I grumble to myself.

"Jesus, Letty," Jake curses under his breath. "We didn't fuck last night."

Raising my arm, I crack an eye in his direction. "We didn't?"

He abruptly rises from the bed, throwing the blanket off. He's dressed in a pair of low-hanging sweats. They do nothing to hide the weapon dangling between his legs, but the thin article of clothing has me believing him a little more.

"No," he hisses harshly. Grabbing a shirt off the floor, he rushes to throw it on. "That's fucking low. Some Keith McCalester level douchery. I know we have our shit, Letty, but I thought you knew me better than that."

I do. But the idea of how vulnerable I was last night—clearly not using my best judgement— terrifies me. "I'm sorry." It's rare I'd apologize to him, but he deserves it. Although this is my first (and last time) being black-out drunk, it isn't the first time I've had to deal with one. If I inherited any of my father's decorum, I'm sure I wasn't easy on Jake through my alcohol-induced haze.

"Like I said, I stripped you down because you were covered in vomit. But only to your underwear. I tried to get you in the shower to hose you down, but you started spewing some nonsense about cursed genetics."

My heart rate increases. "W-what did I say?"

Jake shakes his head. "Nothing really. It mostly came out as incoherent mumbling. I got tired of trying to wrestle you into the bathroom and just let go. *You* stripped off your bra and thong and crawled into bed. I was going to leave you there, especially with how bitchy you were being. But the second your head hit the pillow, you were out cold." Jake runs a frustrated hand through his already disheveled morning hair. "I decided to stick around. The last thing I needed was you choking on your own vomit, or something equally as stupid, and having Tilly pissed at me. But I wasn't about to throw out my back sleeping on the floor either. So, I slept in the bed. We're both adults and at least one of us was of sound mind."

I collapse against the mattress and let out a long sigh. My stomach churns, and not just from the residual tequila floating around in there, but because of the picture he painted. Then again... like father, like daughter.

"Thank you." Jake raises a brow at my sentiment, and I roll my eyes. Of course he's still enjoying this. "For taking care of my drunk ass," I clarify. "I can promise you it will never happen again."

"That wasn't so hard, now was it?"

I toss a pillow at his stupidly smug and handsome face. It should be illegal to look that hot first thing in the morning. "Fuck you, asshole."

"Ah, see, you tried that last night. And as you *don't* recall, I respectfully declined your generous offer."

I grab the pillow from the other side of my bed and hold it against my face. Big mistake... *Of course it has to smell like him.* I'm thankful for the thick comforter hiding how I squeeze my thighs together.

"Well, as pleasant as this has all been," he says, the sarcasm evident, "you should really take that shower now. It smells like a distillery in here. And not in a good way. While you fumigate the room, I will whip up some breakfast." He doesn't give me a chance to reply before he bolts from my line of sight.

I lie there until the stench he's referencing starts to burn the hair in my nostrils. So I get up and strip the bed, including the delicious-smelling pillow. I don't need him lingering in here and further affecting my judgement. I throw everything into a pile with the discarded clothes from last night... and the remnants of my self-respect.

Brushing my teeth—because if I don't get this taste out of my mouth, I'm going to be sick all over again—I stare at myself in the mirror. I look like shit. Thank God I skipped out on the makeup yesterday, otherwise I'm sure I'd have black streaks running down my cheeks. Still, I'm a wreck. I turn away, unable to stomach the sight any longer. Although I thankfully inherited most of my looks from my mom, in the mirror, all I see is my father staring back at me.

Stepping into the scalding shower, I sigh as the water does its best to cleanse me of my shame. I still can't remember the night entirely; everything gets a little hazy after Cassie and Robbie showed up. But words still echo in my mind, things I said to Tilly. They still make my gut twist in knots. Because in the sobering light of day, the reality of it all remains the same.

Tilly and I are on different paths now. We may remain friends, and I will always love her as much as I'm sure she will love me. But, inevitably, she will gravitate towards other married women, women she can relate to. Plan play dates... Talk about nipple creams and stretch marks or whatever moms talk about... The point is, when it comes to running a bar, I'm still on a party schedule. We might both stay up all night and deal with crying babies, because drunks are no better than large toddlers. But when it's over, I'm going to crawl into my bed and sleep until noon or later. Guilt-free. She will still be up, exhausted, at the ass crack of dawn.

The era of Letty and Tilly is over. Those fantasies we had about growing old and being roommates at the nursing home are nothing but that. *Fantasies.* She will have her husband, the twins, and if Jax has his way, a small baseball team by the time he's done pumping her full of offspring. Plus hordes of grand and probably great-grandchildren to care for them.

FRANKIE PAGE

And me? Well, I won't have anyone.

17

Jake

LETTY TAKES HER SWEET-ASS time getting ready. If I were betting on it, I'd say she's purposely taking forever, hoping that I'll leave before she comes downstairs.

No such luck, sweetheart.

Mission Fuck Letty Out of My System is still going at full steam. Drunk Letty, the one without her guard up, was more than ready and willing. But I don't want that one. I want her fully cognizant of the fact that I'm the best dick she has ever *and will ever* have. That if she wouldn't have fucked things up years ago, she could have been saved from a decade of lousy fucks. A sick and twisted part of me hopes Cassie is mistaken and Letty did hook up with Killian. I'd love nothing more than to have that comparison to throw back in his face.

"What's all this?" Letty stands in the doorway of the kitchen. Her long, multicolored hair, still damp from her shower, hangs past her shoulders. And just like yesterday, her face is clean. Usually, she has this heavy black raccoon-eye thing going on that's very punk rock *and her*. This Letty though, she reminds me of the girl I used to know. Both versions are hot, just in a different way. It's like seeing a warrior without their battle paint. She's more approachable.

Not that I don't appreciate a challenge, but it's nice to level the playing ground a little.

"A hangover feast fit for a king." My eyes travel down the length of her body. She's wearing an old band t-shirt that stops mid-thigh. "Or queen."

While Letty attempted to wait me out in the bathroom, I kept dishing up whatever concoction I could think of that would be guaranteed to absorb any remaining alcohol in her system. I might not be a talented chef like Scott, but I can feed myself. Being able to cook something half-decent is a requirement for every firefighter. The few who burn water, yeah, they don't last long.

"That's..." Letty's eyes are wide as she inspects each dish. "... a lot of food. I don't even know where to begin."

With a smile, I pull out a chair for her. "May I?"

She shrugs her shoulders and takes the offered seat. She watches me intently as I prepare a plate for her. Burrito shell in hand, I pack it full of bacon, sausage, a couple of fried eggs, hash browns, cheese, pineapple wedges, jalapenos, a dash of hot sauce, a slice of avocado, and some mushrooms. Then I wrap it up tight and drizzle the end result with maple syrup—a display I think even Gordon Ramsay would be proud of. I put the plate in front of her. And for the final touch, I grab a bottle of Gatorade from the fridge.

Letty eyes it suspiciously. "You're joking, right?"

Why does she always have to be such a bitch? I grind my teeth in an effort not to ask her that same question out loud. Here I am, being nice, taking care of her. Yet she's making it nearly impossible to do so. Letty's scowl matches my own. Arms crossed, she looks away and literally turns her nose at the meal.

Who the fuck does that? Better question. Why does it make me hard?

"I'm not eating that." She pouts.

"Why not? Do you want to be hungover all day?"

"No..." She shifts in her seat, and those big brown eyes look up at me. "But I'm not going to fall for one of your pranks."

"What are you talking about?"

Letty smiles victoriously. "Like when you replaced the salt in the shaker with sugar. Or when you filled the empty marshmallow whip jar with mayo."

I snort at that one. Tilly and Letty couldn't run to the bathroom fast enough. "I promise this isn't a trick. I've made it for myself and some of the guys on more than one occasion."

"Oh," she yells, a finger pointed in the air excitedly. "That time you scraped all the filling out of the mint Oreos and replaced it with toothpaste. No, Jacob Moore, when it comes to you and food, I have serious trust issues."

I forgot about that... It was probably my most epic switch. I got the entire house with that one. Because after I pulled the trick on the girls, I threw the cookies in the cupboard and got my dad. After he was done yelling at me, he put them back on the shelf for the next family member to grab. It was finally my mom who had the last straw. That night, she baked up a batch of chocolate cupcakes, which she proceeded to fill with zucchini. I didn't think they were nearly as terrible as everyone else did.

Understanding her hesitancy, I lean into her space and pick up the burrito. Letty releases a small gasp when my shoulder bumps into hers. Mouth wide, I take the largest bite possible. *It's so fucking good.* I groan as the perfect mix of flavors hits my taste buds. I didn't drink last night, but I really want to now. "See," I tell her when I'm finished. "It's delicious. Try it?" I thrust the burrito in her face.

For a second time today, she looks up at me with those bedroom eyes. Then she licks her lips. I adjust my stance to relieve the pressure from my now half-hard erection. Images of Letty with a similar expression on her face flood my mind, but instead of a burrito at her lips, it's my cock. *Shit*, I need to get a handle on myself. It can't be healthy to have this sort of reaction to someone.

She opens her mouth wide. And the world moves in slow motion as she wraps her pink lips around the food. Taking a large bite of her own, Letty's eyes roll into the back of her head. My dick is all-too-painfully attuned to the teasing moans she releases. It takes a certain level of self-restraint I wasn't even aware I possessed as I watch her delicate throat muscles work to swallow down the contents of her mouth.

There are other ways to cure a hangover, my unhelpful cock reminds me. "Good, huh?" I choke out the question.

"Disgusting," she lies. I set the food down and watch as she brings her thumb to the corner of her lips to wipe off some syrup. I snatch her wrist before she can bring the finger to her mouth.

"If you hate it so much, then why are you licking your fingers clean?" My tongue darts out to perform the action for her. The already delicious combination increases tenfold with the taste of Letty added to the mix. All I want to do now is cover her with all my favorite foods, just to see if they taste this good.

Her eyes are now full-blown black saucers. Like yesterday, that same lust and desire have taken over her. "I haven't eaten in days. I'm delirious with hunger. Desperate enough even that monstrosity seems appealing."

"Is that right?" I step forward and stand between her wide-open, bare legs.

"Yup." She pops the P. "You think homeless people enjoy eating garbage out of the dumpster? No, they are desperate enough to lower their standards."

"Is that what you are, Letty? *Desperate?*"

She studies me for a second before an evil grin spreads across her face. "For you?" She pauses dramatically. "*Never.* I'd rather starve to death."

Letty stands, but I don't let her move an inch. "Really?" I challenge.

"The only chance you had with me..." She leans forward. Apples and cherry blossoms assault my senses. *Why does she have to smell so fucking delectable?* "...was when I was passed out drunk."

The corner of my mouth lifts into a half smile. *Is that what she thinks?* "Wanna bet?"

"You wanna make a sex wager?" Her lips turn up slightly with the question. "Like some early 2000s rom-com?"

My nose runs along her jaw until my lips caress her earlobe. Her thighs clench around my hips when I suck the flesh between my teeth and give it a small nibble. "Nothing of the sort. It's simple." I walk a hand up her thigh. "I'll slip a finger into your pussy. And if it's wet, like we both know it is, then I'm going to fuck you."

Letty sucks in a sharp breath as the tip of my finger draws a line along the hem of her thong. "And if I'm dry as a bone?"

I chuckle at the absurdity. She can claim I repulse her, even compare me to cockroaches and rotten garbage. But those rock-hard nipples and soon-to-be explored panties betray her lies. "Whatever you want," I offer, because it's a nonissue.

Rarely do I make bets I don't know I can win. This isn't about me losing. This is about me giving her a chance to say yes. Letty is more than aware of the current state of her arousal. She doesn't need me to pop her hood and check her fluids. She can feel the moisture trickling from her core. If she agrees to the bet, she knows she'll lose. It's as good as saying she wants to fuck me. But this way, she can blame it on the wager and not admit to what we both know: *she wants this as much as I do.*

"Anything," she verifies, as if it's even a possibility.

"Anything," I repeat.

"Deal," she whispers.

My finger stalls. For a moment, doubt squeezes my chest over the certainty of which she agrees. But I quickly shake it off. My instincts have never led me wrong before. Unless she's the world's best actress with total body control—she's not—there's no way she isn't sopping wet down there. I push aside the scrap of cotton covering my salvation. With a dip of my finger, I will get what I need. The opportunity to fuck Letty out of my system.

Her eyes remain locked on mine as my hand ghosts along her seam. "Ready?" I ask.

Letty makes me nervous when she hesitates. This is her chance to back down. I'd die from the bluest balls known to man if she does. But it's a choice I'd respect. Everything stops as I wait in anticipation. I hold my breath, and Letty sucks in her bottom lip before nodding.

"I need to hear you say it." I won't allow for any misunderstandings here.

"I'm ready."

As though the words are magical, victorious trumpets sound off in the distance. My digit presses forward. *Holy fucking shit.* It takes all my willpower to pull it back again. Like that summer I caught my first thirty-one-inch walleye, I proudly hold up my trophy and present it to her.

"Drenched."

18

Letty

SHAMEFULLY, I WATCH MY arousal glisten in the sunlight and drip down his finger.

The ridiculous bet was nothing but a crock of shit. I knew as well as he did that I was going to be soaking wet. Still, for whatever reason, I didn't back down. Despite knowing the result of the route we were on, I went full steam ahead. For an hour, I want to be selfish. Forget about the rest of the world and do something just for me.

I grab his wrist, like he had mine, and bring the finger to my lips.

"This means nothing," I caution him, looking straight into those sinful hazel eyes. Not that I feel Tral Lake's resident Mr. No-Strings-Attached really needs me to spell it out for him. But as much as he required my verbal consent, I need his. "This is a one-time deal. A secret we both take to the grave. No feelings involved."

"Letty." His voice is deepened by desire. "The only feeling I want is your pussy wrapped around my fat cock." *Good, now that that's been settled...* My mouth envelops his finger. Like a Hoover, I suck it down, savoring my juices and giving him a preview of exactly what I can do. "Fuck," he groans. "Your mouth too."

His arm sweeps the countertop. The buffet he laid out goes flying. Food spills and dishes crash to the floor. He lifts me by my ass and drops me down on the partially cleared-off surface, which is sticky with spilled syrup. I'm certain the cushion under my head is the half-eaten burrito that instigated this whole mess. Jake spreads my legs wide-open. Obviously, he cares about the disaster zone as much as I do. Not at all. *Fucking* should be messy and chaotic, and that's all this is meant to be.

Jake bunches the fabric of my underwear and rips them from my hips. If the act wasn't so ridiculously fucking hot, I'd be pissed since I just bought them. His eyes rake over my slit as he licks his lips.

"I don't have all day," I taunt. "If you're just going to stand there like a teen seeing his first vag, I'd be better off going upstairs and allowing one of my battery-operated—" My words trail off into a moan. Jakes sucks my clit between his teeth and uses his tongue to play with the nub.

"We can grab them," he suggests against the bundle of nerves. "You might need a lesson on how to use them." His tongue fills my channel. *Holy fucking shit.* "With the way this pussy is sucking me down, I think you've been neglecting her." I hate how well he knows me. He resumes sucking my clit. I bite my lip, suppressing any sound of pleasure. I won't give him the satisfaction. Like this, vulnerable and exposed, it's nearly impossible to hide how much I need him. My back arches off the counter when he thrusts two fingers inside me. "Hold back," he says against my clit, his eyes trained on mine. "And attempt to lie to me all you want. But this..." He punctuates the statement with a third finger. "...is one area where you can never deceive me."

I clench my jaw. My natural stubbornness kicks in and makes me want to prove him wrong. It lasts for about 1.5 seconds before I realize this is a stupid argument. The whole reason I'm doing this is for release. It's been too long since I've had an orgasm that hasn't been self-administered.

There's nothing wrong with masturbation, but there's a *big* difference in the overall intensity. It's like I only get half the satisfaction. Because when the euphoria washes over me, I tense up and stop doing whatever's shoving me over that precipice. Someone else, especially someone like Jake who knows exactly what he's doing—well, they take you to that next level.

The delicious tension builds in my core and spreads to all my limbs. Jake's tempo increases as he pushes past my clenching muscles. "Ah, there we go," he praises. "Do you want to come?" I fight my instinct to make a smart-ass remark and nod my head like a good girl. "What's the magic word?" he teases.

I roll my eyes but say it anyway. "Please." His thrusting becomes painfully slow. Seriously, is this bastard really going to torment me? I swallow my pride. "Pretty please." Jake hooks his fingers so they rub perfectly against my G-spot. "Pretty please with sugar on top..." I try again. "*Fuck*." My eyes roll in the back of my head. "Come. *God-fucking-damn-it*, make me come, you asshole... please."

His victorious smile sends a fresh wave of warmth through my system. He latches back on to my nub. The combination of his suction and his curled fingers hitting just the right spot has my body going rigid. Jake's strong shoulders prevent me from closing my legs. My fingers thread through his messy hair. I grasp at the roots. If he's in pain, he doesn't show it. Instead, my reaction encourages him to suck harder. Thrust faster.

I don't fight when the wave of pleasure washes over me. My eyes roll to the back of my head for a second time, and my vision explodes with fireworks. It's cruel that this asshole can bring me to a plane of pleasure I never knew was possible. My body goes lax as the tremors settle. Dazed and bewildered, I make the mistake of looking at him. His expression says: *It's cute that you think I'm done with you.* Because before I can fully come down, he's back at it again. I have no fight left in me as he pushes me over the edge. Twice more.

Finally, he stops. Yes, it's the freaking *Twilight Zone*. While most women have to beg their man for a quick lick, I'm here begging this one to stop. My body feels like jelly and I'm certain my heart is beating so hard and fast that it might explode. Jake gives me a satisfied smile. He knows he got me good, and we just started.

"Sorry," he says. *He's not.* I shiver as his finger runs through the wet mess between my legs, then onto the counter, mixing my fluids with whatever food was spilled along the surface. He sucks his finger into his mouth. For a moment, his guttural moan makes me wonder if he came on the spot. "I was starving and didn't get any breakfast this morning. You see, I was too busy making a feast for a little brat." Jake rips his shirt over his head, his hard, rigid muscles on full display. His body is lean without an ounce of fat. "In order to maintain this..." He gestures to his six-pack and the prominent V that points to the W.M.P.D. Armed, ready, and holstered by his shorts. "...I require a lot of sustenance to keep this delicate ecosystem balanced."

I'd call him on his bullshit... if I had the energy. Another reason to hate him? The guy eats like a stoner and somehow looks like *that*. I take a deep breath and gather what strength I can muster. "Are you planning on fucking me soon? I'm losing my buzz."

Jake laughs before dropping his shorts and underwear, allowing me to gaze upon the device of my very own destruction. For better or worse, when *that* enters me, things will never be the same. I will never be able to look at him without remembering this moment.

Like that hasn't been a problem already? I've never been able to forget our history.

It might be ridiculous, but this is it. A step beyond heavy petting and fooling around. I'm not a nun. I've fucked around with my fair share of guys. Oral and hand jobs are all about pleasure. But this is something else—something I rarely do. Not that I'll ever let him know that.

One time. No repeats. This means nothing. It's just sex.

I'm hypnotized as I watch him stroke himself. "I'm more than ready to go. As you can see." He makes a show of doing a long, slow stroke from base to head. "I was giving you a moment. When I fuck you, I want you to feel your muscles stretch around every single inch."

I gulp nervously. Knees bent and feet flat on the counter, I'm silent as he stands between my spread legs. It's as though whoever designed the house had this exact moment in mind, because his cock lines up perfectly with my core. His smooth head brushes against my lips. Large hands squeeze my thighs as they travel to my waist. He grabs the hem of my shirt and pushes it up. My back arches, allowing him to remove the thin material and toss it amongst the chaos. Without my top, I can better feel the remnants of food I've been lying on as it sloshes beneath me.

He palms both of my breasts, pinching my rock-hard nipples. Leaning forward, he sucks one of them into his mouth. The appendage that should require a conceal and carry permit slides through my folds. *Oh shit.* "Condom," I say in a panic.

He laughs with his mouth still wrapped around my nipple, and the vibrations make me clench. "I'm clean."

I hit him on the shoulder. "I don't care. I meant what I said earlier. Birth control alone is not enough for me. This is a one-time deal. We don't need a little reminder of it running around with its horde of cousins."

Jake reluctantly straightens himself and walks over to a gym bag by the back door. He pulls out a string of condoms, sets them down on the counter next to me, and resumes his position. "I had no intention of sending my men in unarmed," he teases as he resumes licking my breast.

"Good," I moan while he rubs his cock against my tight bundle of nerves.

"*Fuck,*" he groans before reaching for a condom near my head. He tears the foil open with his teeth and spits the top of the packet onto the floor. Within seconds, he's wrapped and ready to go. His palm flat on my pelvis, he lines up with my entrance. "Hold on," he warns.

Slowly, he pushes himself deep inside. And as he promised, my muscles stretch with every exquisite inch. Filled to the hilt, I feel him everywhere. With a hand on my knee, he presses my legs open wider and goes deeper, which I didn't think was possible. My body's already quivering from the leftover sensitivity of my previous orgasms. After a few quick thrusts, I'm panting and prepared for my impending orgasm. Hooking my legs over his shoulder, he increases his pace and leans forward. His Hoover mouth suctions onto the delicate flesh of my neck this time.

A delirious and incoherent string of curses rains from my mouth. I'm so lost to the pleasure I don't know what I'm saying. All I know is he must like it. Because he thrusts harder, faster, as though each syllable is a command for him to do so. "I need you to come," he orders.

"No." I'm not being stubborn. I just don't think I can. While the pleasure is building, the spasming is like nothing I've ever felt before. If I come again, I'm not sure I'll survive it. My body jolts as he ignores my protests and presses a thumb to my clit.

"I said come," he orders harshly and rubs feverishly.

With a scream so loud I'm certain the sheriff's office will bang on the door at any moment, I do as he says and come. The mixture of pleasure and pain has me raking my nails over his back. Jake doesn't slow down or show mercy. I feel him swell larger inside me, but the asshole refuses to come. It's as if he's...

Oh no, he's going to make me do it again.

Jake's evil grin says it all. Like the maestro he is, he plays my body as though it's a well-tuned instrument. The house is filled with a symphony of cries and labored breaths. I clench around him so hard he winces. *Take that, asshole.* And that's the last straw. With a roar of his own, his bomb detonates and drops its payload into the condom (and thankfully not my uterus).

"*Holy shit,*" he pants against my neck as his energy dwindles. He pulls out slowly and cringes as if it pains him to do so. *Serves him right.*

Condom removed, he ties off the latex before throwing it in the trash. Although my bones are officially nothing but gelatin, I sit up. Lightheaded, I go to plant my hand on the counter. Instead, it lands on a cold plate of bacon. It's then I see the full extent of the surrounding chaos. The place is a fucking pigsty. Jake looks around as if noticing the mess for the first time.

With a shrug of his shoulders, he grabs a piece of bacon and takes a bite. "What?" he asks. "It's bacon."

I laugh, or maybe cry. I'm not a hundred percent positive. But whatever I'm doing has Jake staring at me like I've lost it. On my other side, I notice a bowl of raspberries that went unharmed and toss one into my mouth. He looks at me mischievously, before he angles his piece of bacon in my direction, and I take a bite of the offering.

"So..." he drags out in contemplation. "This one-time thing..."

I roll my eyes. "We agreed."

"Oh, I'm not disagreeing." He grins. "I'm just curious about how we're defining *one time*?" He picks up the remaining string of condoms. "Obviously, we aren't limiting it to orgasms, since you had..." He bobs his head back and forth while he does the math. "...five."

"Four," I correct.

"Five." His eyes darken. "I think you lost consciousness while I devoured that greedy pussy of yours."

Heat creeps up my cheeks because he's right. "Fine, five," I give in.

"So, are we saying a single encounter? Day? Until the condoms are gone?" he throws out several suggestions.

I pat him on the chest and hop off the counter. My legs wobble, but he catches me before I can fall flat on my face. *Who knew he could be so chivalrous?* "I need a shower."

He deflates at my response as I grab my filthy shirt and ruined underwear off the floor. He grumbles some inaudible comment as I pad towards the doorway. Hesitating, I glance at him over my shoulder. It would be so easy to invite him to join me, because the sex was just... *wow.*

However, despite his attempts to stretch the definition, I knew what I meant when I said *one time*. I could justify a one-time lapse in judgement. But if we did it again, I would have to declare full-on insanity. I already don't know how I'm going to face everyone today when we go to our reoccurring Sunday lunch.

I wonder if I can get out of it? Blame it on my hangover? Or all the work I need to do at the bar? Which isn't a lie.

No, I can't. Who knows how many of these I have left? Yep, it's time for me to put on my big girl panties and face the music. I had an itch that needed to be scratched—one that Jake took care of very, very expertly. Now that he's eased some of the tension I've been carrying around, I can go back to what's important.

The bar.

19

Jake

I SHOULD BE HAPPY, thrilled, ecstatic.

I'm on vacation (*forced* but time off nonetheless) at my sister's house, surrounded by my family, and snuggling one of the two most adorable babies ever created. Mouthwatering aromas fill the air, compliments of the steaks Jax has on the grill. I got laid for the first time in—well, it's been too long, at least by my standards. Most importantly, I got to fuck Letty. *Finally.* Mission accomplished. Spell broken. Whatever lingering curiosity I had now *satisfied*.

Per my usual MO, it was a one-and-done, meaningless, no-strings-attached, messy, fun, down-and-dirty dicking. Another satisfied customer. It was perfect... yet *it wasn't*.

I should be sitting here, triumphant like the cat who got the cream. Or the brave knight who finally slayed the feared and fiery dragon. Yeah, that one might be more accurate. The point is... I should feel like the goddamn king of the world. Just like Leo. Instead, I feel like someone pissed in my Honey Nut Scooters.

AJ is cradled in my arms while I feed him a bottle of milk Tilly pumped. My gaze keeps wandering across the room to Letty, who's sitting in the living room looking as if she's eaten from *that* same bowl of cereal. Tilly and Cassie are talking animatedly next to her, but she's staring off into the distance, as though those two aren't cackling like a bunch of hyenas.

What's her problem?

She should be on cloud nine. I know for a fact she enjoyed herself. There was no faking those orgasms. *Yes, the self-proclaimed sex god of Tral Lake has had women fake it on him.* Most were from when I was younger and inexperienced. I didn't realize how many of my conquests were just trying to inflate my ego until I witnessed my first genuine full-body-clenching, heavy-panting, calling-out-to-the-gods climax—courtesy of none other than the sourpuss in front of me.

The first time I made her come, it was like heaven had cast a spotlight down on her and the angels were singing my praise. After that, I was addicted. Even made it my goddamn mission to ensure everyone I've been with since sang that same celestial tune. Sometimes I hate the fact that she was my first genuine orgasm, because you never forget your first anything. And fuck, if I don't hate how many of those she still holds...

"Hands-on" orgasm.

Pussy eaten. And not for a lack of trying. I was excited to eat my first pink taco, but the girls at school clammed up the second my head traveled south of the border. But Letty? She drew a landing strip for my tongue. *Literally.* She had herself waxed, leaving only a trimmed bundle of dark curls pointing me to the promised land.

Love. Not that I've ever said the words to her. But at the time, I was very sure that's what I was feeling, and I haven't felt it since. Then again, I've never given anyone the chance to put me in a similar position.

Broken heart. I'll never give her the satisfaction of knowing that fact either.

Yep, you never forget your firsts, no matter how hard you try. I wonder what firsts I was for her? For a foolish few months, I thought I was going to be all of them. As well as her *lasts*. Spots fill my vision and copper floods my taste buds, as I bite my cheek to prevent myself from yelling the question currently running rampant in my mind.

Who the fuck was her first?

This is a small town. How have I not heard any of the standard male locker room gossip when it comes to Letty? As tight as her little cunt was, I'm not foolish enough to think for one second that she was a virgin. So, that means she's been hooking up with the rare gems in this town who don't go around advertising their conquests. Or that the guys aren't locals.

Letty gets up, excuses herself from the conversation, and heads down the hall. Seizing the opportunity, I pass AJ over to Robbie, who still holds a baby like it's a bomb about to detonate. For Cassie's sake, I hope he's more comfortable with his own child.

"I need to piss," I inform him.

"Swear jar," he reminds me.

"I need to tinkle. Better?"

Robbie chuckles, looking a little more at ease with the baby in his enormous arms, while no one else pays me any mind as I rush down the corridor. Surprisingly enough, the bathroom door is unlocked. I slide inside, quietly release the knob into the closed position, and engage the lock. Letty takes a step back from the bathroom sink, putting a hand to her heart as she gasps. Her shock quickly turns to hatred as she realizes I'm the one who followed her in.

"What are you doing in here?" she whispers harshly.

"Who was your first?"

Letty averts her gaze and frowns at the question still burning a hole in my mind. "I'm in the bathroom." She crosses her arms. "You could have walked in on me peeing or something."

"If you don't want someone walking in on you, you should lock the door." I point out the obvious. "Now, stop avoiding my question. Who was your first?"

She presses her lips together in a thin line. "None of your business. Now that that's settled, get the fuck out of here." She gestures to the door behind me.

"That'll be a dollar," I tease. She raises an eyebrow at me. "Swear jar." I'm rewarded with her signature eye roll, which isn't helping the strain my erection is having on my jeans. Not one bit.

"Whatever." The humor that was there a second ago vanishes as Letty turns back to face the mirror. "Can you please go now?"

I step behind her, my hands resting flat against the counter and trapping her in. "Answer the question, and I will." I brush her hair back. Try as she might, my mark is clear as day under the layers of foundation she attempted to apply this morning.

"Why do you care?" she asks breathlessly.

"Why won't you tell me?"

She tilts her head, giving me better access to press my lips along her tender flesh. "Because it's none of your business. Ouch!"

I bite down, creating a second mark. *Good luck hiding that one.* "Tell me." I slip a hand between her thighs and cup her from behind. Again, these ridiculous cut-off denim shorts do little to cover her, allowing me to feel how hot she is. "Who did you give my pussy to?"

Letty's gaze meets mine in the mirror, that spark she was missing suddenly rekindled. *There's my spitfire.* "Your pussy?" she challenges with a smirk.

"Don't fool yourself, sweetheart. I'm only curious as to who got to pop that sweet cherry."

She clenches her jaw. She's pissed. "You really want to know?"

"No, I've only been asking you the same question repeatedly for fun." My tone is laced with sarcasm. "Let me guess... Did you end up tracking down Keith *the douchenozzel* McCalester? Or was it some fuck boy you met while visiting Tilly at college? My bet? It was some meat-headed frat boy, who slammed into you like a two-pump chump."

"For your information, Jakey-poo." I swear my dick doubles in size as she spits out that annoying-ass name. "It *was* while I was up visiting Tilly."

"Ha! I knew it." I lick the column of her neck, tasting her quickening pulse.

"But you're wrong." She gives me an evil grin that should have my balls shriveling up, but it does the exact opposite. *If I get any more turned on, my dick might break.* "It was the lead singer of a band." I stop rubbing her through her shorts, but Letty's having none of that and seeks her own pleasure. Tossing her head back against my shoulder, she closes her eyes and chases her high. "He was so thick and big I thought he was going to split me in two. I never came so hard or so many times in my life." She turns and looks at me, her chocolate-brown eyes now black. Her eyebrow arches when she repeats the singular word. "*Never.*"

She's lying. I know she is. Letty's just trying to piss me off. *She's succeeded.*

"*Tee,*" I growl. She hums an acknowledgement. Based on her increased breathing and frantic movements, she's close. But if this little vixen thinks she's getting off that easy, she's got another thing coming. I remove my hand and she lets out a small cry.

"Hey..." Letty's protests die off as I reach to undo the button on her shorts and slide them down her smooth legs, along with her thong.

"Don't take your eyes off the mirror," I caution before dropping to my knees. With my palm on the small of her back, I push her forward slightly.

"What are you... *oh, fuck*," she mews as I lick her from clit to ass. I catch her looking down at me, instead of the mirror as instructed.

My thumb presses into her puckered hole. She jumps. *I wonder if that's still uncharted territory?* "Eyes," I warn, pressing deeper. "I want you to watch yourself fall apart, then tell me again who made you come the hardest in your entire life."

"*Jake,*" she breathes out for mercy.

"Look down here again, and I will bring you to the brink of the most mind-blowing orgasm you could ever experience and stop before it comes to completion. Then I'll force you to sit through the rest of the day, squirming in your seat and begging for the relief you'll never be granted."

Letty almost snaps her neck to do as I instructed. *Good girl.* I reward her by sandwiching her clit between my fingers, alternating between fucking and licking her with my tongue as wide as I can make it. My engorged cock is jealous because he wants nothing more than to thrust in and out of this sopping paradise. I push Letty to the point where she is practically shaking, desperate for her release, then stop. Gently, I rub her hood while pressing light kisses anywhere and everywhere but the place she needs. I repeat the process until she's nothing but a withering mess.

"Say it," I demand, with my lips vibrating against her bundle of nerves.

"P-please," she sputters. "Let me come."

Nice try, but that isn't what I want this time. "Admit it." I make my tongue wide and flat like a pancake. Painfully slow, I use my entire head to lick her from hole to hole.

Letty remains silent, so I do it again. Her body quivers so violently I have to grasp her hips to keep her standing. "Fine," she moans. *Finally.* "I lied."

"Who made you come the hardest?"

"You." She sighs.

"And the most?"

"You," she growls. "Now—*fuuuuuuuuck...*"

Like the giver I am, I grant Letty her release. I keep hold of her as she almost falls forward to cover her mouth and stifle her scream. Fortunately, with the chaos of the entire Moore clan gathered in one place, unless someone was outside the door, I doubt anyone heard her. Not that I'd care. Wanting to keep this a secret was always her prerogative.

As much as it pains me (it literally fucking hurts to stand—I'm that fucking hard) we've been in here long enough and someone is bound to come looking for us. Besides, she said this was a one-time thing, and I was just looking to prove a point.

That point being: *I win.*

I adjust myself and wipe her juices from my face before walking out of the bathroom. Without a word, I leave Letty to clean herself up. Fake smile plastered on my face, to hide my frown, I rejoin the commotion. Once again, I got what I wanted. I found out who took her virginity and made her admit that she was a filthy liar, yet my gut still churns with unease.

Why does she still have this hold on me?

I make small talk as I plate up my food and pretend I'm not a bundle of nerves about to explode on the inside. As best I can, I focus on my glistening, perfectly charred rib eye. Ignoring Letty, who's still sporting a post-orgasmic glow as well as my angry red mark prominent on her neck, I direct all my focus to this delicious steak that is cooked to an ideal medium-rare. I take a bite, my fist clenching as I attempt to hold back my moan. The juices from the steak mix with the remnants of Letty's pussy still on my tongue.

"That good?" Scott teases, noticing the effect the food is having on me.

My gaze locks with Letty's wide eyes. "Best thing I've ever tasted." While everyone else laughs at my food-gasm, Letty and I both know I'm talking about way more than an expertly seared piece of meat.

20

Letty

FUCK JACOB MOORE.

Fuck him. His stupidly handsome face. And his ability to see through my bullshit. I hate how he makes me want to throttle him *and* ride him, all within the same breath. That jackass knows exactly how to press my buttons—and I mean my *button*. It's cruel and unusual that God would bless someone as annoying as him with the ability to make a girl go from zero to screaming with the flick of his tongue. Or maybe he sold his soul to Satan. Now that I think on it, there's nothing holy about the things that tongue does to my body—well, except for how it sends me to the pearly gates when I climax. Besides that, it's the devil's tongue.

Seriously, does he have any idea how embarrassing it was to walk out of the bathroom and sit with his family, all the while pretending I hadn't just come so hard I went cross-eyed?

Scratch that, of course he knew. It's why he did it. The million-dollar question is why I allowed him to... *Twice.* The first time was understandable. I needed the release I knew he could give me. The second, though? I have no excuse other than I wanted him. A desire I'm not allowed to have.

Knock, knock, knock.

"Go away," I yell. "We're closed."

This is no doubt the worst time for the bar to be out of commission. June is when the tourists and summer families trickle in. The current heat wave has the out-of-towners ahead of schedule. I've already had to deal with two pink-polo-shirt-wearing assholes down here on Daddy's dime, who were pissed when they heard that the main bar in town was closed.

Me too, buddy. Me too.

I told them we would reopen on the 3rd (because if we don't, I might die) and that they could have a free round on me for the inconvenience. After some douche from the newspaper stopped by for an interview, I shut and locked the door and hung a sign up advising people to come back next week.

The pounding on the door intensifies. *Seriously, assholes?*

I rest the mop against the bar and push back my disheveled hair. With the door shut and still no AC, to say it's hot in here is an understatement. Grumbling, I fight with the lock that is sticking because of the humidity and push the door open. I plaster on my fakest smile, not wanting to scare away my customers. While the regulars are used to my resting bitch face, the visiting population doesn't have quite enough time to fully appreciate my charm. Not that I go over the top. This is a lake town, which means we attract all the rich kids with water-sport equipment that costs more than the trailer I grew up in. The guys who come down here from the city make Keith McCalester look like a decent guy (he isn't one). They all think us small-town girls are fanning ourselves, just waiting for a city slicker to pick us up out of the mud and whisk us away to their ivory towers.

Obviously, girls like that do exist in our town—*cough, Madison.* But I'm not one of them.

With their self-inflated egos, the khaki-loving pricks take my disinterest as a challenge. *Kind of like someone else I know.* Granted, when it comes to a certain local firefighter,

I'd say my bullheadedness is less about disinterest and more about self-preservation.

"Sorry, we're closed." My smile falters as the bane of my existence stands before me. "What do you want?"

"What's with the hostility?" Jake gives me a wide, toothy smile.

He must have been spending time outdoors. His skin is sun-kissed, and the ends of his sandy-blonde hair are more bleached. He wears summer well. I've avoided him since he drove us back to his house Sunday after the cookout. It took all my self-control not to strangle him while everyone was still at the table eating.

His completely oblivious family assumed it was classic Jake, melodramatically enjoying his food. No, it was him rubbing in my face what he'd done to me in the bathroom. The heated stare he gave me with every bite of steak had me squirming in my seat. Watching him lick his lips or suck on his fingers gave me flashbacks of the things he'd done with them only moments prior.

Fortunately, everyone was so preoccupied with the twins and giving Robbie shit about Cassie's upcoming ultrasound, where she could find out the gender of the baby, that they didn't notice the fresh red hickey on my neck. Or that I reeked of sex and Jake. Worse yet, I was already extra-sensitive after our "breakfast" this morning. *That,* mixed with his bathroom demonstration, and I couldn't sit still.

Smug bastard knew it too.

On the drive back to his home, and likely in an effort to punish me for the silent treatment I was giving him, he took the long way. Over the bumpiest roads Tral Lake has to offer. I was a withering mess by the time he put the truck in park. I almost couldn't make it to my room. His laughter rang out through the halls as I shuffled my way up the stairs.

Then I scrubbed my skin raw in the shower, but I could still smell his woodsy cologne. Even after I washed the sheets. I swear he must have gone into the room while I wasn't looking and sprayed his cologne on every surface. Or something...

Like I said, *fuck Jacob Moore.*

Speaking of, his giant foot stops me from slamming the bar door in his face. He thrusts an ice coffee at me. "Truce?"

I eye the delicious drink suspiciously. Licking my lips, I fantasize about guzzling down the refreshment. I'm *so* hot and exhausted. The cool beverage, with the extra dose of caffeine I know Scott would have added, is more than tempting. But this is Jake. Nothing is as simple as it seems.

"Did you spit in it?"

He laughs at my accusation, as if it's absurd. *It's not.* He rolls his eyes when he realizes I'm not kidding and takes a sip. He makes a puckered face before offering it back to me. "Fuck." He sticks out his tongue and shivers. "It's like iced jet fuel."

I snatch the drink from his hands and take a giant gulp. It's nitro cold brew from concentrate, and not the stuff they water down, filled with espresso ice cubes. Yes, Scott is a genius. During the summer months, I love my iced coffees, but not when they melt and water down my drink. Scott saw the trend of people making coffee ice cubes and took it to the next level by adding espresso. So now, as the ice melts, I get an extra boost.

"Tell Scott I said thank you." I try to shut the door again, but Jake isn't having it.

"Yeah, what about the delivery boy?" He smirks. "I think he deserves a kiss."

"I think he deserves a swift kick in the nuts." I smile, and he winces at the thought. "Now, if you'll excuse me, I have a week to get this place ready for the inspector."

"Let me help." His offer sounds almost genuine, then I remember what happened the last time he tried to *help.* It ended up with his tongue down my throat and me attempting to drink away the knowledge of how great it felt, which then led to me being so hungover the next morning I knowingly made a pointless bet to fuck him. In summary...

"No."

"Why are you being a stubborn pain in the ass?" he growls.

"Do you really need me to answer that question?" I arch my brow at him. I take his silence as confirmation that I don't. "Goodbye, Jake."

"Wait." He stops me again.

"What now?" I let out a long breath. My patience is wearing thin.

"When will you be home?" He tucks his hands into his pockets and rocks back on his heels.

"Home?" He knows as well as I do that *his* place isn't *my* home. There was a time when it felt that way. But now it's his house. Not my home. Mine is missing part of the roof, courtesy of a stupid tornado.

"Fine. When will you be back at the house? I didn't hear you get in last night or leave this morning."

That's because I didn't. In my attempt to avoid him, I worked so late that by the time I was done, it made more sense to sleep in one of the cleaned-out booths than go back to his house and risk another incident. "Do I have a curfew?"

"Can you stop being a brat?"

No. "Can you stop being an ass?"

Also no. He slams his hand on the door, making me jump. "When are you coming home?"

"Late."

He narrows his eyes at me. He's losing his cool. I shiver at the thought of the last time I pushed him. My traitorous pussy clenches at the memory and encourages me to learn what his punishment will be if *we're* a bad girl again.

"I'm not sure," I say with all honesty. "There's a lot to get done here, plus I still need to work with Scott on a menu and get in touch with my supplier. Cleaning out this shithole..." I gesture to the war zone behind me. "...is taking a lot longer than I thought it would. I need to remove the debris so I can work on getting it back to code. If I don't pass the inspection, I'm finished."

Jake slides down his sunglasses to study the room behind me, then frowns. "Okay."

"Okay?" I'm surprised by his sudden agreement.

"I'll see you later, Letty." He waves as he walks down Main as though he doesn't have a care in the world.

"Sure thing," I mumble to myself while twisting the lock back in place. My shoulders drop as I take in the damage.

There's no way I'm going to have everything done in time.

21

Jake

LETTY IS THE MOST infuriating woman I have ever had the displeasure of knowing.

When we were kids, she crawled under my skin and burrowed herself deep. For over two decades, her sole purpose has been to make my life hell. I still remember the day the she-witch showed up at the playground. Her white dress with the bright sunflower pattern was merely a disguise meant to lure unsuspecting children into her web. Her long dark hair split into two pigtails and tied up with yellow ribbon gave an innocent, yet carefree vibe.

Tilly and I were playing in the sandbox, building one of our signature castles, when this girl with big chocolate eyes came strolling up to us. At first, she seemed shy, a bit out of place. Being the nice kid that I was, I invited her to join us. She studied us both carefully before turning her nose at me and setting her sights on my twin. Sure, Letty might have looked all sweet and innocent. But when she asked Tilly to go play—without me—she knew exactly what she was doing. That was the day Letty stole my sister from me.

Things between us were different after that. For years, it had just been *us*. My twin and me together every day. No complaints. Then, slowly, I was phased out. Cast aside. It was

Letty who she wanted to play dolls with, to build a fort with, watch movies with...

The day I came home from soccer and saw the sign hanging on our bedroom door—the one scribbled in angry red crayon reading: *NO BOYS ALLOWED!* Yeah, that was the day Letty declared war, and the gloves came off. It was one thing to let them have their *girl time*, play with their Barbies without their studly G.I. Joe boyfriends, or to give them a little privacy for their princess tea parties. But when she fully excluded me, banned me from my own bedroom, it was on.

After that, there was no holding back when it came to Letty. The nights that she'd sleep over, and there were a lot, I'd put fake spiders on her face to hear her blood-curdling screams in the morning. Or I'd replace her body lotion with that fake-tan shit, turning her smooth caramel skin this streaky orange color. Tilly was really pissed about that one, especially because she used it too.

For as much as I dished out, Letty gave it right back. Like the time she stole my clothes and towels from the bathroom when I took a shower. Or when she put itching powder in my jockstrap and spread a rumor that I had an STD, using *my discomfort* as proof. Oh, and we can't forget the freshman party on the trail. Letty slipped eye solution into my drink, which left me out in the middle of the woods with the sudden urge to shit myself in front of everyone. I almost didn't recover from that stunt, reputation-wise anyway. Fortunately, the laxative incident in the spirit week boxes for homecoming had the entire Tral Lake football team in a similar mess—myself included. She never admitted it. But to this day, I believe *that* was Letty's doing as well.

Regardless, none of it was as bad as the ultimate prank she pulled on me eleven years ago. Making me believe there was something more between us, then, without warning, ripping the rug out from under me. I've had her. Tasted her. Sated my curiosity, then humiliated her. Left her a wet, withering mess. Forced her to sit through lunch with my family while trying to hide what happened. The ride home was hilarious. I've never seen someone so angry and horny all at once. It was brilliant. Just desserts.

And again, I *should* feel on top of the world. Instead, I felt like shit when I woke up yesterday and realized she snuck out early in the morning, which was only worsened when she never came home and ended up sleeping in her fucking bar.

I can't stop replaying it in my mind. Not the fun, sexy parts—as enjoyable as they've been to relive. No, it's the anguish etched on her gorgeous face that haunts me. While I should be thinking about the video store or going fishing, my mind is consumed by her. Images of Letty alone at the bar, struggling to put the pieces back together. And the fact that instead of sleeping in a comfy bed after busting her ass all day, she hates me so much she'd rather curl up on the worn vinyl cushion and pass out in a disaster zone.

On top of it all, my dick can't read the room. He doesn't seem to care about our past or the knowledge that she hates us. No, all he thinks about is how delicious she tasted, how perfectly she strangled him when she came so hard I thought she was going to rip him off. Yep, the only thing he is concerned with now is how incredible it would have felt without the latex barrier.

Great, there he goes again. She doesn't even need to be in the room for me to get a half chub. I need to fix this—but how?

"Moore," Stone greets me as I approach the group. "I didn't expect to see you here." He tugs me forward and slams a palm against my back in greeting.

"Where else would I be?" Weather and emergencies permitting, every Tuesday we team up against the Tral Lake sheriff's department to shoot some hoops at the court located behind our adjoining buildings.

"Knee-deep in pussy." Derek Lafferty, son of Sheriff Lafferty and my long-time partner in crime, walks up and slaps my shoulder.

"Nope, I visited your mom yesterday." I bend over and let out an *oof*. The bastard elbowed me in the gut. It's not my fault his mom is hot. Being that he's one of my best friends, well, I make certain to remind him of *that fact* whenever the opportunity arises.

"Next time, it'll be your nuts," he warns with a smile on his face. "I heard you're on vacation. Why didn't you tell me? I've got some time off burning a hole in my pocket. We could have gone up north and done some camping."

His statement piques my curiosity. Not that we both don't enjoy the outdoors, but generally, when he takes time off, his brain focuses on where we can cause the most destruction... with our dicks. Like the weekend we went up to the raceway in Brainerd with nothing more than a small duffle bag filled with a change of clothes and condoms. We used our good looks to charm our way into a few tents and bunkered down with some girls for the night. And don't even get me started on when we hit up that nightclub over by the Great Lake. The point is, Derek's primary source of entertainment is fucking. I wonder what little vixen has his attention.

"Sorry, man. I've been busy working on plans for the video store."

"Yeah, how's that going?" he asks while lacing up his sneakers.

"Good. I went over some ideas with Cassie yesterday. She's going to help me review a couple of vendors and some contracts. If everything goes well, she thinks I might have it up and running by the end of July."

"Seriously? I can't fucking wait. You better put a big-ass action section in there," Derek says sternly, but there is humor in his eyes.

"Organized by actor," Metzger chimes in. He's a volunteer firefighter. I mostly see him at our pickup games on

Tuesdays. I don't always get the pleasure of working with him.

"Knowing Jake, I bet his budget is going to be blown on the adult-entertainment section," McCalester adds, in a pathetic attempt to be funny. And we all roll our eyes.

Yep, you guessed it. There is more than one McCalester offspring in this town.

Keith was the eldest son and set to inherit everything, until Derek helped Tilly and me expose the son of a bitch for the predator he was. He has a sister, Evelyn, who is older by a mere ten months. I hardly remember her from when we were kids. At eight years old, she was sent away to some fancy boarding school. Given how small towns love their gossip, word was that Mr. McCalester was so angry his firstborn was a girl he immediately got his wife pregnant again, threatening to keep her with child until she gave him a male heir.

Then, last but not least, there's Huey. Or more formally, Howard. But none of us call him that. He's the youngest and thought to be *accidental* McCalester. He isn't a bad kid. I give him credit for turning his back on the family name long before the shit with his brother. I still remember the day he came to the firehouse asking what he needed to do to join. We thought it was a prank. No McCalester has had dirt under their nails for three generations. Not since they corporatized their farm and now have a full force of underpaid staff to manage their cash crops. But it was his eighteenth birthday, and diploma in hand, he was prepared to be cut off from the family and join the ranks of civil service.

"Huey." Derek drapes an arm over his shoulder and gives him a noogie, messing up his slicked-back hair. "Why would Jake here waste his investment on porn?"

"B-because..." Huey looks around for some help, but everyone adverts their gaze. "I mean, don't all guys watch porn?"

That earns little Huey a round of laughs. Derek pats him on the back and shakes his head. "Why would Jake need to watch that shit when his dick is constantly dipped in fresh pussy juice?"

"Oh." Huey's cheeks burn red. Like I said, he isn't a bad kid. But he's a little clueless sometimes. Not that I blame him. I can only imagine what growing up in his household was like. I'm just glad he didn't inherit whatever dipshit genes seem to plague that bloodline. Keith might have been the first one caught and publicly outed for his despicable behavior, but no one believes he's the only McCalester with predatory tendencies.

"Derek," I scold. "Of course I'm going to stock the store with porn. It would be a disservice to the community if I didn't." He raises an eyebrow at me in response. "What? You think I was just born this good?" I wink at Huey. "No, it started with hours of grueling research, then eventually field testing. I might have a natural talent, but the actual skillset was developed, not God-given."

A few of the guys are trying to hold back their snickers while the others are confused, wondering whether I'm serious or not.

"That's it. As Tral Lake's self-declared sex guru, I decree that if you aren't giving the ladies at least four orgasms each go-around, you must all lock away your Johnsons and study two hours of porn a night—at a minimum. And not the kind where the girl is giving a blow job. No, the ones where the girl is the center of attention." I wave a hand dismissively.

"Fuck off, Moore." Derek chuckles while doing a jerking motion with his hand.

"Three hours for you." I point at Lafferty. Huey laughs, relaxing his shoulders now that the attention isn't on him and everyone is laughing at Derek instead.

"How's Cassie?" Cian asks, coming up next to me after the guys disperse to get ready for our matchup.

Derek mentioned how he was trying to get the guy to come out and socialize a little more. I guess the city native hasn't acclimated very well in the few weeks that he's officially been here as the newest member on the force. I can't blame him. I'm guessing the practically nonexistent crime rate isn't that stimulating for someone with his background. Not that I know exactly what he used to do, only that he's a retired Army Ranger. Beyond that, nothing.

I feel for the guy. Cassie hasn't exactly forgiven him for coming down here and spying on her. I love her to death, but I wish she would put it behind them already. He has enough going on with trying to get used to the change of pace around here. I'm not saying that what he did was cool. Granted, I'd probably do the same for Tilly, except I wouldn't lurk in the shadows, keep things from her, and then rope her fiancé into the entire ordeal. I know his sister is still hurting and hasn't really processed everything that happened at her wedding. I just wish she would cut him a little slack.

"Good. Cassie is definitely keeping my brother on his toes." I grin and Cian nods. One corner of his mouth lifts into a slight smirk as I pat him on the back. "She'll come around."

He shrugs. "It's fine. I'm kind of glad." Now it's my turn to quirk my eyebrow at him. He looks off into the distance. "Cassie spent most of her life catering to others' expectations. Not standing up for herself. It makes me happy to see her flex the backbone I've always known she has. She'll forgive me when she's ready and not a moment sooner. Us Murphys are notoriously stubborn."

"Sure thing, man." I love Cassie, but the Murphy clan is an odd bunch. Suddenly, a bolt of genius strikes me. An ability to hit two birds with one stone. "You know, I might have a way you can make it up to Cassie."

"How's that?" he asks, clearing his throat.

"With some good old-fashioned elbow grease and community service." I flash him a big smile. He tilts his head and pauses, waiting for me to elaborate.

"Are you ready to get your asses handed to you?" Derek dribbles the ball behind us. He attempts to catch me off-guard with a quick pass. But knowing him as well as I do, I see the move coming and catch the ball midair.

The abrupt thump to my palm strikes another brilliant idea. Not only could it earn Cian some favor with his sister, but it could also benefit these guys, and most importantly, help me with my current situation.

"How about we make things interesting..."

22

Letty

I OPEN MY EYES and my first thought is why is it so sunny? The second is why *the fuck* is it so sunny? Frantically, I feel around on the nightstand and locate my phone. I tap the screen several times but it doesn't wake up. After holding down the button on the side, the useless device finally displays an empty battery icon with an angry red line.

I forgot to plug it in.

I got home extremely late last night. I didn't plan on being at the bar that long. I was already exhausted, and sleeping in the booth didn't help any. My plan was to work on cleaning until eight or nine, then come back to the house, shower and eat, sleep in a comfortable bed, wake up early, and repeat. What I didn't count on was Ted showing up around three with a claims adjuster. I thought meeting with the health inspector was nerve-racking. But this second guy was downright terrifying. No smile. Barely spoke two words. Just a bunch of disapproving hums, clicks of his judgmental pen, and snaps of his all-seeing camera.

Jax helped me take a gazillion images of the damage before I started any clean-up, which he kindly ran over to the bar for me. Again, the adjuster wasn't impressed with anything we said or did. Even Ted was uneasy and hightailed it the second the man and his negativity were both gone. My stomach was flipping with unease over the entire exchange, so I kept busying myself at the bar. Before I knew it, it was three in the morning and it hardly looked like I'd accomplished much of anything. I must have been so out of it last night that I didn't think to charge my phone and just fell asleep. I'd been using it for music all day and the battery was already down to five percent.

In a rush, I jump out of bed and take a quick shower. Although I'm going to get covered in grime again today, I need the refreshing water to perk me up. I don't bother doing anything with my hair and throw it up in a wet knot on top of my head. The hot pink is toning down a little and needs to be touched up soon—*after* I save Harper's and get it up and running and preferably when I'm safely back in my own place.

I'd hate for it to look like I murdered a unicorn in Tilly's bathroom. Or I guess it's Jake's bathroom now. No matter what, or who it may belong to, this will always be *her* room. Cassie might have lived here shortly, and Tilly's old furniture might be long gone. But at the heart of things, the sentiment remains. Glow stars that don't shine quite as brightly still cling to the ceiling. That hot-pink stain on her gray carpet from when we spilled nail polish forever freezes that moment in time. The walls are slightly discolored where she used to have pictures hung up. And tape residue where she had a Backstreet Boy's poster until it mysteriously disappeared—along with her CDs—stares back at me from across the room.

Sure, some things may have changed on the outside but the memories of this house are lasting.

I practically run down the hall and pause by Jake's door. Sucking my bottom lip between my teeth, I contemplate knocking. As much as I hate to admit it, I really could use the help. I'm not exactly sure what time it is, but it has to be at least early-morning hours. Most days, I'm gone before he's even able to leave his bedroom. *To avoid him.* So I don't know what time he usually wakes up. My mind battles with itself. A part of me says to take his offer to help. The other part says this is Jake, and the price of my pride might not be worth it. Especially if I can't keep myself under control and fall victim to his charm again.

Harper's, I remind my wounded ego. *That's all that matters.*

The bar is my home, my future. I've worked too fucking hard to lose it all now. Resolute, I knock on the door and wait patiently. I don't hear any movement so I try again. After a few more moments of silence, I slump my shoulders and continue down the stairs. I half expect to see him in the kitchen with some smug, victorious grin on his face. Except it's empty. The only sound in the house is the soft blowing from the air-con. The clock on the oven reads half past ten.

Shit, I'm really behind. Whatever. Clearly, he has better things to do with his time than just lie around the house. *Like finding a new pick-up spot for his next victim.* Ignoring the way my gut churns at the thought of him with whatever chick he's currently seducing, I jog to the bar. Usually, I would stop at the café and grab a pick-me-up to get me going, but I've already lost enough time today. I need to finish wet-vacing the remaining water and get the floors dried. Clearing out the unusable appliances will have to wait until I can get some extra hands. As long as they're covered and marked *not in use*, and the dishwashing and handwashing areas are clean, I should be fine... hopefully.

I halt dead in my tracks, with the key hovering near the lock. It's muffled, but I can hear the distinct sound of men talking and laughing on the other side of the door. Tral Lake isn't a crime capital by any means. We are still one of those towns where you can leave your door unlocked and not worry. Occasionally, you'll get some dumbass kids who commit a little vandalism or steal. But it's very rare to witness anything major.

It's not like up in the Twin Cities where you hear about multiple murders, assaults, rapes, and robberies on the regular. I even read this one article talking about how every car lining a specific street had its windows smashed in. Things like that don't happen here. However, I'm a little more cautious during tourist season. A majority of the visitors are well-to-do families seeking escape for the summer, or college kids looking to party and enjoy a little wakeboarding. Still, these people aren't local. I don't know them.

The hairs standing up on the back of my neck have me on full alert. Someone is in my bar. And I don't know how many *someones*. I can easily assume at least three, possibly more. Did those entitled frat boys come back? Decide to raid what little booze we have left in stock? *Those fuckers.* One of the Laffertys is probably going to yell at me later, but I won't let these assholes think they can barge into my place and mess it up more than it already is.

Quickly and carefully, I corner the building and grab a broken table leg from the debris. It sounded like the intruders were up front. To have the element of surprise, I sneak around the back. The door is already propped open with a rock. I take a deep breath and peek down the hall. The coast is clear, so I stay close to the wall and inch towards the bar. Though the commotion is getting louder as I near the open area, the blood pumping fiercely through my veins has muffled the sound. I can't hear what they're saying or doing, only that someone's definitely there.

I tighten my grip around the table leg and count. *One. Two. Three.*

I round the corner with my makeshift weapon raised high, ready to bash the first asshole's head in. I doubt I'll be able to take them all. But I'm not going down without a fight. I approach the closest shadowy figure. My mind is so focused on striking I'm not actually seeing what's in front of me. Squeezing my eyes shut, and with a roar, I let out my best battle cry and swing as hard as I can. My motion is stopped. I hit something. At least I'm pretty sure I hit something...

"What the fuck, Letty?" A furious voice growls at me. I open my eyes and am met with one very pissed-off Jake holding the other end of the stick.

Like a fish in open air, my mouth bobs up and down a few times. I mean to apologize, but I can't seem to find the words. "What are you doing here?" I say instead. My blood settles, my focus clears, and finally, I look around the room as everyone's face comes into view. There are a few guys here from the fire department, along with Lafferty Junior.

Crap... I knew I was going to get my ass in trouble with one of them. Derek stands in the middle of the bar with his arms crossed, his eyes bouncing between me and my intended victim. Jake rubs his fingers through his disheveled hair. "This is what I get for fucking helping," he grumbles mostly to himself, but I catch it.

The table leg is snatched from my grip. Cian holds it up with an open palm, as though he's stepping away from a rabid dog. Then my eyes begin to dart around the room more carefully, and I recognize some sheriff's officers amongst the crowd of firefighters, as well as Mack from the garage. My cheeks burn with embarrassment at the realization. These guys have been busting their asses in here since... well, I'm not sure how long. But the bar looks nothing like it did when I left a few hours ago.

"You did all this?" I whisper.

Jake tucks his hands in his pockets and glances around casually, as though he's just noticing for himself. He shrugs. His hazel gaze remains locked on mine, each of us silent while daring the other to speak. I'm at a loss though.

Why is he doing this? Why are they all doing this?

"Of course he did," Mack says, slinging an arm over Jake's shoulder and giving me a cheeky grin. If it wasn't for the grease permanently stained on his fingers, the mechanic could pass for any of the other summer beach bums roaming around here. His shaggy hair is pulled back and secured. He's already sporting a golden tan from being out on the water as much as he can squeeze in. While the rest of the guys are here in jeans, shoes, and t-shirts, Mack's wearing board shorts with tropical flowers, a button-up shirt, and sandals. He's the odd man out, appearing more ready to surf the waves than clean up this shithole.

"Why?" I ask Jake, but Mack answers for him.

"When he told us the only way we were going to get our bar back was by pitching in, how could we say no?"

"I can't pay you," I blurt out. Realizing how stupid and unfair that sounds, I shake my head. "I mean, I don't have money. But when we're open, you guys can have a few rounds on the house." I'd offer to cover their tab for a month, but I've seen how much these guys can put back. We're going to be pushing it as it is. I can't risk losing income from my regulars, even during the summer.

"Don't worry about it, Letty." Derek drapes his arm over my shoulder. Jake's eyes leave mine and focus on where his buddy's touching me. "Payment isn't necessary. We take care of our own."

I hate how my chest squeezes at the sentiment, and I have to fight the tears now threatening to fall. Sure, I might have known Jake, Mack, and Derek since we were kids. But it's a small town, and we were all in the same classes. While Jake and Mack have been friends for about as long as Tilly and I have, the rest of the guys just frequent the bar. We've shared a few laughs and had a couple of drinks, but never would I have considered them friends.

The closest among the sea of faces would have to be Jake, and that has more to do with his sister than the man himself. He clears his throat. "Can we talk outside?"

Even though he's asking a question, it comes out gruff and more demanding than anything else. Mack chuckles, pats Jake on the chest, then nods for Derek to join him. Nonverbal male communication is definitely a fascinating thing to witness. Jake leads me through the door with a hand possessively on the small of my back. I don't miss the few snickers as we leave.

"You need to go," Jake demands.

All those warm and fuzzy feelings I just had evaporate in an instant. Tapping my foot, I rest my palms on my hips and narrow my gaze at him. "And why's that? This is my bar, in case you've forgotten."

Jake's eyes rake up and down my body in response. I fold my arms across my chest, hoping I look tough over him realizing that I'm really just covering how my nipples pebbled. The upturned corner of his mouth has me believing I was a little slow on that front.

"I grabbed the to-do list from your office. I have a mix of guys willing to help out here for the next few days to make sure everything is ready."

"Not that I don't appreciate the assistance, but this is my—"

"Letty." I squeak at the depth of which he says my name. "I know it's your bar, and I believe it when you say you can do it all by yourself. But don't fight me on this. You have more important things to worry about than cleaning out the mess in there."

"What's that?" I ask softly. My mind is swirling. I don't know what to make of his gesture. Or his intentions, for that matter.

"For starters, you have an appointment to get your nails done with Tilly." I open my mouth to object, but he raises a finger. I guess he isn't finished. "That was her idea when I stopped in to talk with Scott this morning. Something about how you were both supposed to have some girl pampering before the storm ruined everything. So that's her demand, not mine. Between you and me, she needs some adult-only time with her best friend. After that, you and Scott are going to sit down and go over menus and logistics for the Fourth."

My first instinct is to argue. That's typically the reaction I have to almost anything he says. But I can't seem to find it in myself to fight with him. Besides preparing for our inspection, there's a lot more that needs to be done. Things only I can do. Ted could handle some. But at his age, he's best behind the bar, making small talk with the older regulars. He's a mascot, and he knows it. Plus, how can I turn down my best friend?

"Okay," I agree.

"Really?" He raises an eyebrow, waiting for the punch line.

"Thank you." As though some demon has possessed my body, I push up on my tippy-toes, press a soft kiss to his rough cheek, and immediately realize how stupid that was. I don't look at him. I can't. Instead, I turn around and march over to the bookstore.

23

Letty

Resting my elbows on my knees, I cradle my head in my hands. For what I can only guess is the hundredth time, I reevaluate everything again.

Bar cleaned up and put back together—*check*.

As promised, everything on my list from the inspector plus more was completed. The bar area is the cleanest I think it's ever been. All the damaged and broken furniture is gone, the debris and shattered glass picked up. Honestly, if you hadn't seen that there was almost an inch of standing water in there, you'd never know. The kitchen is immaculate. They even removed the bad equipment for me.

When he's not volunteering at the fire department, Tony Metzger works for this restaurant company that recycles used oil and inedible meat products. He's a technician and had all the equipment on hand to clean out the buildup of grease the inspector found. At this point, all I need to do is find replacement equipment and we can reopen for food service.

How these guys went above and beyond for me made leaving that horrific framed newspaper—the one with a blown-up image of Jake carrying me out of the bar after the storm—that much more bearable. I'd remove it, but considering most of the work was done by our town's emergency responders, displaying that moment of glory felt like the least I could do for them. Thankfully, no revealing pictures from that day have surfaced. I hope whatever weasel took some (because I'm certain someone did) reserves those images for his private spank-bank. But that's a matter for another day...

Menu plan finalized—*check.*

Scott had most of that figured out and really didn't need me for it. I mean, he's eaten at Harper's how many times over the years? He knows what my customers want. He's also snuck in a few new things that he's excited to try. As long as someone can get a burger and fries with their beer, I told him the rest is up to him. Chet's been over at the new restaurant, helping Scott get set up.

Sadly, I'm going to need to look for new kitchen and waitstaff when we reopen. Chet said he's getting too old and that this break has been a sign he's ready for retirement. Simon, the asshat, decided to test his luck in the Twin Cities... without notice. I only found out after I called to ask him if he was coming to meet us, when he didn't show like he was supposed to. Luckily, Jax, given his new love of cooking, agreed to help. I still have a few busboys, but I'm down to only one waitress (Kat, who works seasonally) and one backup bartender. Which, let's be honest, Ted isn't what he used to be. Not during a rush at least. He'll be perfect for the beer garden, but I need real help for the holiday chaos.

That's future Letty's problem.

Scott has talked to a couple of his baristas about waiting tables in the evenings, since we aren't offering lunch service. Cassie hooked us up with this crazy ordering system that allows us to take an order and put it into our phones. It then sends it across the street to the guys in the kitchen. They'll cook the food, and we found a couple more kids to help run everything over.

If we can sustain like this until the insurance check comes in, I think we'll be set.

Besides what Scott's taking to cover the salary for his staff, all the profits are going back to the bar. He and Cassie negotiated awesome rates for the food. Scott partnered up with some of our local farmers and Cassie got a steal on the rest. She even brokered me a discount on my liquor order when she mentioned who her brother is to my usual supplier and how Killian can provide me a list of at least three other vendors with better rates and product.

Short of stocking the bar, which I can't do until after we get our all-clear from the inspector, and putting up our festive decorations, there is nothing left for me to do but sit and wait. And fucking pray to whomever is listening that Tuesday goes off without a hitch.

What if the inspector isn't happy? Or he can't make it? Or another storm happens, and the plywood and tarp currently securing the roof aren't enough?

"What's wrong?"

I jump when Jake's palm rests on my shoulder. I was so lost in my thoughts I didn't hear the sliding door open. "Seriously." I place a hand over my chest to slow my pulse. "You need to wear a bell or something."

Jake gives me a half grin. "Sorry, sweetheart, breathless is just an effect I have on the ladies."

I launch one of the outdoor lounge pillows at him. "Full of yourself much?"

"Doesn't change the fact it's true." He shrugs, and I roll my eyes at the arrogant bastard. "What are you doing out here anyway?"

I cross my arms and cock my head. "Am I not allowed to sit out here?"

He takes a deep breath and looks at the sky. "No." He squeezes his eyes shut and rubs the bridge of his nose. "That's not what I was saying. It's just..."

I wave him off and stare out into the backyard. I've always loved this yard—it's nothing like mine growing up. Our grass was only ever mowed when the lot manager issued us a warning. There were no flowers, just dandelions. The beauty of the tree line was tarnished by piles of scrap metal and other hunks of junk Dad stashed out back. You know how they say the grass isn't always greener on the other side? Well, whoever started that bullshit was clearly standing on the *greener* lawn. Hell, the Moores' grass is without a doubt lusher and more vibrant. Not rough and scratchy, like the crap we had over at the lot.

I'm startled again as the cushion sinks and fingertips begin digging into my shoulders.

"What are you..." My question trails off with a groan as Jake presses into a painful knot.

"You looked tense," he states.

You think? "Of course, I'm tense." Doesn't he understand my future depends on some random insurance guy coming in on Tuesday and giving me the green light?

"I thought everything was all set and just waiting for the inspection." He continues to massage me. I hate how good it feels, yet I don't have the willpower to ask him to stop.

"It is. But..." It's so hard to think with his strong fingers digging deep into my muscles, working out tension I didn't even realize I had.

"But...?"

I let out a sigh. Not only because of the magic he's working, but also because of my failing resolve to keep everything to myself. "There is nothing else I can do. Everything is out of my control, and I fucking hate it. My fate rests in the hands of some stranger, and I have two days to stew while imagining all the worst-case scenarios."

"What do you do for fun?"

"Fun?" The concept seems foreign to me. Not that I don't know how to have a good time, but I don't exactly have any hobbies either. I guess I could try the book Tilly gave me. But the last thing I need to read is romance.

"Yeah, what do you do to blow off steam?" he presses. I turn my head, look at him over my shoulder, and quirk an eyebrow. His eyes darken in understanding. "What else?" His voice drops a level as he gulps.

"Get my nails done with Tilly, which we just did."

Jake frowns. "Really, that's it?"

I shrug. "What do you do?" His hooded gaze darkens again. "Besides the obvious," I clarify.

He chuckles. "Lots of things. I go running." *Of course he does.* "Fishing, bowling, watch movies."

"Oh." My cheeks burn with shame. I've spent so long only seeing the playboy that I forgot about all the other stuff. I guess it's easier to hate the persona than it is the complete individual. Especially when, deep down, you don't hate him at all. But you must because it's the best kindness you can offer.

Jake pinches his brows together as I stand and turn to face him. His legs are sprawled on each side of the chair. He leans back on his elbows and looks up at me. The posturing, mixed with the thin material of his athletic shorts, does little to hide the bulge nestled between his legs. At my continuous gaze, his dick grows firmer and jumps.

A smile spreads across my face as I think of the perfect activity to help take my mind off things for a moment, while also leveling the playing field. "Drop your shorts," I order.

"What are you doing?" Despite asking my intentions, he doesn't hesitate to remove the article of clothing. His already hard and thick cock springs free, dripping precum like a tear of joy.

I kneel on the chair and position myself between his legs. "Taking control," I say, looking deep into his eyes as I wrap my hand around his length. "I need it."

"Really? Because I'm pretty sure you enjoyed when I was in control... *Fuuuuuuccccccck.*" His cocky statement trails off into a moan as I squeeze him firmly. His eyes roll to the back of his head.

Leaning forward, I close my lips around his tip and lick off the bead of juices sitting there. Jake must be rubbing off on me, because his taste alone has my center throbbing. I'm not one to shy away and generally swallow when going down on a guy. But let's face it, sometimes it can taste awful. Of course, he just needed to have an additional check in the plus column.

Realization that it's the first time I get to do this with him encourages me to make it the best he'll ever have. I don't know why he wouldn't let me go down on him during our brief fling, but I'm not letting him stop me today. Based on his grunting as I swallow him to the back of my throat, I don't think that'll be an issue. My eyes—now trained on him—pool with tears as I hold him as deep and for as long as I can. Once black spots fill my vision, I release him and use my lingering saliva as lubricant while I stroke him. As soon as oxygen fills my lungs again, I go back to the work at hand: licking, sucking, massaging his balls, and stroking him. It isn't long before his balls clench and his fingers thread through my hair.

"I'm going to come," he warns through gritted teeth, and I'm surprised by the courtesy. Not that I can't tell, but most guys aren't as considerate. At least the ones I've been with. Lips wrapped around his head, I suck as hard as I can. He bites his knuckle, repeatedly murmuring, "Shit, shit, shit." The hand in my hair nudges me downward.

For the first time since I started, I allow him to take control and push himself deep into my throat. Seconds later, his cock pulses as warmth trickles from the tip. He flinches once before I release him with a pop. I push the remaining droplets seeping from my lips back into my mouth and suck on my finger. With a growl that sounds more animal than man, he sits up and crashes his mouth to mine, tasting himself on my lips. Reaching between us, he rubs me through the soaked material of my sleep shorts.

"These need to come off." He issues the feral demand.

I tilt my head back, giving him better access to my neck as his ferocious kisses move there. Based on the sucking and small bites, I know he's going to leave me with little love marks—again—and I couldn't care less. I whimper when he stops rubbing me. That sound is quickly replaced with a shriek as he lifts me up, spins me around, and drops me against the back of the chair.

How is he still this hard? Despite coming just moments ago, he's still fully erect. I'm so distracted by the sight I don't realize he's stripping me down, leaving me in nothing but the bikini top I'm wearing in lieu of a bra. *Laundry day.*

Roles reversed, I now sit with my legs spread wide for him. He licks his lips as he stares at my glistening pussy. I barely have a moment to brace myself before he dives in and consumes me like a starving man devouring his first and possibly last meal. My fingers thread through his hair, pushing him to exactly where I want him. The mix of his licking, sucking, and fingers has my body convulsing in no time. I clench around his fingers as he takes my clit between his teeth and sucks as hard as he can.

The fucking bastard is trying to kill me.

I'm a panting mess when Jake pushes to his feet again. My juices shimmer on his chin in the sunlight. It takes me a moment to realize he's retrieving a condom from his pocket.

Of course, this is Jake. He's always prepared. If I wasn't still high from my orgasm, I'd probably be pissed by that fact.

Wrapped and ready to go, Jake scoots in behind me, his cock pressed firmly against my back as he leans forward and sucks the lobe of my ear between his teeth. "Lift your ass. I want you to fucking ride me," he orders, sending a fresh wave of warmth through my body.

I rise up, my arms supporting me from behind and my feet on each side of the cushion. He helps me balance as he slides below me. I have to lift my leg, one foot at a time, to get into position. Like sliding together the pieces of a puzzle, the tip of his cock lines up with my spread-open pussy. Then, with his hands on my hips, he impales me with a single hard thrust. I cry out with both shock and pleasure at the sudden intrusion. He allows me only a second before continuing.

"Hold on," he whispers. And I do. Jake is relentless as he fucks me from below. The sounds of our bodies slapping combined with heavy breathing fill the backyard. He's hitting a spot that has me cross-eyed. If it wasn't for his bruising grip, I think I would collapse.

My muscles squeeze as my climax approaches, but Jake doesn't let up. He thrusts harder and faster. His palm touching my clit makes me jolt. I hadn't realized he moved his hand. At first, I think he's going to press down to push me over. Instead, he does something different. He flattens his hand and vigorously rubs his palm back and forth over my clit, just as hard and fast as he's fucking me.

An unfamiliar sensation takes over, and I don't know what to think as this foreign pressure builds. "*Fuck...* Jake... You need to... stop," I pant. He does the exact opposite and picks up his pace. The sensation intensifies and I'm not sure I can handle it.

"Don't you fucking hold back." He grits his teeth, sounding as strained as I am.

"Please..." My plea morphs into a soft scream. As though the levee breaks, I let it all out. Euphoria takes over and colors burst behind my closed eyes.

All my strength zapped, I collapse with my back against his chest. Jake lets out a soft *oof*. When I open my eyes, my face burns red with embarrassment over the amount of liquid on the chair. Sitting up while still nestled within my walls, Jake wraps his arms around me and nuzzles into my neck, pressing soft kisses against my hair. "Losing control can be fun sometimes."

It can be, but it can also be dangerous.

"Don't." He holds me tighter at the realization I'm ready to bolt.

"Jake," I say with a sigh.

"Tell me you didn't enjoy yourself."

"You know it's not that."

"Then I don't see the issue." *That's the problem. He never has.* "It's just sex, Letty."

I bite my lip in contemplation. He rocks his hips, and I let a moan slip free. He's a machine. He's already growing hard inside me. "Seriously?" I groan. "Did you pop a little blue pill or something?"

He chuckles into my neck as he offers more of those soft kisses that have me clenching him. "It's called stamina." His words tickle my ear before he sucks on my lobe. His finger traces around my clit. "At this rate, imagine how much I could do to that greedy pussy. I promise the last thing you'll be thinking about is the bar when I'm buried between your thighs."

His offer is appealing. I know this is bad, that I should run far away from him. But it seems tempting fate is a habit of mine. And, just like the booze I know I shouldn't drink, I give in to my vice. To prove to myself I will never be an addict. This is me taking what I want, and I can—and *will*—walk away when I'm ready.

"No one can know," I point out the obvious. It's one thing to play cosmic roulette. Another to advertise to the world that I'm a pathetic idiot. Especially when my best friend, his sister, is involved. I love her, but Tilly can't find out that I'm no better than all the other girls in this town. The ones I've spent years making fun of. She'd never look at me the same.

Jake hesitates before releasing a deep sigh. "No one will know."

24

Jake

LIKE A CREEP, I stand at the foot of Letty's bed and watch her sleep. For whatever asinine reason she came up with in that little head of hers, and despite how many times I made her come, she decided that she wanted to sleep alone. Some bullshit about needing *actual* sleep.

She's lying flat on her stomach, her head turned to the side and her hair fanned over her pillow. She must be a rough sleeper, or overheated during the night, because her sheets and blankets are kicked onto the floor. I angle my head to get a better view. While one leg is straight, the other is bent, leaving her spread wide-open. The thin strip of her underwear leaves her exposed to my greedy eyes.

This wasn't my plan. But not one to turn down a golden opportunity, I gently climb onto the other side of the bed. Then, I lie flat on my stomach with my nose centimeters from the sweetest thing I've ever tasted, before pulling the fabric farther to the side and exposing her fully. Letty lets out a small mew as I give her a long lick from bottom to top. I repeat the motion several times. Half-asleep and on instinct, she rolls to her back. She lifts her hips as I slide her bottoms off. I bury my head between her legs and watch her face as I make my tongue wide and thrust it in and out of her. I smile into her lips as she forms a small O with her mouth. Moaning, she rocks against my face. Her back arches off the bed as I replace my tongue with two fingers.

"Do you like that?" I ask, sucking her clit between my teeth.

"Uh-huh," she murmurs almost inaudibly. I pick up my pace, thrusting my fingers faster. Letty matches my speed and threads her hands through my hair. "Don't stop," she says breathily, spreading her legs wider. I'd tongue fuck her daily if she'd let me. Next time, she's going to ride my face. "Oh," she breathes, and squeezes her thighs so hard my eyes my bulge out of their sockets like in *Total Recall*. Fuck, that would be one hell of a way to go. I'd proudly etch "death by pussy" on my tombstone—especially this particular one.

"Do you want to come?" I tease.

"Yes," she pants.

"Tell me whose face you're going to come on."

"Yours."

"Letty," I warn, before sucking her clit between my teeth the way I know she likes.

"Oh, fuck," she cries, desperately seeking the right amount of pressure to push her over.

"I love eating this pussy," I torment. Her body freezes for a split-second before she resumes seeking friction. "I could do this all day, without ever letting you come." I had other plans, but this is a suitable alternative. "Now, tell me." I turn my fingers so they curve upwards and press right against her G-spot.

"Oh... *Tom*." Letty yelps as I bite down a little too hard on her clit. Her glorious thighs might muffle things slightly, but I know for a fact she just said someone else's name.

Who the fuck is Tom?

"Ouch," she whines, sitting up to look at me. Those large chocolate eyes are filled with mischief. "Jake, what are you doing here?" I bite down again in response. "Fuck, stop doing that."

I release her but don't move. I don't know who the fuck this Tom guy is. But I will make sure the only name to ever part her lips again is mine. "Who's Tom?"

"Better question: what are you doing in my room?"

My third finger slips into her tight channel. I see the whites of her eyes as she bites her lip. "You've been awake since you rolled onto your back. You know damn well what I've been doing in here. Now, who the fuck is Tom?"

"I don't know what you're talking about," she scolds. "I was sleeping innocently while having the most wonderful dream about Tom. Ugh, his tongue is made of magic. I was about to come harder than I ever had, when you—"

Letty's eyes go wide as I sneak a finger into her puckered hole. I don't repeat my question. My face says it all. Whatever game she's playing isn't cute. I've used my skills to get the truth from her before, and I'm not above doing it again.

"Tom Hardy," she shrieks before collapsing back onto her pillows. I remove my fingers and pounce on top of her. She squeals with laughter. "Ouch, that thing hurts when it's not stabbing you in the delightful spots." She's referring to the raging morning wood that's poking her in the stomach.

"He wants payback for the little stunt you just pulled."

"Yeah, are his feelings hurt?" Her eyes sparkle with humor. It takes my breath away. It's like being transported back in time.

While Letty will occasionally smile on the outside, there's always this hint of sadness behind it. The first time I ever saw her smile, truly smile, was when we were lying out in that clearing over a decade ago. We were watching the clouds float past as we talked about what we would do if we left Tral Lake. The places we'd go and the things we'd see. Her eyes lit up like this when she talked about going to Disney.

All the warmth of that memory is washed away as what followed it comes crashing back.

This is just sex, some no-strings fun. We're just getting our fill so we can move on, I remind myself.

"Hey, is everything okay?" Letty sounds genuinely concerned as she rests a hand on my cheek.

"Yeah." I shake away the unwanted visions.

"You sure?"

"Yes, I'm just a little disappointed." Her eyebrows draw together in confusion. "Do you know how many times I came into this room to wake you and Tilly up on the weekends when we were in high school, and saw this pussy on display for me because you insisted on sleeping in these tiny shorts with your legs spread wide? Years... I've fantasized about burying my face between your thighs and having you wake up screaming my name *for years*."

"Is that right?" She chuckles.

"It is, and when I finally had my chance, you ruined it... with Tom Hardy. What's so hot about him anyway?"

"What's *not* hot about him?" she scoffs.

"He's short."

"Everyone's short, compared to this family of giants." She has a point. I'm still wondering what growth hormones my parents fed my brother Robbie. "Anyway, what were you doing in here... besides the obvious?" She glances at the window. While there's a small stream of light peeking through, it's still dim outside. "What time is it?"

"Five."

"Five!" She hits me with a pillow. "Why in the hell are you waking me up at five in the goddamn morning? I hate mornings. It's why I'm a bartender, so I only get a glimpse of them before I go to bed."

"Well, I figured after last week with you getting up and leaving around this time every day, you must have reconsidered."

"You're an ass. What do you want at this ungodly hour?"

"Oh, I wanted to give you enough time to get up, shower, and grab your swimsuit."

"Where are we going?"

"That's a surprise."

"I hate surprises." Even as the words leave her mouth, her eyes are bright. She's excited.

"Don't care." I scoot back down between her thighs and throw her legs over my shoulders.

"What are you doing?"

"Finishing my breakfast."

25

Letty

"Nope. No way. I'm not doing it." I cross my arms over my chest and shake my head vigorously.

"Come on, it's not that bad," Jake attempts to justify again.

"That thing is massive," I screech.

"It's not that big," he says, glancing at it with a shrug.

"Not happening." I turn my nose and look away.

"Tee." He drags out my nickname. "You owe me."

I grit my teeth at his guilt trip. The same one he's been giving me all morning. Yes, recruiting the guys and helping me out at the bar was amazing, and I do owe him. But he can't seriously expect me to do... *this*. The sound of screaming reiterates my point.

"I'll do anything else." I stand firm.

"How do you know you won't like it if you don't at least give it a try?"

Is that his justification for everything? There are several things in this world I know not to try, because common sense says I shouldn't. "I don't need to drink battery acid to know I won't like it. This is no different."

"Please," he says, giving me giant hazel puppy-dog eyes and the sexiest pouty lip I've ever seen.

"Jakey-poo," I whine, thrusting my cleavage forward. He struggles to maintain eye contact and quickly fails when his gaze lands on my breasts, which are hardly contained in the black spaghetti-strap top I'm wearing. "I'm sure there are other things we could do instead. Fun things. *Wet things.*" I trail my finger down his arm.

Whatever daze I have him under isn't strong enough, and he shakes it off. "No, I want to do Wild Things." Jake presses a palm to my back and pushes me through the gates of hell. "Come on, it's our turn."

"You know, if you wanted to kill me, there are easier ways for you to do it."

The clerk snickers at my comment. I doubt I'm the first girl to ever be pushed forward by her boyfriend. Not that Jake's my... Never mind, the point is the guy probably sees this all the time. My pleading will do nothing to crack the armor he's built around his heart—courtesy of his job.

"Uh-uh, no way." I dig my feet into the ground. "If you're gonna make me do this, I won't be in the front."

"You enjoyed being in the *front* yesterday," he says suggestively.

"That was different, you asshole. People aren't meant to do this."

"Of course they are. People all around the world do it every day. It's perfectly natural."

"There's nothing natural about this."

"It might be scary at first, but I promise you're going to enjoy yourself. You're probably even going to beg me to do it again."

"Wanna bet?"

His eyes grow bright with the challenge. "Fine, name your terms."

Shit, it's rare that Jake makes a losing bet. Still, there is no way he's right about this. I know myself, and there's no way I'll like it. No matter what he says or does. "*When* I win, I get to shave your head."

"Deal," he agrees with too much confidence. He has no doubts whatsoever. Did his years of bringing me misery somehow make him an expert on my innerworkings? "When I win, you have to buy me mint ice cream."

"Seriously?" There's no way that's all he wants.

Jake leans forward and whispers in my ear, "That I'm going to eat out of your pussy." He gives my lobe a quick nibble before pulling back to glance down at me. My thighs clench at the thought. "You're hoping I win the bet now, aren't you?"

"No." *Yes.*

"Deal?"

"Deal," I say, taking his hand and allowing him to lead me to my execution platform. The clerk's face is bright red, having more than likely heard the entire exchange, as he verifies the bar is secure. His poor virgin mind is probably on overload. "I can't believe you're making me do this," I mutter again, looking forward at the tracks that will lead to our sudden death.

"It's exciting, isn't it?"

"No, it's not. Especially not when all I can think about are those awful death movies you and Tilly used to make me watch. So many kids died on these things."

Jake rolls his eyes. "If you recall correctly, there were several different ways people died in those movies."

"I know that. I was scared shitless for a week, paranoid that everything was going to kill me."

"Don't worry, Letty. Compared to others out there, this roller coaster is tame. It doesn't even have one of those loop-the-loop things."

"No, just a two-hundred-foot drop." With any luck, my heart will give out before we plummet to the ground. A whistle blows and our car begins to roll forward. *Just like in those movies.* I squeeze my eyes shut, my pulse racing as we slowly approach a steep hill.

"Wow, this view is incredible," Jake says breathlessly. "You can see the entire park from here. Come on, Letty, look."

I open my eyes as we reach the top and the nose of the car breaches over the highest point of the track. Jake lets out a victorious laugh when he realizes he got me to look at the most terrifying part. And it's like we're kids all over again, watching some stupid horror movie he and Tilly picked, as I huddle under a blanket in the Moore family living room. Jake always used to say something to make me peek before someone popped out of a corner, then he would laugh as I screamed. And so would my traitorous best friend.

My heart drops when we bend forward and face our demise head-on. I let out a squeal as we nosedive with a speed of seventy miles per hour. I scream as we go up, down, and twist. The sound echoes through a dark tunnel after which we finally come to a halt. I'm panting as the bars unlock and rise to let us out. Jake's golden hair is blown back and a giant smile is plastered on his face. I look down and realize I must have held his hand the entire time. When I loosen my grip, I can see my nail prints in his flesh.

"Well?" he asks. Instead of replying, I crash my mouth to his. Jake threads his fingers in my hair and deepens our connection. I almost forget where we are until a nasally cough interrupts us. We both peer up at the same pimply faced kid from earlier.

"I-I'm sorry... but..." He gestures to the line of people behind him. A few bystanders are clapping. Jake exits the car first, then reaches down to help me out, refusing to let go of my hand.

"So, what's next?" he asks as we walk down the stairs.

I glance at the giant roller coaster, which seems far less intimidating now that I've ridden it. I look up at him through my lashes. "Can we do it again?"

Jake's smile grows before he pulls me close to press another kiss to my lips. "I told you so," he whispers. Then he tugs me along as we push past the little gate and run back to the front of the line.

26

Letty

Chewing on my thumb nail, I obliterate what remains of my manicure. Gel polish usually lasts longer, but it's no match for my nervous habits.

True to his word, Jake has helped to keep me distracted. Going to Valley Fair yesterday was incredible. I think I rode every roller coaster at least twice. Then we made our way to the water park and hit up some attractions there. As fun as the thrilling rides were, I think my favorite was the lazy river. Despite all the noise of the surrounding parkgoers, we could just lie in our little raft, float along, and soak up the sun.

When he stopped at the convenience store to get "road provisions" on the way home, I was pleasantly surprised with his purchases. In the pickup's bed, under the stars on a back road, he gave me the experience of a lifetime. When he mentioned eating mint ice cream from my pussy, I didn't imagine that he actually would. *Oh my god*, it was... well, I don't have the words.

As it stands, Jake already eats me out like he's starving. Mix in the sensation of the cold cream, followed by the heat of his skilled tongue, and I can never look at a carton of Kemps the same way again. Not without thinking of him. When he kissed me, my juices entwined with the cool mint and *him*.

Another wonderful memory I will unfortunately carry with me forever. It was the best day of my entire life. Even if it wasn't one of those larger theme parks I've had my sights on for as long as I can remember.

I've always wanted to go to Disney, but it wasn't for the rides. I wanted to see the characters and explore. It might be shocking, *especially given my bright and sunny personality*, but I love Disney princesses. When I was little, my mom and I would watch every movie on repeat. We would sing the songs and dance around the house. She told me about a place where I could meet all the princesses and have a tea party. She even promised she'd take me there when I was a little older. Then she got sick, and one day, she was just gone...

A year later, the Moores made plans for a family vacation and invited me to come along. Honestly, looking back at it now, I think the only reason they planned the trip was to help distract me from the upcoming anniversary. Initially, it worked. I was so excited I didn't realize mom was gone until I went home to tell her about the invitation. Once the shadow of her absence was cast over the trip, I couldn't imagine enjoying it without her. I didn't care about the amusement park, the princesses, the food, or any of it. It was just something I was looking forward to doing with *my mom*.

Staying behind is one of my biggest regrets. It at least makes the top three. I should have gone. But back then, my mind could only think of how much I'd miss her. However, now that I'm older, I wish I would have enjoyed it in her honor. I even saved my tips for two years, intending to make the trip after graduation. You know, like as one last hoorah before Tilly had to go to college. I figured we could plan something later in July, since there was no way Jake would ever let her miss their shared birthday. But Dad killed any and all hopes of that happening.

With what I saved, plus the graduation money I got from the Moores and the collection Ted gathered from the patrons at Harper's, I had more than enough. It almost seemed like destiny. Jake and I were... well, we were *something*. And Tilly and Jax were together. We could have had a blast, except dear old Dad had other things in mind. I came home to find the house torn apart and the box of tampons I hid my savings in lying amongst the wreckage. Every penny I pinched and was gifted for the entire two years, gone in a single drunken rampage. Sadly, that was only the tip of the iceberg.

I opened a new account not long after that incident, since I was an adult and didn't need him as a cosigner anymore, only to find my credit was riddled with debt he took out under my name. That little treat was like the gift that kept on giving. Collection notices and paycheck garnishments. At almost thirty, I should have been building credit history, maybe making a few mistakes along the way. Instead, my young adulthood has been spent cleaning up his mess.

My text tone dings, and I'm shaken from my miserable past into my miserable present.

Jakey-poo: How's it going?

I sigh, noticing the time. The inspector is an hour late. I was hoping the text was from the insurance agency, saying someone was on their way or something. Nope, just Jake again. It's not that I'm ignoring him. I just don't know what to say. The guys worked their asses off, and it all might be for nothing.

Ted left about fifteen minutes ago to grab us some lunch from the café. I growl and stomp my feet as I pace through the bar. Muscles coiled tight, I'm ready to combust. Every ounce of tension Jake worked out of my body over the last couple of days has returned with a vengeance. The weight of all of this is suffocating.

The food and liquor we ordered are supposed to be delivered tomorrow. In the unlikely event we don't get the green light, Scott assured me he'd be able to use the food. Something about a pop-up restaurant—I don't know. It isn't like the booze will go bad. We have the permits to serve at the beer garden for the parade, so the kegs won't go to waste either.

The past couple of days with Jake have been fun. More fun than I've ever had. It's like for the past thirteen years I've been working myself to the bone, never really taking any time off. The exception being that year Tilly convinced me to join her and Cassie for spring break. While it was fun, it wasn't anything like yesterday. I already spent my days surrounded by drunk idiots (still do) and spring break wasn't much different.

Most of that trip, I acted as their designated bodyguard to make sure Tilly and Cassie didn't get date-raped by some frat douche. The only chance I got to relax was the couple of hours spent lounging on the beach, while they recovered from their hangovers before the partying started all over again.

Like I said, I was with my best friend, so of course I enjoyed it and was excited to spend time with her, especially since I hardly got to see her while she was away at school. It was also nice to watch her have some fun, considering she'd been so sad about her breakup with Jax. But yesterday was different; it was freeing. Though it probably had something to do with Jake's carefree personality rubbing off on me.

I stop and turn at the sound of the front door opening. My shoulders drop when I realize it's just Ted coming back with our sandwiches. "Come on, kid, you need to eat." He gestures to the table. My stomach grumbles as I get a whiff of the food. With a sigh, I collapse in the seat and tear open the wrapper to my sandwich. "You know, kid, I've been thinking..." I pause with my lunch hovering in front of my mouth. As much as I want to sink my teeth into it, I have a feeling whatever nonsense Ted's about to spew is going to require my full attention. "Maybe this is a sign."

"Stop." I set my food down and hold up a hand. "This isn't a sign or fate or anything else, Ted. It's life. I was dealt a shitty hand, and I've grown accustomed to disappointment. But don't try changing my mind. I want this place. As much as it will fucking suck if the asshole doesn't show up today and we can't open for the holidays, I will figure it out."

"I know you will, but there's so much you could do with your life. With your determination and business smarts. You could put it all to better use. Your mother, God rest her soul, would turn over in her grave if she knew you were wasting away here."

"Ted," I caution. "I'm not wasting away."

"You are, and it's my fault. When Samantha begged me to fire you—"

"Mrs. Moore did what?" I ask, slamming my hands on the table in shock. Ted jumps, then nods with his gaze cast to the floor. "What did she say?" I wrap my arms around myself.

He laughs, shaking his head. "Oh, Samantha was pissed when she heard I hired you. Came marching into the bar one night demanding I fire you at once. That she'd give you a job at the café or bookshop instead."

"I remember that..." I trail off, and Ted scrunches his brows together in confusion. "She never said anything outright. But not long after I started, she offered me a job at the shop with more money than I was making here. Hell, probably more than she paid anyone else. She wasn't all that pleased when I said no."

Her jaw about hit the floor when I turned her down. She didn't say it, but the disappointment was etched on her face. It broke my heart to let her down like that. But I couldn't handle the embarrassment that my dad would have caused. His reputation wasn't a secret. However, hearing about the town drunk and being exposed to his toxicity were two different things. I couldn't handle the day I'd have to cut out early to scrape him off the floor somewhere. Like when I was interrupted during one of my finals with a page from the principal's office that there was an *emergency* at home. That was my dad's code, meaning he was out of booze and I needed to pick him up a bottle from the store on the way over.

Small-town conveniences. Clark from the liquor store had no problem selling me booze and smokes long before I was ever legal. They all knew where it was going. So, yes, the Moores knew who he was. But I don't think they really understood what that meant.

Ted shakes his head with a sad laugh. "She was angrier after your daddy passed."

I open and shut my mouth, unsure how to respond. "Did she say why?"

Ted shrugs. "Samantha meant well. You weren't quite the same after he died, though, and she was worried you'd follow down that path. I think her goal was to keep you as far from this life as possible."

I get it. She feared I'd suffer his fate. I mean, the whole town saw how well he handled my mother's death. It wouldn't be hard for her, or anyone, to assume I'd drink myself into oblivion like he had. As I proved the other week, I'm not above hitting the bottle when shit gets hard. But what she and everyone else saw wasn't grief; it was guilt. Guilt for moving out, and not being there to take care of him. Because, despite being a mean son-of-a-bitch when he drank, he was still my father.

Guilt for not checking on him when he didn't show up to Harper's for a few days. But after the sheriff had been called and escorted him home the last time, I didn't think too much on it. Dad had become belligerent, screaming about how the least I could do was give him free drinks and food since he was going to starve to death. *Because of me.* That they turned off the power at the trailer and it was my fault for not paying my share, even though I moved out months prior.

Guilt for not crying when Lafferty Senior called me down to the coroner's office (per procedure) to identify and claim the body of my bloated father. From what they determined, he had passed out drunk on the floor and choked on his own vomit. Not that he was long for the world by that point. According to the autopsy, he had advanced liver failure.

Guilt for the relief I felt upon realizing we were spared the medical debt from the care he would have needed. As well as the time I would have wasted at his bedside, attempting to comfort him in his final days. Guilt for the weight lifted off my shoulders, knowing he was no longer a burden for me to carry. The only grief I suffered was when they demolished and ripped out the trailer. The county gained it as part of liquifying the estate to pay his debts. Not that I wanted it. He'd trashed the small space over the years, and it didn't even resemble the pleasant home we once used to have. It was more the symbolism that got to me. One more piece of *her* lost.

"So why didn't you fire me?" I ask, hoping to steer my mind away from the rabbit hole I was spiraling down. I have enough to worry about. Reliving negativity won't do anything to help me now.

Ted smiles. "I tried, but you kept coming back to work. Eventually, I gave up trying."

"That explains it." I chuckle. "I thought you were just trying to teach me a lesson about hard work and determination."

"Well, if that's what you got from it, then that's exactly what I was doing." Ted nods to my meal. "Now eat up, kid."

We eat in peaceful silence, whatever point Ted was going to make about me giving up on this place long forgotten. I appreciate everything he's done for me. Taking me under his wing and teaching me all I know. Giving me an actual home. It might be unconventional, dirty, occasionally rowdy, but I wouldn't change a thing. The Moores meant well and always had their door open for me. I just never felt like I belonged in their Beaver Cleaver sitcom home. I still asked to use their bathroom whenever I was over.

Just as I take a giant bite of my hoagie, the front door of the bar opens, and the inspector walks through. I almost choke as I try to swallow quickly and stand to greet him. "Sorry I'm late," he apologizes as he glances around. "I had another inspection before this one, and it ran over."

"No worries." I scan the table for a napkin but don't see one. Discreetly as possible, I wipe my hands on the back of my shirt. "I'm just glad you made it."

"Well, let's take a look, shall we?"

27

Jake

SITTING ON THE COUCH, I keep glancing from my phone to the door. I figured Letty would have been back by now. Or at least texted. I don't know how much time these things take. But it can't be this long, can it? It's almost seven at night. There's no way they do inspections that late.

What if she got denied? Fuck, I didn't think about that. No, no way. I might not know shit about running a bar, but we made that checklist our bitch. There is no way she didn't get her approval.

Then where is she? Better yet, *why do I care?* I shouldn't. We had our fun. I helped her get things ready for the reopening and kept her mind at ease while she waited for her inspection today. Granted, it wasn't all one-hundred percent chivalrous. I got to live out a few of the fantasies that have been floating through my mind over the years. Why can't I get her out of my head?

Is it because there are still more? That I haven't had her every which way yet? Do I just keep getting my fill and hope to find the threshold soon? Because it's there; it's always there. Do I plan on being some bachelor for the rest of my life? No, I don't. I'm sure one day I will meet *that* girl and settle down. Have a kid or two, maybe a dog. I guess it depends. The point is I'm not some guy saying he'll never be tied down. I'm not against commitment. I just haven't found the right woman yet. There was a time I thought I had, but that was nothing more than a hormonal eighteen-year-old's pipe dream.

You're older now and things change. I shake my head at the ridiculous notion. Things don't change that much. We were kids, and I got caught up in the moment—a byproduct of having parents who found their soul mates in high school. My brain short-circuited, and I misinterpreted my natural horniness for something more. Like love.

I never thanked her, but I should have. For ending things before I did something stupid. Such as, confess my feelings. *Fuck*, she would have never let me live that down.

Nope, this is just some fluke. Boredom. Convenience. Fucking her brains out is more about maintaining my sanity than my overall desire for her. Soon, Harper's will be up and running again, and she'll be there all day. The roof will get repaired, and she'll be out of my hair. Everything will be back to normal. Letty, the sexy bar maiden. Me, the charming playboy.

It's what I want. Hell, what we both want. But if that's the case, then why does the thought of her not being here feel like a thousand pounds crushing my chest?

I grab my phone again—*seven thirty.*

"Damn it, Letty," I grumble to myself as I rise from the couch. Knowing her, I bet she got the approval to open back up tomorrow and is probably at the bar, alone, scrambling to get things ready. Not that she'd ever ask, but I should help.

I open the front door, keys in hand, but stop dead in my tracks. Unable to move. Letty stands there, her eyes wide and her teeth biting the handle of a plastic bag that rests on top of two pizza boxes she is currently balancing in her arms. One hand's extended, as if she was trying to get in, but struggled to work the doorknob without dropping everything. I can't hold back my laughter at her expense. In true Letty fashion, instead of knocking or seeking assistance, she tried to do everything on her own.

She frowns. "Are you going to move?" she grinds out with her teeth still clenched together.

I step aside to allow her entry. She rolls her eyes at me before walking through the door towards the kitchen. I take a moment to appreciate the sway of her hips and how the denim of her jeans hugs the curve of her ass... *perfectly*. Instead of wearing the cut-off shorts she's been tormenting me with for the past week, she went with a pair of pants covered in slits and holes—one of them below her left butt cheek, giving me a sneak peek.

Shutting the door, I follow behind her. Letty places the pizza on the counter, then drops the bag down. Is that what took her so long? Also, she doesn't have a car. Did she seriously walk the whole way with everything piled on top of her?

"How'd it go?" I ask, sniffing around. My stomach rumbles and I realize, uncharacteristically, I haven't eaten today. While my appetite demands to know what deliciousness she brought home, my brain won't allow me to enjoy it until I know if this meal is celebratory or in consolation. Unfortunately, Letty isn't giving me any clues. Her face is blank.

I scratch the back of my neck. It's rare that I can't get a read on someone. But Letty is a paradox. One moment, I can tell exactly what she's thinking. The next, nothing. It annoys me and makes my dick hard, all in one go. Sucking her bottom lip between her teeth, she lets out a deep breath. Her big chocolate pools never leave mine. My heart plummets as her shoulders drop and she looks away.

"You can't be serious?" I shout. No way. That place was fucking cleaner than it's ever been. How could Ted be allowed to operate for all these years in that grease fire waiting to happen (seriously, after Jenkins cleaned the grease trap, we were shocked that the place hadn't gone up in flames already) but now she's getting shut down?

Letty's lip twitches and her eye ticks. Suddenly the room is filled with laughter—*hers*. She bends in half, holding her gut. "*Oh my god,*" she wheezes. "You should've seen your face."

I stand there slack-jawed, feeling like an idiot. Clearly, I'm missing something. Letty straightens herself and wipes a tear from her eyes. *It can't be that funny.*

"Sorry, that wasn't the plan. But I couldn't resist." She takes a calming breath. "The inspector was late. He had a couple of small notes that we corrected onsite. But I got my all-clear."

"So, you get to reopen tomorrow?"

"Yup," Letty says, but not with as much enthusiasm as I was expecting. Granted, she's never been the giddy schoolgirl type.

"Then what's all this?" I point to the stuff on the counter. "I assumed you'd be there, prepping for tomorrow."

"Already did." Her face flushes. "There wasn't much to do since we aren't serving food. It only took a couple of hours to get everything stocked and ready to open. Tomorrow morning, I will just need to stop by the café to pick up my garnishes, since I can't prep them at the bar. This...?" She looks behind her. "I don't know. It's stupid, and in no way equivalent to what you guys did for me or for allowing me to stay here. But... I wanted to say thank you. It was last minute, and this was the best I could—"

I crash my mouth to hers. Effectively stopping her rambling. My fingers thread through her hair as I pull her closer and deepen the kiss. While my cock can think of several ways she can show her gratitude, the loud rumble of my stomach kills the mood. Reluctantly, I separate from her. "The pizza smells amazing."

"Oh, yeah," she replies breathlessly, as though she'd forgotten.

"Did you walk home with all this?"

Letty snorts. "No, Ted gave me a ride after helping me prep."

I'm relieved, knowing she didn't cart this across town or set up on her own. "What'd you get?"

"Pepperoni." Of course, Letty and her boring pizza toppings. She was always the weird one who'd be happy with just cheese. "For me," she clarifies. "I told Dax that the second pizza was for you and to go hog wild."

Excitement floods through my veins. Dax is a cool dude, and knows me well enough to make something amazing. He recently took over his parents' pizzeria after they retired. I approach the counter and open the top box to reveal Letty's lackluster pizza. She laughs as I quickly cast it aside. I open the cardboard lid of the next one, and I swear gold light emits from the contents and angels sound their trumpets. The aroma alone has my mouth watering.

"He said it was something new," she mentions. "He got some special honey-apple barbecue sauce from Eli. I guess he put it on there, along with smoked chicken, caramelized onions, and..."

"Rhubarb." It takes me a minute to figure it out, but now the scent hits me.

"Yeah, it sounded disgusting. But usually that translates to delicious for you."

"You just need to be more open-minded," I comment as I grab a slice. Letty, like the responsible adult she is, walks around the counter to grab plates while I sink my teeth into this bad boy. The flavors explode on my tongue like little bombs going off. It's the perfect balance of sweet and savory. The rhubarb mixed with the basil practically blows my mind.

"Do you two need a room?" Letty snickers behind me, paper plates in hand.

I turn and offer her a bite. "Try it."

She wrinkles her nose and shakes her head. "Ew, no."

"Come on, trust me." Why does she always have to question me?

"No, you have the taste buds of a stoner."

"That doesn't mean I'm wrong."

"Rhubarb doesn't go on pizza."

"Says who?"

"The same people who say pineapple doesn't. It's fruit."

"Tomatoes are fruit." I grin, and Letty huffs in annoyance. I love when she gets worked up, especially when I know I'm right. "I'll make you a deal." She quirks an eyebrow at me. "Take a bite. If you don't like it, you can pick the movie."

She knows how serious an offer this is. Over the years, we've had many battles over what to watch in this house. Not that she has terrible taste. It's the principle of the matter. Granted, I know if she wins, she'll pick some princess flick, hoping to annoy the piss out of me. Too bad for her I don't hate the movies as much as I pretend, especially the ones with a catchy soundtrack. It's just part of the routine. I love to hate the things she enjoys because when Letty is angry, she's as cute as a ferocious little kitten.

"But if you like it—*like I know you will*—I get to pick," I explain with a grin.

"No," she groans, crossing her arms and pushing her breasts up to peek over her low-hanging tank top. They might be covered by a sports bra, which she conveniently put on since she's wearing a man's muscle top that has wide-arm openings. However, the perky little fuckers look extra tempting like that. I can't see them, but I would bet my left testicle that her nipples are hard. They always firm up when she's angry at me.

Huh, I wonder if that's why I enjoy pushing her buttons so much...

"You're going to pick some movie that has a guy getting his face ripped off." She hates horror flicks, which always made forcing her to watch them that much more satisfying. Since Tilly loves them too, it was never hard to outvote Letty.

"See? This way, I'll know you're not lying." I take a step closer to her, put the slice to her lips, and look into her eyes. "If you hate it, we both know the pleasure you'll take in not only being right, but also getting to force me to watch one of those old Disney films that bore every child into naptime."

"Hey!" She pushes firmly against my chest, catching me off-guard. I have to take a step back to balance myself. *Like I said, ferocious kitten.* At first glance, you'd think she's nothing but sweet bubblegum with a touch of punk rock. Loud, but ultimately harmless. However, push her too hard, and the claws come out. And those scratches sting. "They don't put kids to sleep. They're classics."

"I'll give you that. They are classic and will always hold a special place in cinematic history. But they are snooze-fests, and you know it." She pinches her mouth together, obviously annoyed by how right I am. "Anyway, back to the matter at hand. What do you say, Tee? Ready to expand your horizons?"

"You're that sure of yourself?"

"I am."

Not breaking eye contact, she opens her mouth wide, and of course my cock grows, wishing he could switch places with the bubbling cheese. She takes a bite and chews, defiance written across her features. She wants to hate it. But her dilated pupils betray her. I won.

"You suck," she groans before going in for another bite.

I let go of the slice, and it flops down, hitting her in the chin. She keeps hold of it with her teeth before grabbing the other end of the crust. I connect with her shoulder as I walk past. "Skip the plates. Grab the box," I call out as I exit the kitchen. "I'll get the movie cued up."

Quickly, I rush to the small collection we have on hand. Mom, not wanting our movies on display for the world to see, had dad build a custom chestnut bookcase in the living room that spans the length of the wall. As you can imagine, it's filled to the brim with books. Mostly older decorative ones that only Tilly or Dad would ever read. But the bottom section, with the cupboard doors, is equally packed with Blu-rays and DVDs. I have each section organized by genre with some bleed over. The chick-flicks Scott loves only get a couple of shelves, while horror takes up about three sections. The second largest being action. We even have a small kids section for Letty, since she was the only one who was into them. Like the rest of the makeshift Moore clan, Jax included, she got her say in movie night. I take only a minute to spot my visual torture device and our entertainment for the night.

I pop in the disk and conveniently hide the cover so she can't see what I picked. Plopping down on the couch, I rest my arm over the back and get comfortable as I wait for her. It isn't long before she enters with *one* pizza box on her open palm and a couple of beers tucked under her arm. She sets everything down and takes a seat next to me. I start up the film while she leans forward and grabs us each a slice. Food in hand, I anxiously wait for her to peer up at the screen.

Over the years, I've taken pleasure in tormenting her with horror movies. In watching her squirm and cover her eyes during all the good parts. But nothing ever compared to the complete and utter horror on her face when we first watched this one.

"I really hope you didn't pick anything gory," she remarks. "I'd prefer not to watch someone get disemboweled while we're eating. Granted, a normal person wouldn't want to see that *ever*."

"I promise it isn't *gory*," I say with a wolfish grin.

"I'm struggling to find that comforting." *Just you wait.* It isn't long before the title screen appears, revealing exactly what I picked. "*No,*" she cries, "you didn't."

"Oh, yes, I did." The warmth of victory floods my veins.

"Please, anything but this. I'm not even above the whole *guy having his face ripped off* thing right now."

"Nope, too late. Movie's started. We have to finish—that's the rule."

Letty's nostrils flare as she takes a deep breath, before her shoulders drop and she finally concedes. We may be adults and no one else will ever know. But even after their deaths, we wouldn't dare break one of Mom and Dad's rules. The ones they drew up in order to maintain civil living in a house full of rambunctious children and their friends. These conditions kept things fair and the bloodshed minimal. Once a movie is started, it must be finished by all parties involved.

"That's a low blow, even for you."

"Come on, Letty, it's just a movie about spiders."

She shivers at the mention of her biggest eight-legged phobia. Oh, yes, Letty might get creeped out and hide through most horror movies. But in everyday life, she is beyond terrified of spiders. So much so, she doesn't even have the courage to get close enough to kill them. Out of all the crap she was exposed to as a kid, *Arachnophobia* is the one that sunk deep into her psyche and had her paranoid for weeks.

"I hate you," she mumbles.

"I know," I reply with a smirk before pulling her closer.

I sit here comfortably and enjoy my new pizza with her tucked into my side. How natural it feels doesn't escape my notice. Letty and I have watched countless movies in this room over the years. But never just us and never sitting together on the same couch, at least not without Tilly between us. I glance down at Letty, her eyes wide and glued to the screen. At the first sign of a spider, she yelps and buries her face into my chest. Her repeated declarations of hatred are muffled against my shirt, but I can hear them. I shake my head and laugh, enjoying this more than I probably should.

"Don't worry, Tee." I rub her back. "I won't let any of the big bad house spiders get you."

"Fuck off," she says a little louder. But contrary to her statement, she nuzzles in deeper and holds on to me tighter.

FRANKIE PAGE

This might be my new favorite movie...

28

Letty

DESPITE NOT GETTING A wink of sleep last night, thanks to fucking Jake and his horrific choice in movies, I feel like a million bucks. How money can feel like anything is beyond me, but I didn't make up the phrase. Needless to say, I feel *fan-fucking-tastic*. It may not be back to normal, but Harper's is open. Looking nicer and cleaner than it ever has before. We are packed to the brim with regulars and tourists. Scott has his crew here doing a practice run for our limited lunch hour. We figured it would be best to work out any kinks in our system today versus tomorrow when I know we will be twice as busy.

Since the parade goes down Main Street, which will block the road between the bar and café, we are only offering evening service for food tomorrow—besides a small supply of prepackaged snacks. Granted, most people will be out in the street watching the festivities anyway. It will be a while before everything is cleared up. Nonetheless, that is my biggest concern tomorrow.

After the parade, they keep the business district of Main blocked off to vehicles. There is a giant street party, and I'm worried about the servers being able to run orders over. Everything will be packaged in disposable to-go containers, but still, I hate the lack of control. Scott assured me he has everything set with the city, and that they are doing a small barricade to make a walking path. But I know how people can get, especially when they are drunk and rowdy.

Take a deep breath, I remind myself. *It could be worse. We could be closed.*

Regardless, we will have the beer garden tent out on Main, but that doesn't compare to the revenue we see inside the bar. You'd be surprised how many people look to escape the shenanigans outdoors, avoid the sun, relax, and cool off. The only lull we'll have after the parade tomorrow is during the fireworks show. But as soon as that's wrapped up, the party moves in here.

It's chaotic. Loud. And I probably won't have time to sit, eat, or drink all damn day, considering my only back up (Ted) will be manning the beer garden. Either way, it's going to be a fucking blast. The high I get from days like these can only compare to the roller coasters we road at the fair. I guess, much like Jake, I too am an adrenaline junkie. However, where he gets it from that death-defying shit, I get it from being pushed to exhaustion's limit and the gratification from knowing (after the madness has settled) that I survived.

"Holy fuck," Kat, my seasonal waitress, comments.

She's been helping out for the past three years whenever she's home for summer break. Thank fuck I don't have to replace her today. It's sad knowing this is probably her last season. Unless I'm lucky and she switched to a longer degree, this is going to be her senior year. And she'll be bound for some fancy city job, way overqualified to sling drinks and burgers all day.

"This is insane." She gestures to the phone in her hand. "When we get the kitchen back up and running, can we keep this?"

"That good, huh?"

"Seriously, there are picture buttons for food. Not to mention, no more excuses from Chet's old ass. No more *if you wrote clearer...* or whatever shit he comes up with when he gets an order wrong."

"Ugh," I groan. "Don't bring up Chet." She quirks an eyebrow at me as I load up her tray with a couple of long-necks. "Just one more staff member I'm going to have to replace."

"That isn't a terrible thing. You could use some hotter men in this place. I'm thinking someone tall, dark, and handsome. Oh! With tattoos and a fractured past. Then, one night, when you are both working late—"

She squeaks with laughter as I whip a towel at her. "You're as bad as Tilly."

The girl just shrugs with her tray in hand. "What? You spend all day here. If you're ever going to get some, it's going to be with someone at work. So far, you have two ancient dudes and a couple of busboys who I'm not even sure have seen their first pube yet."

"I get enough," I clarify, without going into detail. Then again, now that I'm back at work, our little arrangement (as fun as it was) is over. Especially considering his hunting ground is once again *open for business.*

I bite the inside of my cheek as my chest squeezes at the thought of watching him in here, picking up his new flavor of the week. I did it before. It took a while to tune it out, but I did. Luckily, with Harper's reopen (partially) and Jake going back to work after the Fourth, we should hardly see each other until I move out. We'll get back to normal soon and forget whatever temporary insanity consumed us this past week. Besides, if I add up all the orgasms I've had in the past nine days, I'd hit my quota for the year. My vagina needs a break.

Okay, that's a lie. Even after being thoroughly serviced on the couch last night, to make up for the terrible movie choice, she clenches the second his name, face, tongue—any part of him—flits through my mind. He's corrupted me. I have had spontaneous flashbacks of the things he's done to me three times already today. *So far.* Jake has always had an enormous appetite for food and sex. I just never realized they went hand in hand.

"Yo, sweet cheeks," some douche at the other end of the bar calls out. To keep myself from stabbing him in the eye with my paring knife, I repeat my internal mantra, reminding myself that they bring in the money and I won't make any if I go ahead and kill all the tourists. "When you're done painting your nails, how 'bout you do your job and get me a drink?"

Kat rolls her eyes before giving me a sympathetic smile and walking over to deliver the tray of beer. She knows how it goes. The regulars usually never say or do much. You get the occasional drunken asshat, but when you're the main bar in town, they tend to be on their best behavior. I'm not sure if I got soft over the past couple of weeks, but the way some of these guys have been acting today... it leaves my stomach in knots. It's probably a good thing I haven't eaten yet.

I shake off the negativity. This is my bar. My town. I might rely on their patronage to keep things afloat, but they rely on having a place to conspire with their douchey counterparts.

Bracing my hands on the bar, I lean forward to better hear their order. I don't miss how jackass number one's eyes travel down my shirt. I let him get his fill. It usually shuts them up. Not to mention, better tips.

"Sup?" He gives me his best set of bedroom eyes. He bumps shoulders with jackass number two. *God,* do girls really fall for this shit in the cities?

I keep my face blank, my tone flat. "What can I get you?"

"How 'bout your number?" He high-fives his buddy. As if that was the cleverest line ever uttered to a girl in a bar. *Oh, how my panties are damp—not.*

I smack my gum and blow a bubble. It makes a dramatically loud pop in the noisy space. "Okay, now that you got that cliché out of your system, what would you like to drink?"

"Aren't you feisty?" number one observes. A couple of customers wave me down at the other end of the bar. As much as I love playing around with assholes like these two, I don't have the time for it tonight. Pushing myself off the bar, I squat down and grab a couple bottles of whatever trendy crap my supplier dropped off. Skillfully, I pop the tops on the ledge of the counter and slide the bottles over.

"That'll be fifteen," I demand with my hand out.

Number two pulls a twenty from his wallet and places it in my palm. I go to retract, but he holds on. "Keep the change, *señorita*," he says in a horrific accent that tells me he took the two years of mandatory Spanish in school and only learned enough to visit Cancún, in hopes of picking up an unsuspecting local.

I open my mouth to respond when a deep voice interrupts me. "Is there a problem here?"

Jake and Derek tower behind them. The tourists versus the locals, appearing like night and day. Jake is in pale-blue denim with a tight white t-shirt—the lightness of his wardrobe mixed with his sun-bleached hair makes him seem that much tanner—while Derek is Mr. Tall-Dark-and-Broody. Pre-Cassie, the sheriff's officer would definitely hold his own in a brooding contest with Robbie.

His dark hair is styled in that *I look like I just got out of bed but I actually spent an hour twisting the ends so they're perfect* way, and he's wearing a black shirt with dark-gray slacks. It's the epitome of good cop, bad cop. Which is funny since Derek is one. A good cop, that is. He may have a future starring in the next Batman movie, but the guy is one big softie.

The air is sucked from the room when Jake's burning gaze goes from the tourist's hand on my wrist up to my face. And I'm not sure if this ridiculous guilt in the pit of my stomach is because I've allowed some other male to touch me in his presence. Or because I'm off my game in general and allowed this guy to touch me in the first place. I'm stronger and faster than this. The last thing I need is Jacob Moore coming in here like Prince Charming and looking to rescue me. I've reached my quota this year. That photo hung up on the wall is proof enough. I can't allow myself to fall into a routine of relying on him.

I snatch my arm back, along with the money. "Nope, no problems here. They were just leaving," I say as a demand to them and a clarification to him. Number one is about to object, but number two does some telepathic guy speak. They take their beers and walk to an open table. Jake and Derek slide into the now vacant spots. I don't bother asking what they want and grab a couple of beers off the tap.

Derek glances around the place. "It's packed in here." Ah, yes, Officer Lafferty is also Captain Obvious, though I appreciate his attempt to break whatever awkwardness Jake is sending my way. The douchenozzles are gone, but that fire is still in his eyes, and it's burning me from the inside out.

What the fuck is his deal?

"Where's Ted?" Jake bites out. Derek chuckles before taking a sip of his beer, looking anywhere but our way. I don't blame him. The tension is enough that even I want to escape it.

"At home," I state. I'm about to walk over to a group of waiting customers, when a strong grip grabs me again. "What is with people thinking they can just touch me?" I yell at him.

Realizing his mistake, Jake lets go immediately and lifts his palms. "Sorry, it's just..." He lets out a sigh and rubs the back of his neck. "Why isn't Ted here? You're busy. Have you even taken a break today?"

"Ted's old," I justify. Jake's deadpan stare tells me that isn't excuse enough. "And he's slow. It's why he started having me take over. He'd just be in my way. Not to mention, he's got to run the garden tomorrow. So, I told him we'd handle everything here so he could rest."

Jake should know better. Ted has been deteriorating for a while. Not just physically, but mentally. Many of the past-due notices I found were simply because he forgot to pay. He'll mix up orders, not take money or take too much. I trust the regulars enough to not take advantage. But the tourists? No way, especially assholes like dumb and dumber over there.

"Now, if you'll excuse me, I got some customers who have been patiently waiting. Be back in a moment to freshen your drinks." Before I walk away, I turn around. "Oh, and tap's on the house. For all your help." Not giving him a chance to reply, I resume serving up drinks.

The next couple of orders go smoothly. Thank fuck not all of our tourists are as bad as the guys from earlier. While I harp on a specific set of people who come down to spend the summer on the water, there are a few good ones. Turning to grab a bottle of vodka from the shelf, I run into a hard chest. My senses go on high alert, before I notice the white shirt and the scent of his cologne mixed with something that is just naturally *him*. But before I let my libido cloud my judgement, my big-girl brain takes over.

"What are you doing back here?" I ask, one hand resting on my cocked hip while the other pokes him in his deliciously hard, muscular chest.

No sexy thoughts. Not right now. I have a long day ahead of me, and I'd prefer a pair of dry panties to get me through it.

"Helping," he states, as if that answers anything.

"With what? Do they teach bartending at the firehouse?"

"No, but I've seen—"

"Don't even tell me you learned all you need to know from *Cocktail*." That stupidly handsome grin of his tells me I'm right. "No way." I shake my head. "I know I make it look easy, but it's not. I've had years of practice."

"I never said it was easy." He crosses his arms, his biceps flexing the sleeves of his shirt. "But look at this place. I don't think I've ever seen it this busy before. You need help."

I sigh. He's right. I could use the help. But I need experienced hands, and not the kind he has. I'd suck up my pride and call Killian, but I doubt he's in a much better situation. Not that he's located in a densely populated tourist area, but either way, holidays pack bars.

Jake looks good; he's dressed up for a night on the town. He and Derek both are. Their intentions are obvious. "I don't want to interfere with your *plans*." I nod to the sheriff's officer. "Like you said, the place is packed tonight. Lots of fresh outta-town meat for the two of you to divide and conquer. So much pussy, so little time." My bitchyness knows no bounds. This is what I agreed to, yet here I am, biting his head off the second I see him back in his role.

Once again, I'm stopped by someone grabbing me as I turn to walk away. Except, this time, I don't have but a moment to feel annoyed. Because that look he's giving me is something else. I clench every muscle in my core and pray no one can notice that I'm mere seconds from combusting. Nostrils flared, face red, he's pissed or wants to throw me on the bar and fuck me senseless. Or maybe both. I don't know why he's angry. The other, well, that might just be my own wishful thinking.

"Stop," is all he says. I don't know exactly what he means, so I stop everything. Even breathing. His eyes darken as he steps into me.

Suddenly, we're no longer in my crowded bar, filled with people all looking to me to quench their palates. The loud chatter and booming music dies out, and all I can hear is my heart pulsing. This is a terrible idea. Almost worse than deciding to allow him between my legs. It terrifies me, the thought that once I let him in, I'll never want him *out* again. And out he'll be. He'll leave, even if I have to be the one to end it again. As much as everything's changed, *nothing has*. I can never be what he wants. Despite knowing this is a disaster waiting to happen, there's also no turning back now.

"Fine," I concede. "I'll mix. You handle the beer."

Victory shines in his eyes. He leans down and my heart stops. Fear that he is going to kiss me has my feet rooted to the ground. It's already bad enough that he's here, behind the bar. It's no secret that he's helping. But if he kisses me in this room, everyone will see it. And by the end of the night, everyone will know. Including Tilly.

He creeps closer, his face next to mine. Once again, he shouldn't be doing this, but I lack the will to stop him. Just as I think our lips will caress, he pulls back and presents a rag, now clutched in his hand. "I'll get started down there." He winks before walking off. The bastard knew exactly what I was thinking, and he allowed me to think it. He *wanted* me to think it.

To my surprise, we seamlessly manage the bar. Each of us taking drink orders, Jake on top of pours and grabbing bottles, and me mostly mixing. Two hours pass, and I almost don't realize it. Typically, I hate sharing the bar with someone. Like I said, Ted is slow and usually in my way. My hyperawareness of Jake's proximity, combined with my need to avoid any additional physical closeness with the town playboy, has been to my benefit.

"Wow, you work fast." Kat snickers as she grabs her drink order. I notice her nod to Jake, and I draw my brows together, confused. "I know it was my idea, but I didn't think you'd act so fast and get some actual man candy in here."

Our earlier conversation comes back to mind. My fist clenches around the bottle as she gives Jake that wide-eyed ogle most girls offer in his direction. "Don't you have a table to serve?" I bite out harshly, and immediately regret it when shock registers on her face.

Her eyes dart from me to Jake and back to me again, before a knowing smile spreads across her cheeks. She grabs her tray. "Sorry, boss, didn't realize he was spoken for." With a saucy wink, she pivots on her heels and walks away.

Looking over, I realize the ultra-observant Captain—or better yet, *Lieutenant* Obvious, AKA Derek Lafferty—is still chilling at the bar as he chats with a few other regulars. His keen observation of what just transpired doesn't go unnoticed, especially as he glances away and laughs into his beer.

I'm well and truly fucked now.

29

Letty

I'VE NEVER BEEN SO thankful to be legitimately swamped in my entire life. Last night around midnight, we died down, which isn't unusual. That late, we typically only have those looking to party hard or hook up. All the families have gone home and are long asleep. The lull in customers gave me the excuse I needed to kick Jake out. He'd helped enough, and without a swarm of drink orders to occupy our silence, it left too many opportunities for us to talk or interact. There were only so many times I'd need to *get something* from the back, before he'd catch on that I was avoiding him.

Then, the fact I didn't get the last drunk out until about two thirty—even though last call was over—helped prolong the inevitable. I didn't have as much cleanup since we only had glassware for washing. But I still needed to wipe everything down and make sure the decorations were ready for today. I didn't get back to the house until about four in the morning. Jake was passed out on the couch, as if he waited up for me.

He is coming back to help me again today, which I appreciate but also feel bad, since this is his last day off. He has to be at the fire station to start his rotation early tomorrow morning. If he's going to be up late, he should be out celebrating with the rest of the town. Not stuck here. With me. At least I convinced him not to come in until after the parade. And only to help with the evening rush.

The food service went off with almost no issues yesterday. If anything, we suffered a few growing pains. I'm hopeful tonight will go just as smoothly. The menu was perfect and exactly what we needed to keep butts in seats long enough to have a couple of rounds.

Everything is going well. Too well.

My dad, the drunk bastard that he was, used to say: *if something seems too good to be true, it is.* Though his rambling was usually in reference to my mother, as he reminisced about how he was duped into believing what they had would last forever, he wasn't wrong. Just like Harper's. Finally, my dream was within reach. Short of some legal paperwork, the place was mine. Then the skies opened up and an actual act of God nearly destroyed it. This isn't me being religious—it's how the insurance company is classifying it. Since we don't live in a well-known tornado area, we didn't have coverage for it.

Yeah, that was the small gem I found in the business email this morning. I guess the adjuster sent it over yesterday, but I didn't have time to check. Unfortunately, it's something I'm going to have to deal with later, after I talk to Ted, or maybe even run it past Robbie. I didn't understand much of what it said but it sure didn't sound good...

For the time being, I just need to focus on surviving the holiday and one more day elbow-to-elbow with Jake. I'm terrified that after two minutes alone, I'm going to be begging him to tear my clothes off with his teeth.

Speaking of the devil, Jake strolls in, dressed much like he was yesterday. But instead of a plain t-shirt, he's wearing one branded for this year's Fourth. It's tie-dyed in blue and red with the town's logo across the chest. I'm wearing one too. It's actually a town charter requirement for all open businesses to wear these during the festivities. Lucky for me, they never specified the condition in which it needed to be worn. Mine is cut off at the waist, exposing my midriff. Neck torn open wide, it hangs off my shoulder, leaving my lacy red bralette exposed. Paired with my high-waisted stonewashed cut-off shorts, I look like I'm ready for summer fun. I'm just glad that when I skimmed through the apparel catalog, I found a pair of black and white nonslip sneakers that almost look like Chucks. All the other options had the appearance of those ugly orthopedic doctor shoes.

Jake's heated gaze travels up and down my ensemble. He shakes his head and chuckles. "I shouldn't even be surprised. Yet I am."

"What's that supposed to mean?"

"Nothing," he teases. Walking past me, he stops. The slight shock from a set of fingertips grazing the edge of my shorts makes me jump. "I think you cut a bit too much off this pair," he growls in my ear. His breath sends a shiver down my spine, and my skin goosebumps. "How am I supposed to focus when every guy here is going to be looking at your ass tonight?"

I take a step back, turn, and shake the lustful thoughts from my mind. *Letty, you need to be strong and stop this before it gets out of hand—more than it already has.*

Defiantly, I cross my arms over my chest and pivot to face him. I remind myself this isn't Jake Moore, the guy who's recently been making me come so hard I'm transported to an alternate plane of existence. Nope, this is Jakey-poo, my best friend's annoying-ass twin brother, who once covered my bed with fake spiders while I was sleeping after watching the most horrific movie of my life.

"Same as you've done every night before," I deadpan. "Focus on any other ass in this room. You have your pick. Because *mine* isn't your concern."

Jake frowns and rubs his forehead, which appears to be wrinkled with confusion. "Did I miss something?" he asks quiet enough for only me to hear.

"Yes." The crease in his forehead deepens. "No." I sigh, dropping my shoulders. I bite my lip and shake my head. "Look, this isn't the time or place." *It isn't.* This is my busiest night of the year, and I don't have time to explain to Jake what he should already know. "Let's just make it through tonight. We can talk later."

He drops his hands, tucking them in his pockets. His narrowed gaze makes my heart clench. "No, it's cool. I get it. I might be stupid, but I'm not oblivious," he bites out sharply.

My mouth opens to object. To clarify. I don't know... I want to say something to deflect the daggers he's shooting at me, except I can't. Instead, I bite my tongue as he storms off. Déjà vu slams into me, nearly stealing my breath away.

The sound of tapping startles me awake. I glance around my dark room but see nothing. Closing my eyes, I prepare to go back to sleep when the tapping becomes more incessant. I get up from my bed, head over to the window, and pull open my curtains. Jake stands outside, glaring up at me from the ground. I push open the three-tiered glass panel.

"What are you doing out there?" I whisper harshly and look at my door. Only hearing the muffled sounds of Dad's TV and his loud snoring, I turn back to Jake. Fortunately, I left my dad passed-out drunk on the lounger. It would take a nuclear explosion to wake him, and even then, I'm not positive it would; however, I wanted to make sure this wasn't one of those rare nights where he stumbles awake and rampages through the house.

"Why?" Despite the added height of the foundation under our trailer, Jake's head reaches the bottom of my window. Through the small opening, his alcohol-heavy breath wafts into my nostrils. His glassy eyes look up at

me, as if pleading for a response. Something reasonable that would help him understand.

"Jake." I sigh.

I hate seeing him like this, even more because I'm the cause of it. Further proof I'm doing the right thing. If he's like this just because I ended things after a brief summer fling, how much worse would he be if we continued? If we let these budding feelings grow beyond our control. Or worse, what if I give into whatever happily ever after I know he has rattling around in his brain, then suddenly leave him one day, just like Mom left us? I shake the thought from my mind before the tears have a chance to fall. I need to be strong, strong enough for the both of us.

"Go home."

"No." He stomps his foot, grounding himself into place. "Not until you tell me why. What did I do?"

"Nothing." A glimpse of hope shimmers in his eyes. And I need to snuff it out before it spreads like a wildfire consuming my will. "It was fun, but summer's over. It was just a fling."

"You know damn well it wasn't just a fling." His voice rises, and I glance around. The lights from the unit next door remain off—thankfully.

"It was. We were just having some fun. Blowing off some steam."

"Bullshit."

"You know it's true." That clenching in my chest tightens. The pain is almost unbearable. I need to make him believe it, squash any lingering hope he might have. "Look, the orgasms were great. Truly top-notch. But you know as well as I do that's all it was. We were bored and horny. Summer's almost over, the real world is starting, and this..." I let out a long breath. "...the expiration date is long past due."

"Why are you lying?" His brows furrow. "It was more than that. What about—"

"Jake, stick to what you're best at. Your tongue is good for one thing, and it isn't pillow talk." The words make me want to vomit, even as I say them.

Jake's nostrils flare and a vein pulses in his neck. Clenching and unclenching his fists, he stares up at me. The fire burns in his eyes, but not the one of hope or love. No, these flames are cold and hate-fueled. In all the years we've bickered and got on each other's nerves, anger or hatred would never be a word I'd use to describe it. One look, though, and I know anything that we have or had or could have had is gone. And not just these past couple of months, but everything from before.

He opens his mouth, no doubt to sling an insult or two my way. I deserve whatever lashing he has in store. Instead, he closes his jaw, grinds his teeth, and looks down at the rough patch of grass beneath his shoes. Then he shakes his head before turning on his heel and walking away as he waves a hand dismissively. I'm not even worth the final blow.

There is nothing left to say.

My heart shatters as his figure retreats into the tree line leading to the main trail that runs through town and back to his house. Each step he takes smashes the broken pieces, obliterating them into pulp. Nausea and exhaustion take over. When Jake is finally out of sight, I turn and drop to the floor. Hugging my knees tightly to my chest, I breathe deeply and stave off the tears that want to fall. I won't cry because, ultimately, we dodged a bullet. We're better off this way.

Lesson learned: love fucking sucks.

The evening rush is heavier than originally expected. Every seat is full, and people are standing where they can. Even the streets are packed. Scott's barricaded path has held up so far, which is great, given how much food is being ordered. A few of the specialty items sold out almost instantaneously. Well, the ingredients to make them anyway. Scott had these Reuben balls, which were amazing, and then this apple pie fritter thing that made your eyes roll back in your head. The only hiccup was having a temporary waitress bail out on us last minute. So I've had to both man the bar and take orders out on the floor. Nothing I haven't done before. But as quick as Jake has picked up on things, he isn't equipped to fully cover for me. *But he's better than nothing.*

The silver lining of it all is that I've been too swamped to think about Jake. Beyond anything work-related, that is. If I had a second to breathe, I'd go down a rabbit hole of wondering what he's thinking... if he's mad... Then scolding myself for caring, because this was my idea. If he's paid me any mind, beyond when I was providing him instructions, I certainly haven't seen it. No heat from his gaze or little smirks cast my way, which is another blessing since Tilly and the boys stopped by briefly after the parade.

Unlike last night, there was no sign that anything has been different between us lately. Things were so chaotic I hardly got to say three words to them before she took everyone home. So, even if there was something in the air, I doubt she would have noticed. Lucky for Tilly, their house has a clear view of the fireworks tonight from the convenience of their deck. Robbie and Cassie are going to join her there. I don't blame them. Robbie isn't exactly Mr. Social or a party guy, and at twenty weeks pregnant, Cassie isn't interested in dealing with a wave of people.

Even though I'm happy we could be open today—the revenue and tips alone will go a long way towards making up for the profits missed while we were shut down—I'm ready for tonight to be over. My body and mind are equally exhausted. As soon as I can lock the doors, I'm curling up under my comforter and refusing to open my eyes until at least 2:00 p.m. tomorrow. Ted is going to open in the morning, since he gets to cut out early when the beer garden closes. Which is great, because we usually don't get busy until the evening after the holiday anyway. Everyone is too hungover to function. Or, if it's nice, they're out on the water, soaking up the rays while I get a chance to finally breathe.

"Yo, sweet cheeks."

I turn to see who's calling out. *Great!* It's Thing One and Two from last night. Oh, and look at that! They've multiplied. Studying the additions, I realize why the guys looked so familiar. They're with Captain Douche—the tourist who freaked on me last week for having the bar closed. Just my luck. They're at a table, and would normally not be *my* headache to deal with, but being a waitress short has me in their radar.

"Hello, gentlemen." I laugh to myself. They're nothing close to resembling men or anything gentle. "What can I get for you guys this evening?" I plaster on my fakest smile and use my best customer-service voice.

Thing One whispers something to his counterpart, who then mutters to the bastard at his left. They're all snickering while the fourth guy, the one who freaked the other day, well, it appears I have his full smarmy attention. Clasping his hands together, he leans forward on his elbows. His beady eyes rake up and down my body. I hate creeps like him. He gives me that vibe, the same one that Keith gave off. In the past, I would disregard it as an allergy to privileged little boys who live off Daddy's credit card. Realizing that, ultimately, they're harmless. But after what happened with Keith, and what he attempted with Tilly, I've been more cautious. This guy, well, he sets off all my alarms and makes my skin crawl.

"What's your name?" he asks, and it takes all my willpower and then some to not vomit at the half smirk he throws in my direction.

"Letty," I offer professionally. Glancing at the table, I notice they already have a bottle of the hipster brew and several shots. "Do you guys need some burgers? Or how about a plate of nachos?" I toss out a couple of food options to move this along. Their eyes are already bloodshot and glazed over—probably three sheets to the wind. Their faces are red with pale outlines that showcase where their sunglasses have been. Alcohol and too much sun never mix well. Grease to soak up the booze will do them some good.

Number Four licks his lips. "*Leticia,*" he says with an overtly fake accent.

"Oh, yeah!" The one in the middle speaks up for the first time. "Like that hot chick from *The Fast and the Furious.*"

"Hola, señorita," Thing Two slurs.

"Amanda," I correct sarcastically, with some southern accent I pull out of nowhere.

It's going to be one of those nights. It used to happen a lot back in the bullying days. Because my mom was Hispanic (my dad was not) and I'm her spitting image, everyone assumed I spoke Spanish or alluded to some other stereotype. Like Taco Tuesday being my favorite lunch choice for school. Or kids asking me to help with their Spanish homework.

First off, yes, Taco Tuesday was my favorite. But because it was better than the meatloaf surprise or the mystery chicken casserole they served most days. *Everyone* loved Taco Tuesday.

Secondly, I speak as much Spanish as I can remember from my Minnesotan public school years, because of the district's requirement that everyone *had* to take two years of a foreign language. Which I failed, by the way, because they too assumed I was fluent and threw me into advanced courses. My mom, who did speak Spanish, died when I was eight. And unless she was teaching me a song or a specific recipe, we only ever spoke English. She never liked to make my dad feel excluded from the conversation.

"She might be cuter than that chick in the movie, but she definitely has the attitude," remarks douchebag number three.

"Are you guys going to order?" I huff out. Hip cocked to the side, I rest my hand on the curve of my waist while tapping my foot. My patience is running thin, not that I have much for their type in the first place. I still have to get the last table's drink order. Not to mention, two more groups of people came in. "If not, I have other tables waiting."

"That's no way to talk to a paying customer," number four taunts. "I think I'd like to speak to your manager. Unless..." His eyes go dark, and a chill runs down my spine. "... you'd like to come sit on my lap and make it up to me."

My nails dig into my palm as I hold back my urge to ruin this pretty boy's face. "I *am* the manager. Oh! And also the owner." I give him a victorious grin. Okay, maybe not on paper, but for all intents and purposes, I own this place. And Ted won't contradict me to an asshole like this.

His eyes travel around the room to the other waitresses, who, like me, are all wearing the town shirt with a pair of shorts or a skirt. "Ah, that explains the Coyote Ugly vibe going on here. How much to get a show?"

"Wouldn't mind a private viewing," one of them adds, though I'm not sure who. I'm so pissed I can hardly see straight. My blood is pumping in my ears, drowning out the chatter.

"You guys have had enough." My tone is flat and stern. "I'd appreciate it if you got the fuck out of my bar and never returned." I move to walk away. And I'm surprised at the punishing grip squeezing my wrist and pulling me down into the offending asshole's lap.

"Listen here, you little bitch." Number four's liquor-fueled breath suffocates me as he growls in my ear. I struggle to get up, but he moves his hand to my throat and squeezes, restricting my breathing. Something hard in his pants rubs against me, and I pray it's his wallet. Or anything other than what it probably is. "I don't know how you do things in this Podunk shithole. But no one talks to Brad Masterson like—"

The room spins as I'm ripped from *Brad's* grasp and tossed into the arms of Kat. Screams erupt and echo off the barroom walls, along with the sounds of pounding flesh. Rubbing my throat and rasping for the oxygen I lost, I turn to see what's happening. If I wasn't having a problem breathing before, I sure am now. Brad is lying on the floor with Jake kneeling over him, the firefighter's fist repeatedly hitting the tourist in the face. A wave of different emotions floods through me. But the one that outweighs the battle in my mind is how hot Jake looks beating this guy's ass.

He's not usually the violent type. I've seen him take more punches than he's dished out. Not that he can't fight, *obviously*. It's more that he never feels strongly enough to do anything beyond defending himself. Like that time Jax punched him, Jake never once raised a hand to strike back.

"Okay, man." Derek pulls Jake off the bloody mess on the ground. The sheriff's officer is in full uniform, meaning he was either patrolling and came in when he heard the commotion, or someone called. "I think he's had enough." Derek rubs the back of his neck as he looks from Jake to Brad, now crowded by his goons.

"Aren't you going to arrest him?" Number one screeches as he points to Jake, who is still huffing like a wild bull.

"That's bullshit, Lafferty," someone yells.

"The jackass was holding Letty against her will," another patron adds. I don't know who's standing up for us because my eyes refuse to leave Jake.

"Letty," Derek says, and based on his tone, I think he might have said my name a few times before I heard it. Reluctantly, I look from Jake to Derek. "Is that right? Did this man assault you?"

"Hey," one of the goon's cries, "the only person assaulting anyone is that asshole."

"They were being crude," I rasp out. "I asked them to leave when he..." I gesture to a blubbering Brad on the floor. "...grabbed me and wouldn't let me up."

"He was choking her," an angry voice in the crowd yells. "Look at her throat."

Derek's eyes narrow in on what I'm sure are a pair of red handprints marring my skin. He pats Jake on the shoulder before squatting down to talk to Brad and his buddies. "Listen here." He removes the toothpick he was chewing on. "You guys are going to go back to wherever you were staying and sleep it off." One guy opens his mouth to object, but Derek doesn't give him a chance. "If you even think about pressing charges, I can promise you *she*..." He points to me with the small piece of wood. "...won't hesitate to do the same. And with a bar full of witnesses, let me just say you won't like the outcome. How about it, Letty? Do you wanna see any of these boys in jail tonight?"

As much fun as it would be to watch these assholes get carted off and have to beg Daddy for bail money, I don't want to get Jake in trouble. I've caused him enough as it is. "I don't want to see them. Ever again." I make my intention clear: *they aren't welcome back in my establishment.*

"You heard the lady." Derek pulls Brad up by the collar of his bloodstained polo. "Now, settle whatever bill you have. Leave a tip, plus enough to cover the damages."

"But he—" one goon starts.

"He defended a female who was being assaulted and held against her will?" Derek spits out.

"It's fine," Brad says, struggling to push himself off the ground. His friends help him get to his feet. Grabbing his wallet, he draws a few hundreds and tosses them on the table. "Let's get out of this shithole. The beer tastes like piss."

"The bar's owned by a fucking cunt anyway. I'm going to leave a one-star yelp review. I have over eight thousand followers. You'll be out of business in a month."

My knuckles burn as they collide with the speaker's jaw. Pain is radiating up my arm, but I don't care. Because it felt fucking great to hit the asshole.

"Are you going to let her get away with that?" the guy whines, holding his cheek.

"Did you see anything?" Derek asks one of the regulars, then turns to another and asks the same. Everyone stands around, refusing to look at the guys, while shaking their heads in unison. "I think it's time you boys got out of here."

"Are you okay?" Jake's hazel eyes bore into me as he cradles my hand.

I nod, unsure of what else to say.

"Why don't you take Letty to the back and clean her up," Derek prompts, patting Jake on the shoulder. "I'll make sure those guys get back to their cabin, then have one of the other patrols verify when they leave town."

30

Jake

MY MIND IS REELING as I escort Letty to the bathroom. Along the way, I grab the first aid kit she keeps behind the bar while Derek helps get things under control in the dining area. It's packed, and she was already shorthanded—at least most of the people here tonight are locals. With the fireworks starting up soon, things will clear out long enough for us to get cleaned up.

What the fuck happened?

One minute, I was behind the bar watching the interaction. Letty with her hip cocked... I could tell she was pissed. Next thing I knew, the guy had her in his lap with a hand around her throat, and I was jumping over the bar to get to him. After that, all I can remember is seeing red. And not just metaphorically: his blood, the marks he left on her slender throat and wrist, the welts on his face, the cuts on my knuckles and now hers.

In the bathroom, door locked, I guide her to the sink. Silently, I rinse and inspect her wounds. The cuts are shallow. All they need is cleaning and ointment. With the way she gasped when making contact, I was worried she broke or sprained something, but so far, she hasn't made a peep. She watches our hands in a daze.

"Does it hurt?" I ask to make sure she isn't just in shock.

"Not really," she whispers. Her brow bunches together as her eyes focus on my knuckles. "Oh no, are you okay?" She turns those chocolate pools on me. They remind me of the river in *Charlie and the Chocolate Factory,* and I wish I was that fat little boy so I could fall in and drown in them.

"I'm fine." My hands look worse than they are. They will be sore for a couple of days, but nothing major.

"No, you're not—"

"Letty," I say sternly as she scrambles to look through the first aid kit. She halts, glancing back at me. I reach up and gently brush the bruise he left on her neck. She winces, and my desire to beat the guy's face in reignites. "What happened?" I grind my molars as she looks down at the floor.

"Can we just drop it?" Her shallow tone squeezes my chest.

"Please," I plead, taking her face in my palms and nudging her chin upwards so I can look at her. "Talk to me."

"It's nothing I haven't heard before."

"That doesn't make it okay."

"I never said it was okay." The bite in her tone returns and has me half-hard. "It's just not new. In school, people said the same shit. Sometimes worse. The point is, I would have to care for it to affect me. What bothers me is..." The hesitance returns and she struggles to look at me, but I won't let her turn away. "...*he touched me.*"

Her eyes swell with tears. I pull her head into my chest and hold her close. "It's okay, spitfire. I got you."

We embrace for a few moments, her hugging me tightly while I brush back her hair. Eventually the sobs stop, and she is pulling away to wipe the moisture from her cheeks. "Thank you."

I scratch at my temple, unsure what I'm being thanked for. She should be pissed. I just caused a major disruption in her bar, plus more damage. I didn't think, just reacted. If Derek hadn't stopped me, I'm not sure I would have done so on my own.

Her fingers trace my jaw. "No one's ever stood up for me before."

That grip she has on my soul tightens. I know it's wrong for so many reasons, yet I can't stop myself from threading my fingers through her hair and pulling her lips to mine. I expect hesitation after everything that just happened. Add in what she said prior—that *once again*, without reason or explanation, she decided this was over before it could even start—and a smart man would walk away. Let her be. Then again, I'm not the smart twin. So, instead of running, I delve my tongue deep inside her open, eager mouth. My hand snakes down her sides. I take her luscious ass into my palms and grip her firmly. With a groan, she rocks into me, and all common sense (not that I have any) is gone.

Lifting her up, I set her on the ledge of the counter, step between her welcoming thighs, and grind my painfully hard cock into where it wants to nestle. It's only been a couple of days since he was last embraced by the comfort she offers. Still, he's desperate to return *home.*

In the months—almost a year—since my parents' deaths, I've felt lost. The world has been passing me by. Everyone is moving forward while I remain stationary. Tilly and Jax, Robbie and Cassie... Hell, Scott might not have found his soulmate yet. But he is sure as shit looking for her, on top of manifesting his restaurant dream. All the while, I've been stuck in the past, living with the ghost of things that used to be and hoping everything would go back to normal. But that's the problem: it's impossible.

Mom and Dad are gone. Tilly moved out, happily married with twins of her own to raise. Robbie and Cassie found each other and are starting their life together. Scott will join them all soon. Me? I thought if I kept the same routine, it would get better. That I would feel like myself again.

Being with Letty is the first time I've felt the thrill of anything in so long, even before the accident. It isn't just the amazing sex, or how the list of things I want to do keeps growing. It's the things I want to do *with her*. Not just the sexy stuff. Granted, those are high up on there. Simple things: like not hiding, going to dinner, and being able to touch and hold her. Or use up more of my vacation time and get away. Just the two of us. And not in secret.

There is a lot I want when it comes to Letty. But above all else, I want *her*. If she won't let me tell her that, I know other ways to show her. We move in perfectly synchronized chaos to remove the scraps of material keeping me from where we both want me to be. I make work of her shorts as she unbuttons and lowers my jeans. During all of which, our mouths remained joined. The only thing escaping is our labored breaths. My cock springs free. Her soft hand firmly grips my throbbing cock just as I slip a finger into her drenched pussy.

Oh shit... The sensation makes me realize there is one major problem with the course we're on.

Letty stalls her skilled stroking. "What's wrong?"

I rest my forehead against hers. Like a heat-seeking missile, my dick can feel her from here. "I don't have a condom," I groan.

"You're kidding." She lets out a long breath.

"Nope," I confirm. My finger strokes her wet slit. After a moment of silent sulking, she tugs me forward. My hands grip the counter, and she lines me up with her entrance. "Are you sure?"

Biting her lip, she looks up at me and nods. "Yes, I'm on birth control and I trust you."

My cock grows twice as large at the notion. We—*him* and I—have never gone bare before. *Ever.* Not even with the few girls we've had repeated sex with. It's been offered and begged for occasionally. But honestly, until the other week when we were in the kitchen and I got a taste of what it could feel like, I didn't have any interest. Out of all the things I have done to a body or have had done to mine, this seemed like a level of intimacy too great for anything casual and fun. The ultimate form of trust.

I reach between us and take control of sliding the head of my cock up and down her lips. Letty lets out a small gasp each time I bump her clit. "Last chance to back out."

"Jake," she moans. "If you don't fuck me with that thing—" Her words die off into a silent scream as I slam home with force. Other than my first time, I don't think I've ever wanted to come in one thrust. It's so warm and soft in here. I never want to leave. No doubt remains in my mind. This is home.

"Hold on," is the only warning I give before I pull out just enough to plunge into her again. She grips my shoulders with surprising strength. As her nails slice into my flesh, I increase my tempo. *Goddamn it,* I never want this to end, yet I know I won't last much longer. I'd be more embarrassed if I wasn't holding on by a thread. I have a four-orgasm minimum. However, if she's only going to get one, it's going to be the best one ever.

Sneaking my thumb between us, I play with her clit. Having every crevice and fold burned into my memory makes pushing the buttons I need easy. She's coiled up tight, strangling my cock. A light breeze could push her over the edge. Instead, I give her a gale-force wind. I repeatedly push her to that precipice and pull back just moments before she explodes. Her panting is mixed with pleas and curses. As a tear rolls down her cheek, I increase my pressure and grant her the release we're both desperate for.

"Oh, fuck, Jake..." she screams. The distinct sound of fireworks pops in the distance. And the timing couldn't be more perfect. My balls tighten and I come so hard I can't breathe. I might have missed the grand display outside, but I'm enjoying a show of my own creation. "That was—" she exhales.

"Incredible," I finish for her. Nuzzling into her neck, I remain seated inside her, enjoying every second of feeling our combined fluids as they slowly leak onto the porcelain. For the first time since I was put on leave, I'm not looking forward to going back to work tomorrow. I'd much rather convince her to stay in bed with me. Like this. All day.

Knock, knock, knock.

"Umm..." Derek clears his throat. "You guys might want to finish up and get back out here." Letty's face goes pale at the realization that at least one person, if not more, heard us just now. Though we are linked, I can feel her mind pulling away from me.

"Don't," I plead before kissing her. "Stay with me."

"I need to get back to work." Letty's pulse quickens as she glances at the door, that orgasmic glow now gone.

"That's not what I mean, Tee." Her meltdown stops, and she looks at me again. "I mean, stay with me *here*." I tap her head. "And *here*." I tap her heart. "Don't crawl back inside and close me off." Each second she takes to consider her answer twists the knife in my gut.

"Okay, Jake." She softly presses her lips to mine.

Though she's saying what I want to hear, as I slide out of her, the sinking feeling that this will be the last time I'll ever get to feel her warmth roots in my mind. I just fucking pray to whomever is listening that, this one time, my instincts are wrong. That I am paranoid and misreading the signals because of all the excitement tonight.

31

Jake

"MOORE," STONE YELLS SHORTLY after throwing a sponge at my head. It lands with an annoying precision and splashes me in the face.

"Dude," I say, wiping the suds from my temple. "What the hell?"

"You're the one who zoned out," he accuses. *Fuck, did I?* "I know you were on vacation and things got exciting last night at the bar," he teases. "But you need to get your head back in the game."

He's right. Today has been a mess. The incident has been the talk of the town. Not the part where Letty and I fucked in the bathroom. Derek didn't confirm or deny if he heard anything. But the smirk he suppressed before he left was sign enough that he did. Thankfully, he's not one to spread gossip. No, all day people have been stopping by to ask about the brawl at Harper's. Through the town's game of telephone, the story is that I took on five guys with one hand tied behind my back. Or some shit like that.

Although the drop-ins have disrupted our normal routine, which is already difficult the day after a huge town holiday event, no one is complaining about the goodie baskets that have been delivered. Of course Patty dropped off the largest, filled with so many sweets from her shop that I'm certain she's trying to give us all diabetes. Inside the care package, she made a special batch of my favorite fudge and labeled it: *for Jake only.*

"Sorry, what were you saying?"

"Letty," he repeats, and I freeze at the mention of her name. I hold my breath and wait for him to continue. "She's hot. I was thinking about asking her out."

"Who's hot?" Derek asks, stopping next to the rig with a coffee in hand.

"Letty," Jenkins adds. "Stone is considering asking her out."

"Is that right?" Derek states. He angles his head so that he's looking at Stone over the rim of his aviators.

"Yeah, I don't know." Stone shrugs. "I kind of thought we shared a moment."

"A moment?" I ask.

He waves his head back and forth in contemplation. "I mean, she smiled at me."

All the guys make sarcastic "oh" sounds, as though that is the most definitive proof of a moment they've ever heard.

"Brave man, if you ask me," Jenkins adds before throwing a wash rag at Stone.

"Brave indeed," Cian chimes in as he towers over us all. Unlike Derek, whose posture is casual as he sips his cup of coffee, Cian's is squared-off and intimidating. The guy looks like he's about ready to burst from the seams of his uniform. I wonder if they needed to custom order one that large?

"Why's that?" Stone spits out, obviously annoyed with all the teasing. Being the newest member of the fire station, as well as a newcomer to Tral Lake, he gets the most shit from the guys.

"Because, last I heard, she and my brother were a thing." Everyone goes silent. Cian might be the latest addition to the sheriff's office, but his reputation has spread like wildfire. Which includes his famous brother. The only one not looking at him is Derek; his eyes are glued to mine in question. I shrug my shoulders and get back to cleaning the truck. I bite my tongue to keep myself from correcting him. Not that I care, but Letty would.

We can't keep this hidden anymore. I'm sick of it. If these guys knew the level of intimacy I've shared with her pussy, they wouldn't say shit like this.

"Good luck with that, man." Jenkins pats Stone on the back. "I was going to say you're brave because Letty isn't a bunker bunny. She'd chew you up and spit you out. Believe me, short of Jake here, all of us at one time or another have tried."

"Why haven't you?" Stone asks me.

Before I can respond, Huey chimes in. "Oh, those two have hated each other since they were kids."

"Hate is a strong word," I clarify.

"Wasn't it you who started that rumor freshman year? The one about how her vag was so rank your mom had to air-dry her underwear whenever she spent the night?" Derek ponders, rubbing his chin. "I'm pretty sure you even told one guy that if he was going to go to Tuna Town to make sure he brought tartar sauce."

I wince at the memory. That was a real dick thing to say. "She's the one who spread the rumor about me having crabs after putting itching powder in my jockstrap. I simply retaliated." Everyone laughs at my expense, including the usually expressionless Cian. "Fuck off." I snap my towel at Derek's leg, which only makes him laugh harder.

"So, what you're telling me..." Stone wipes a tear from his eye. "...is that Jake ruined it for the rest of us?"

"Pretty much," Jenkins confirms.

"Your blank scorecard has nothing to do with me." I point to Jenkins. "You're the idiot who had one too many and thew up down the front of her shirt on your twenty-first birthday. That is way more unforgivable than any prank I did when we were kids."

"I agree," Derek says, his mouth half turned up in a smirk. "They have more of a *sibling* rivalry." *Asshole.* I knew he heard us last night and the last thing *that* was, was brotherly.

"Regardless." Jenkins reins everyone in. "If she's fucking Kill, the KO Murphy, dude... I mean, come on. Sure, the whole man in uniform gets the ladies almost every time. But there is no competing with a guy whose hands are classified as lethal weapons." Stone opens his mouth to object but is quickly cut off. "Retired or not. Unless your cock was blessed by the gods and you're hiding the fact you're a billionaire, there is no competing with that."

Jenkins is an idiot. Letty isn't some superficial piece of ass, looking to add to her repertoire. Not to mention, she already verified they weren't a thing. And she doesn't lie.

So, you had crabs? Practical jokes are different.

What about that summer? Those couple of months together? You damn well know it was more than a fling. Yet that's what she played it off as before dumping you. We were stupid kids.

And now? Things are different. We're older, mature. We have over a decade of life experiences under our belts now. Last night, that was something new. Nothing about that was fake. She trusted me. Gave herself to me fully. After the incident at the bar and Derek potentially hearing us, I was certain she'd pull back. But when she came home, she crawled into *my* bed. I can still taste her on my tongue, having ate her for breakfast before starting my shift this morning.

Just like I know she'll be passed out in my room when I get home tomorrow morning. And soon after, I'll be balls-deep in that pussy.

Never have I rushed so fast to get out of the fire station. Though I was delayed by a few minutes because, of course, the next shift had to give me shit about being on vacation for a couple of weeks. Then the Captain brought in doughnuts and coffee for everyone, and I ended up sitting around and chatting. It's later than I planned, but checking the clock and seeing it's only eleven, I'm sure Letty's still asleep.

No big deal. Just a slight change of plans. Instead of greeting her with my cock when I crawl into bed, it's close enough to the time she'd normally get up that I'll make a brunch buffet. I stopped by the market and grabbed some fresh berries and maple syrup. All of which, I plan to spread across her body and lick clean, before fucking her senseless in the shower.

I quickly set everything on the counter before tiptoeing upstairs. I open my door. It's the first room on the right. My dick jumps in anticipation of seeing her fanned out across our sheets with her ass cheeks sticking out of whatever mini shorts she's still wearing. *I really hope she slept in one of my TLFD t-shirts.* Except... the bed is empty.

Huh? I guess she felt weird sleeping in my bed alone. No worries. I travel to the end of the hall and slip inside her room. Again, she isn't here. *Where is she?*

"Letty," I call out as I frantically check every room on the second floor. Unable to locate her, I run downstairs, in case I missed her doing laundry or something. I plop down on the couch, out of breath, and scratch my head. *Did she need to go to the bar early?*

A small folded piece of paper on the coffee table catches my attention. My chest squeezes with dread and a chill runs down my spine. With icy fingers, I reach for it. I hardly glance at the scribbled words before shooting up from the couch and taking the stairs two at a time, until I'm back in her room. I throw open the closet doors, then rush to the en suite. Drawers fly across the room as I open each one and toss it in the air. *They're empty.* Everything is gone.

Desperately, I look at the note again, praying it says something—anything—else. Yet the same sentiment remains scratched in black ink: *I'm sorry. I can't do this.*

Crumbling up the paper, I toss it on the floor and stomp downstairs to grab my keys from the table. The door slams shut behind me. I get in my truck and peel out of the driveway.

I'm going to find Letty and sort this out. When we were young, I let her push me away with whatever lie she had to tell herself. *Not this time.* If she doesn't want me, then she's going to look me in the fucking eye and tell me *this* was nothing. Even then, I'm not sure that will be sufficient. I doubt anything will be.

32

Letty

You know in those old western movies when the bartender is wiping down the counter, and suddenly, there's a swoosh of air. The chatter and music die out. The bargoers lift their gazes to focus on whatever caused this shift in energy. Then there is a tall, looming figure standing at the door with his eyes laser-focused on his target, and you know a duel is about to take place.

That's Jake right now.

I knew this was coming. Honestly, I'm surprised it took him this long to get here. I half expected him to be sitting at the bar waiting for me when I came in. Irrationally, I was disappointed. What kind of cunt packs her shit and runs while someone's working? Leaving behind nothing but a note with six brief words and no explanation. Only to pout when that same man isn't lying in wait at the most obvious location to find her. Jake should have burned that note, along with the sheets I slept on, and forgotten I ever existed. It's the least I deserve.

On top of it all, he should tell Tilly what an evil bitch I am. That would be true justice. Taking away my best friend and leaving me with nothing.

The sea of patrons parts as Jake stomps towards me. His narrowed glare doesn't waver from the object of his contention. He's on autopilot. "We need to talk," he growls out, his nostrils flared.

Probably. Talking would be the mature thing to do. *But we can't all be perfect.* "I'm working," I state the obvious.

Jake leans forward and speaks through clenched teeth, "Now. I'm not stepping foot out of here until we talk. The choice is yours. Out here for the whole town to hear, or back in the office. Just you and me"

Low blow, Jake. Of course, he'd threaten to air our dirty laundry in public. Again, I deserve it. But self-preservation has me nodding to Kat, who's probably heard the entire exchange.

"I'll be just a minute," I inform her as she comes behind the counter.

She looks from me to Jake and back again. "I don't know about that," she replies with a smirk.

I roll my eyes and head to the office with Jake hot on my heels. I hardly get two steps through the door before it slams behind us, making me jump.

Just the other day, the intensity of his stare in this small space would have my panties wet. But he isn't looking at me like he wants to devour me. No, it's more like I'm the villain in this movie, and he's finally come to confront me.

"Talk," he demands, crossing his arms over his chest. Taking a step away, I yelp as my thighs hit the desk. Jake doesn't back down. Instead, he stalks into my space and traps me between his corded arms. "Letty, I told you. I'm not going anywhere until you tell me what the fuck is going on."

My nostrils flare as I take a deep breath. How much clearer can I be? I left. We're done. "Can't you read?" My defensive bitch mode activates. Backed into a corner, my claws come out on instinct. "Sorry, I forgot—" I wince as he slams his hands on the desk.

"Cut the shit. I read your shitty-ass note. What I want to know is... why?" The anger that was radiating off him moments ago diminishes. His hazel pools beg me to stop fighting with him. To be honest.

"What is *this* to you?" I ask, swallowing down my lump of dread. It's one thing for you to think you know something, entirely different to hear it's reality.

His brow furrows at the question. "What do you mean?"

"You and me, where do you see this going?" I clarify.

His thumb gently caresses my cheek as he stares into my eyes. He lets out a relieved breath as though this is exactly the moment he was waiting for. "Everywhere." My heart plummets as he continues. "Marriage, kids, growing old, all of it."

"Is that what you want?" I push.

"With you..." He sighs, resting his forehead against mine. "It's all I can see." My eyes burn as my worst fears are confirmed. "Tee, don't cry." He wipes away the traitorous tear rolling down my face. "I know I've got a reputation, but I promise I'll never cheat or whatever other terrible thing you're thinking right now. This is it. All I want is you, only you."

He presses his lips to mine. I want to return the kiss more than I want to take my next breath. But I can't. If I do, I'll never stop.

For years, I tempted the fates with booze. Each day, proving that alcohol needed me; I didn't need it. That I didn't inherit my father's weakness. The problem with dependency is that it isn't always the most obvious affliction. Most think of drugs, food, risky behaviors, even exercise.

Congratulations, Dad, I'm a chip off the old block.

I, Leticia Ruiz Frost, am a fucking addict. And my bad habit is Jake. Although I inherited my father's genes, I won't repeat his mistakes. I'm stronger than him. For that reason, I fight every instinct I have and don't give in.

Step one: admit I have a problem.

Step two: pray to whoever is still listening to restore the sanity I lost weeks ago when a tree crashed through my roof.

Pulling back, Jake looks down at me, his brows squished together in confusion.

"I don't want any of that," I confess. "I don't want to get married and pop out a litter of children."

"Well, not right now, at least not the kids. But—"

"Not now and not ever." I keep my eyes focused on his and speak slowly and clearly, so he doesn't miss a word. "Jake, I never want to have children."

"With me?" If any part of my heart wasn't broken, it is now. How could he ever think that the problem is him when it's obviously all me?

"With anyone."

He narrows his eyes. "Don't patronize me. Come on, Letty, you've never held back with telling me how useless you think I am before. Why now? What? You think they'll be stupid like me? Or that I'll be a terrible father? Forget them in a parking lot someday or some shit?"

"It's me, you fucking jackass," I scream and push him back. Jake looks at me, his eyes wide. "I can't have children." He focuses on my abdomen. "Not physically, asshole, *ethically*." I rub my temples. I've never talked to anyone about this. Not even Tilly. "Let's say we have a beautiful child together and then I die? Leaving you both alone and broken. Would you take care of her? Or would you drown yourself in a bottle and leave our daughter to fend for herself?"

"Fuck, Letty. Is this about your dad? I would never—"

"He wasn't always that way. Not many remember, but I do. He used to be a good father. Happy, loving, caring, everything a girl could want. That version of him died with *her*. He loved her so much he couldn't live without her. Not even his daughter was enough to keep him going. Jake, *I* wasn't enough. Instead of a bullet to the head, he put a bottle to his lips."

"Letty—" Jake's expression is pained as he rubs my arms.

I push forward and ignore his pity. "Or worse, what if I pass my shitty genetics on to our child? She inherits my mom's cancer or my father's alcoholism? Don't tell me it's unlikely or that it's a one in a million chance. Because it's hereditary. My grandmother—my mom's mom—also died at a young age from cancer. My great-grandmother too. My dad, well, this town knows he comes from a long line of drunks, who all either died of liver failure or some other alcohol-related accident." I inhale deeply before continuing. "You deserve a wife, someone to raise a family beside, to grow old with. Not a damaged mess with a fast-approaching expiration date. I'm doing you a favor. Saving you from a life of pain."

"Letty," he says my name as a demand, taking my face between his large palms. "I didn't know."

"Now you do."

"Let's talk about this," he pleads.

"There is nothing to discuss."

"No? It sure as shit seems like there is a lot we need to *discuss*," he growls.

"What? Suddenly you don't want to get married and have kids?" I bite out.

"Fine, we don't have kids. Marriage?" He shrugs his shoulders before giving me a half grin. "That's debatable. None of what you said is a deal-breaker."

"Jake." I sigh. "Less than two minutes ago, you said those were all the things you wanted."

"Yeah, and that's when I thought it was what you wanted too," he growls. "Don't you get it? I lov—"

My finger pressing to his lips prevents him from finishing the sentiment. "Please," I warn. "You don't mean it."

"Don't you dare tell me how I feel."

"I'm not." I attempt to reason with him. "You might think you do. But, one day, you'll wake up and realize what a mistake this all was. Your family was always so good to me.

I can't dishonor your parents and betray their kindness by tying you down to my sinking ship."

"My parents loved you. My whole family loves you. Why wouldn't they want us together? Letty, you aren't making any—"

"Your mom hated that I worked here. She even approached Ted, begging him to fire me because I wouldn't quit and work for her. If they were alive, they'd never approve of us. You're a Moore, Jake. A golden child of this town. And I'm... just *me*." I shake off his hold and step around him.

"What if that's enough?" Jake is grasping at straws as he grabs my hand and turns me to look at him. "What if you're enough?"

"I can't be." I detach myself from his hold and walk around to the other side of the desk to put something physical between us. "Maybe you think that's true. Right now. But eventually you'll realize what a mistake this was and resent me. You and me, it's a slippery slope. It's better if we end this before we go past the point of no return."

"The other night—"

"Is exactly the kind of shit I'm talking about. We had sex without a condom."

"You said you're on birth control."

"Look how well that worked out for Tilly?" I remind him.

"Okay, never again. Or I'll get snipped—whatever you want."

"That's not the point, Jake."

"Then what is?" he yells, waving his hands in the air.

"That you are doing whatever I want without thinking about your own needs. I've had years to carefully consider this. Come to terms with my decision. You've taken all of two seconds to make a major life-altering choice, based on *my* fears."

"I might've only had a few moments to consider whether or not I want to have children, but I've had years to come to the realization that I want you."

I'm so frustrated I want to scream. He's not seeing the big picture. "It's also the fact that, for a moment, I was stupid enough to think that maybe the risk was worth it. All it took was one second of letting my guard down, and I could have destroyed you."

"Letty, you're being too hard on—"

"No, I'm not being hard enough. This is over. It has to be."

"Can we—"

"Just stop," I yell. He looks at me, his eyes pleading. Desperate. "I want you to go."

"You don't mean that."

"I do. I want you to go. We're finished here." The best way to move past your addiction is to cut it from your life. Remove the temptation.

Jake looks like he is going to protest again. Instead, he drops his shoulders, turns, and walks out the door, slamming it behind him. A second later, I let go of the breath I've been holding since he walked into the bar. My strength is zapped, and the tears I've held back flood my face. I don't know how long I've been sitting like this before I feel two arms wrap around me.

"Shh," Scarlett whispers, pulling my face into her chest. I forgot she was going to stop by today. She offered to drop off the key to my room, after she got everything set up at the Inn. "It's going to be okay."

"Why does it hurt so much?"

"It always does," she murmurs, brushing my hair back.

33

Letty

My pulse races as I step through the door of Harper's. I've been working for Ted since I was sixteen and I've never been called to his (my) office before. Considering he asked me to come in early, before opening and my usual shift, I know something is up. Maybe the douche and his buddies from the Fourth pressed charges. Or that threat one of them made about writing a bad review actually did damage. No, Ted wouldn't call me for that. My guess is he's pissed that I left early on a Saturday night, leaving our waitress in charge of the bar during one of our busiest weekends.

I just couldn't do it. I could barely put one foot in front of the other today.

This is the right thing to do. I repeat the mantra over and over in my mind, hoping that if I say it enough, this ache in my heart will lessen. My emotions are all over the place right now. One moment, I'm a mess of tears. And the next, I'm ready to storm out of the hotel. Back to his house and beg on my knees. Ask him to forgive me and give me another chance.

The start of my period didn't help matters at all. I always become extra hormonal and on the edge. Now I'm a nuclear bomb ready to implode. I was lucky that I had Sunday and

Monday off as usual, otherwise if I knew we had the staff to cover, I would've called out anyway. I needed time to get my shit under control.

Straightening my spine while presenting confidence I don't feel, I enter the office. Ted looks weird sitting at my desk. It's been years since he has. Especially with papers spread out in front of him. "You can't be serious?" I cross my arms and groan. "I never call out. Ever. The one time I leave a little early, and you're going to write me up."

"What are you talking about, kid?" He raises a bushy brow at me, then glances down at the paperwork. Rolling his eyes, he gestures to the seat. "Sit down."

I plop into the chair. "This is bullshit," I huff.

"I'm not writing you up." He shakes his head. "I don't even know how I would."

"Oh," I say, feeling a bit embarrassed. Fucking hormones. I need to relax. "Then what's all this?"

"I spoke to the claims adjuster yesterday."

"And?" I remember the email from last week. I meant to ask Ted about it but got distracted with everything going on. Ted sighs before shaking his head. "You have to be shitting me." I slam my hands on the desk.

"They are classifying it as a total loss."

"No! We have to talk to them."

"There is nothing left to discuss. The case has been closed and a check's been cut."

"What does that mean?" I swallow down my urge to vomit. This can't be happening. Not after all the work we did—*Jake did*. His name makes that sick feeling worse. Like an idiot, I told myself I could get through this as long as I had Harper's. My home. Now I have nothing. I'm going to need to find a job.

Except for helping at the bookshop now and then, I have no other experience. Maybe this isn't the end of the world. As much as I try to convince myself that Jake and I will move past everything, that we will get back to a normal where we can be in the same room, I know that won't happen. Not this time. It might have been brief, but it felt like we lived a lifetime these past few weeks.

"This check is for you." Ted slides it over. I read the amount. It's what I saved up to give him as a deposit.

I push it back. "No, I can't take this."

"You're going to need it to start over." He eyes me sympathetically. "You'll need this too."

I study the paperwork more carefully and realize it's the deed. "What's this?" I ask, even though I already know. The better question is why.

"It's yours," he states. "If you still want it."

"I don't understand," I murmur in wonder as I stare at the official document.

"Look, kid, I'll be honest with you." I glance up from the paper to Ted. "I wanted to sell a long time ago. Not just the bar, but the house as well. The winters are too cold, and it's been shit for my arthritis. Not to mention, I know the old noggin isn't what it used to be. The insurance paid off the mortgage and the lien on the building. I spoke with Bill Avery. He's been eyeing up my land for a while. It sits on a mighty fine access point for them to expand the housing development. He's been asking me to sell for some time now, and I've turned him down. Until this morning."

"You sold your house," I yell in shock.

"I did," he verifies. "Not only did I get more than enough money to move my old ass to Arizona, but I also made a deal with Bill. He's going to bring his guys in here and repair all the damage, including restoring the upstairs. I also ordered new kitchen equipment, so when you reopen, you'll be able to do so fully."

"When I reopen?"

"Of course, kid. These guys won't be able to work with people standing around drinking. You're gonna have to shut down."

"For how long?"

"Luckily, I've been in talks with Bill. He has most of what he needs on hand and is going to start renovating tomorrow. He says you can reopen in a week—*two tops*. I've already talked to the rest of the staff."

"But the tourists..."

"That's not your problem, Letty," Ted scolds. "I need you to promise me you won't let this place run your life. You need to live. Get out of here for a while. See what's beyond these county lines. There is a whole big world out there, and you're going to miss it. Here." He slides me another envelope.

"How many papers are you going to give me today?" I chuckle while sniffling back my tears. As I pull out a plane ticket and brochure to a resort, my brows draw together. I look back at Ted.

"Kid, I've known you practically your whole life. Telling you to go on vacation isn't enough. I talked to Jax and asked if he could recommend somewhere to send you. He did me one better and set you up with an all-inclusive resort package at some fancy new place that just opened. Everything's taken care of. Go, enjoy a few days on the beach, relax—you know, all those things young people do. When you get back, there'll be plenty of work waiting for you. This will all be yours. You've helped run this place for a while now. But I promise it will be different when it's yours."

"Mine," I clarify, still in shock.

"Yes." He snatches the deed from my hands and holds it up. "But not until you get back from your vacation. Even then, if after some time away, you decide to take that money and do something else, you can. Selling this place won't be an issue once it's repaired. So, take the time. Make sure this is the life you want."

My chair slides back as I get up and round the desk. Leaning down, I wrap my arms around Ted. "It's what I want," I assure him. Then, dropping my hands, I look back at him with a giant smile. "I hope you're ready to sign that paperwork when I get back."

"Believe me, I'm looking forward to it."

34

Jake

I SIT ON THE back porch and stare off into the distance at the vast farmland, picking the peel off my beer. I haven't set eyes on Letty since last Saturday. And not for a lack of trying. Knowing her as long as I have, I gave her time. Hoping she'd realize that this doesn't need to be all or nothing. I went to Harper's on Wednesday. It's the one place I could make her talk to me, except I was met with a "closed" sign. Bill Avery and his crew were onsite, working upstairs and finally fixing the damn roof.

Another benefit of a small town? I knew she was staying at the hotel and went there. Again, a swing and a miss. Scarlett told me that Letty was gone and refused to elaborate. Which then sent me storming to the bookshop to interrogate Tilly and get details about what was going on with Harper's. Luckily, my sister's a Chatty Cathy with shit sometimes. So, without asking, she gave me the rundown. And that's when I learned Letty was on vacation.

At first, all I wanted to do was ask where, buy a ticket, and work this shit out. But then reality set in. She left. It might not be forever. But it still didn't change the fact she left town and didn't even tell me. And the realization that *this* is actually over set in.

Here I am. Alone. And she's God knows where. Probably fucking a cabana boy. My first thought was to show her two can play that game. I even recruited Derek and Mack for a typical boys' night out. It ended with Derek and me chilling at the bar, watching basketball finals, while Mack proceeded as normal.

Since that didn't work—to keep occupied and preserve my sanity when I'm not at the fire station—I've been kicking ass at the video store and getting it ready to open at the end of the month. It's badass. Heavy black curtains and runner lights on the red carpet make a path along the interior. It looks like a movie theater. In the corner, I set up a couch and projector, along with a popcorn machine and a mini-fridge stocked with pop. Ever since the theater shut down years ago, kids in town have little to do. Now we have a spot where they can come and chill. I even hired a few high schoolers to help work the shop for me, since I can't be here all the time. Although it was my idea to open it, this place is way more for them than me. The kids are cool too. Both big movie buffs and have a ton of theme nights planned.

All of this kept my mind off *her*. Today, though, nothing is helping to ease my anxiety. According to Tilly, *she* got back yesterday. I assumed (like any other Sunday) she would be here. I was prepared to corner her in the bathroom again. Not sure why or what I was going to say...

Part of me wants to convince her this can work. That she's wrong. The other part wants to interrogate her about what she did while she was gone, wipe her memory of whoever touched her, then leave her a withering mess again as punishment for leaving me. Maybe a mix of both. She once told me there was only one thing my tongue was good for...

If I don't have the right words to speak, I have at least twelve appendages that are experts at communicating exactly what I want to say. Except she's not here. And for once, Tilly hasn't been forthcoming with details.

"What's up?" Jax asks, taking a seat next to me.

"Not much," I reply. My shoulders drop and I take another swig of my beer.

"You sure?" He turns to look at me.

I shrug. "Yeah, just been thinking."

"About?"

"Life." I sigh.

Jax chuckles. "Anything in particular? Life is a pretty big thing to be thinking about."

"How'd you know?"

"Sorry, dude, you're gonna have to be a little more specific."

"That you were in love with Tilly? That you were willing to give up your dream to be with her?"

Jax lets out a long breath before taking a drink from his bottle. "First, I've always loved your sister. It just took time and maturity for me to realize how much. Second, I didn't give up my dream."

"No judgement," I clarify, "But come on, Jax, we all know you never wanted to settle down here."

"When I was young, no, I didn't. There was this entire world out there I wanted to explore. I resented Tilly for pushing me away. But now I realize she was right. If I would have stuck around, I'm not sure we would have made it. Or have been half as happy as we are presently."

"Okay, so then what changed?"

"I don't think it was one specific thing, but a sequence of different things. Ultimately, I realized my dream was only half-fulfilled. Sure, I got to see the world. However, every place I went, I'd always have her in the back of my mind. Always thinking how much Tilly would love this... or enjoy that. Or imagine her reading a book on the beach while I snapped pictures."

"If that was the case, then why'd you stay gone for so long?"

"Because I was an idiot." He laughs half-heartedly. "Scared. Eventually, so much time had passed without contact I didn't know how or *if* she'd even see me."

He doesn't need to say it. If my parents wouldn't have died last year, he probably wouldn't have come home. At least not yet. And by the time he finally did, who knows if Tilly would have taken him back or even been married to someone else? If it wasn't for that tornado, I'm not sure Letty and I would have ever gotten together again either. Was this the universe giving us a second chance? Or was this just closure?

But none of it feels resolved to me...

"I think I'm lonely," I admit out loud for the first time.

"Man..." Jax laughs. "I'll give you the same advice your sister gave me."

"Yeah, what's that?"

"If you're lonely, get a fucking cat."

"What?" I chuckle.

"Yup." Jax pops his P. "When I told your sister I was lonely and wanted to be with her, she turned me down flat and told me to get a cat instead. She said that loneliness wasn't the same as *wanting to be* with her. Honestly, I didn't understand what she meant until I had to leave again."

"What's the difference?"

"Wanting someone versus needing *the one*."

35

Letty

I STARE AT THE calendar reminder displayed on my phone, the birthday cake icon glaring back at me, before glancing up at the house again—July 15th. In the past, I've always enjoyed the festivities associated with the date. But today? I dread it.

Walking up the stone path to Jax and Tilly's home, I take deep, calming breaths. This will be my first time seeing *him* since I told him my deepest, dirtiest, shameful truth. If it wasn't for the fact that Harper's would officially be mine tomorrow, after I meet Ted to sign the paperwork and do the walk around for the remodel, I'm not sure I would have come back.

The resort was gorgeous. The meals, the music, everything was perfect. I was expecting overrated cafeteria food when I saw it was all-inclusive. Not that I'm a picky eater or anything. It was just what I expected. I've never been so wrong in my entire life. Fresh tropical fruits. Crisp veggies. There was some shredded pork dish that I couldn't stop eating. For three days, I did nothing but eat, swim, and nap on the beach. I even took time to read a couple of the books Scarlett packed for me. And I now understand their *appeal*.

However, as with all good things, it had to end. Hell, knowing me, a day longer and I would have gotten bored and started crawling up the walls. This experience was perfect. I didn't really understand what Ted was saying about having "a world outside Harper's." But now I do.

During the plane ride home, I made myself a promise to leave the confines of Tral Lake at least once a year. One week, just for me. Fuck, maybe I'll throw a dart at the map and let chance choose my next destination. That's the plan after I finally see Disney World anyway. Maybe I will visit every location worldwide, then pick random vacation spots from then on. Or have Jax do it for me, since he's the expert. Honestly, I don't care. The point is I've seen this world everyone keeps talking about. And that small taste wasn't enough.

"Are you ready?" Scarlett asks, walking up behind me.

"Yes." *No.*

She hasn't asked. Or even said anything. Yet somehow I'm sure she knows something happened between Jake and me. Then, by the state she found me in at the bar, she also knows it didn't end well—whatever it was. I'm grateful that she hasn't pried. Nothing against her, but *if* I was going to talk about what happened, that conversation was reserved for Tilly.

I feel like shit as it is. For a second time, I had something going on with Jake and never told her. It's bad enough that she's his sister. What makes it ten times worse is that she's my best friend too. I've always told her everything (at least the things I'm willing to discuss). I don't have a clue how I'm going to make it through their birthday party while pretending everything is fine.

Because it's not. It will be eventually. But at the moment it's all still too raw.

It's why I skipped out on the usual cookout yesterday. Luckily, my excuse of being jet-lagged and tired from traveling the day before was believable enough for her. I'm not ready to face Jake. Not yet. I'm praying to whomever is listening that there will be so many people here he won't even notice me. Although it'll make me want to vomit, maybe he'll have a date or whatever he calls them. If he's moved on, back to his routine, it'll be easier for me to return to my old habits as well.

"I love this dress," Scarlett says. "It's so weird to see you in one. But you look amazing."

"Thank you." I saw the dress in a shop. It's nothing fancy. A simple white spaghetti-strap summer dress with an oriental lily pattern. It reminded me of the dresses Mom used to buy me.

"Very tropical-chic," she comments. We enter the backyard, and I breathe a sigh of relief.

One: As I assumed based on the volume of cars out front and parked along the shoulder of the county road, there are a lot of people here.

Two: Upon my immediate survey of the crowd, I don't see Jake. Though I'm not stupid enough to think he'd skip his own birthday party. Twenty-nine years and they've celebrated each one together.

"Letty!" Tilly shouts, unwittingly announcing my presence. She jogs over from the few people she was talking to, wraps her arms around me, and squeezes tight. "I've missed you so much," she murmurs before pulling back to examine me. "Wow, Florida looks good on you. Did you get a lot of sun? Or is it the dress making your skin seem tanner? Regardless, did you have fun?"

"Hi, Tilly." I chuckle. As happy as I am to see her, the guilt of keeping secrets from her is eating away at me. Obviously, *now* isn't a good time to tell her. That being said, I need to rip off the band-aid and hope for the best. "Happy birthday."

"Thank you." She hiccups, and I get the scent of alcohol.

"Are you drinking?" I whisper the question. Last I saw, she was still breastfeeding.

"Yes." She giggles. "Jax got a margarita machine and might have upped the tequila a bit, so be careful. Don't worry, I pumped," she clarifies, before taking her breasts in her hands and squeezing them together. "I was worried I wouldn't be able to keep up with the twins, but these puppies are genuine milk factories. Jax had to buy a chest freezer to store the overflow." She snorts. "*Chest.*"

"Okay." I chuckle, shaking my head. I haven't seen her this light and carefree in a long time, even before the accident. It's great seeing her happy. For that, I will put on my biggest, brightest, fakest smile. And ignore Jake and anything Jake-adjacent for the day. This is Tilly's birthday, and as her best friend—if she doesn't hate me after we talk—it is my job to help her ring in another year with a bang. "So, how 'bout one of them margaritas?"

"Jax," she hollers across the backyard, "we need two more, please."

He gives a thumbs up, dispensing two drinks and walking them over. "Here you go, ladies." He hands us our cups, presses a kiss to the top of Tilly's head, and drapes an arm over her shoulder, pulling her closer. "How was the resort?"

"Perfect, thank you. Seriously, I've never been or stayed anywhere so nice before."

"I'm glad." He smiles. "Hey, would you mind writing up a small review or something we can include in the editorial?"

"Sure." *Woah.* I take a gulp of my drink, and based on the volume of tequila, it seems Jax might be looking to get started on the next set of twins. From the TMI conversation I overheard between Tilly and Cassie, I really hope he knows that not only is it too soon for her to try for another baby, but sex in general is off the table. "If you ever need a civilian like me to travel to some of these spots and give their untrained opinion, I would be more than happy to oblige."

"Seriously?" He seems shocked by my offer.

"Of course. I'm hoping to make annual vacations a thing. So, if you've got a place for me to go, I'm your gal."

"I might take you up on that. We've noticed a decrease in traffic. People want genuine opinions about places from real vacationers like them. Not from an experienced traveler, who goes to ten or more resorts in a month."

"I get that," I comment. "Well, if you need—"

My statement is cut off by two arms wrapping around my waist from behind. My blood runs cold as lips are pressed to the side of my neck. But the smile plastered on Tilly's face has me realizing there is no way this is who I think it is. The scent of his minty cologne registers as the shock fades. I glance down, and instead of seeing the tropical design Jake has inked across his forearm, there're two heavily tattooed arms attached to two equally tattooed hands. All decorated in a myriad of themes, which shouldn't go together but somehow do?

"*Mo mhuirnín,*" Killian whispers in my ear.

"Aw," Tilly squeals. "Surprise!"

"It's your birthday," I say through clenched teeth and a forced smile. "It's me who should be surprising you."

"Nonsense." She grins from ear to ear. "I know you two have such busy schedules, and when I told him about my party—"

"Killian, you made it!" Cassie yells excitedly as she waddles over. Robbie is on her heels, holding a plate of fruit.

"Of course, I did. I couldn't pass up the chance to see my baby sis," Killian says to Cassie. "And I couldn't wait to see you again," he growls in my ear, continuing to play the role of some love interest I don't have.

Bastard. Cassie's steel eyes light up with amusement at the display. *Does Robbie know he married the devil in disguise?* Maybe this is a good thing. It'll keep me distracted from Jake and whatever bimbo he's decided to eat his birthday cake off later.

"What're you doing?" I say just loud enough for Killian to hear.

"Cock-fighting," he replies, nuzzling into my neck.

"It's so great to have everyone here." Tilly claps her hands. "We should get a big family photo. Who knows the next time we'll all be—"

Tilly's excitement dies off into a look of shock and horror. I almost fall backwards, but Killian lets go of me, and I manage to stay on my feet. I turn around to see what happened. Killian stands there with a devilish grin, as he wipes the small trickle of blood from the corner of his mouth. Jake's fists are still raised like a madman, his chest puffed out as he stares at Killian.

"Jake!" Tilly screams. "What's your problem? First the fight at the bar, now this?"

"I'll give you that one," Killian says to Jake. "But only one. If you wanna fight, I won't take it easy on you." Jake moves to throw another fist. And Killian, the skilled fighter that he is, dodges the attack and lands a strike to Jake's ribs. Although he lets out a small *oof* from the contact, it's clear that Killian is holding back, despite his previous claim. "You don't wanna do this," Killian offers again.

"No, I think he does." Robbie chuckles. He's not helping the matter.

I turn to look behind me, and that's when I realize most of the party has given them a wide berth. I'm the only one who remains close to the action. Jax, Tilly, Scott, Robbie, Cassie, Scarlett, Derek, and Cian are right behind me. Everyone except Tilly is watching with apt amusement as though they have ringside seats. Scott passes Robbie some cash. None of them short of my best friend have any interest in stopping this.

Jake throws a quick jab and gets Killian in the jaw again. But whatever victory he experienced is short-lived as Killian lands another solid punch. Both are now sporting matching bloodied lips.

"Jake, stop it!" Tilly screams again. "Why are you doing this?" His eyes betray our secret as they dart to mine. Tilly follows his line of sight. She scrunches her forehead in confusion before making an O-face in realization. "Letty?" Tilly whispers her question. She shakes her shock away. It morphs into disappointment as she frowns at me. "How long?"

Behind me, I hear the sound of Jake and Killian resuming their fight. I turn to look at them, then back to Tilly, who is still waiting for a response. She has her hand resting on her cocked hip as she taps her foot in frustration.

I'm conflicted. Do I attempt to break up a fight that *shouldn't* even be happening? Considering Killian and I are not—nor have we ever been—a thing. That's before adding in the fact that Jake and I are no longer anything, and based on Tilly's expression, will remain that way. Or do I attempt to fix my damaged friendship before it's destroyed beyond repair?

I suck in my bottom lip as I look back and forth.

"Stop it!" I shout to Killian and Jake. They both pause mid-blow. Surprisingly enough, Jake has Killian on the ground with the advantage. From the few hits I saw Killian take, though, he's been allowing Jake to maintain the upper hand. I'm not sure why, but I'm grateful. Like the psychopath he is, Killian is still sporting a shit-eating grin, even with the blood splattered across his face.

A small hand grabs my shoulder and spins me away from the guys. "Did you sleep with Jake?" Gulping while unable to utter the words out loud, I cast my stare towards the grass. "How could you?" she admonishes.

"Tilly," Jax cautions, but she isn't hearing any of it and shakes off the comforting hand he has placed on her shoulder. With both palms raised, he takes a step back to join the rest of the onlookers.

"I'm sorry," I finally whisper. I'm ashamed of myself and don't know what else to say to her.

"How long?" Tilly presses again.

"A few weeks." I swallow hard. "This time."

"This time!" Tilly exclaims.

"Senior year, that summer, we..." I don't know what to call it. Dated? We never really went on a date. Even this time—short of the trip to the amusement park—all we did was have sex and hang out.

"Seriously?" Tilly throws her hands in the air before combing her fingers through her flowing hair. "How could you?"

"Wait, Tilly." Jake steps in. "That's not fair—"

"And you!" She directs a finger at her twin.

"Tilly..." I stop her from saying something she might regret later. She's drunk, which isn't normal for her, and it's the first time since before she was pregnant. She can hate me if she needs to. But I won't let her ruin what she and Jake share. "It was my fault, my idea." Tilly glares at me like she doesn't believe a word I'm saying. She looks like she's about to respond, so I cut off her train of thought and plow forward. "But it's fine. It's over now."

"You had sex with..." She points to the man in question. "Jake! You hate each other."

I rub my temples. "It's complicated... but it doesn't matter. Like I said, it's over. It was just sex. Things can go back to normal now."

Jake looks at me, shaking his head before throwing a hand in the air and waving me off. "Fuck this," he murmurs, and stalks in the opposite direction.

Shit, that came out wrong. "Jake," I call out after him. But Tilly stops me.

"I might not know what's been going on between you two. But that..." She gestures to Killian and then the gate. "...doesn't look like *nothing*. Were you cheating on Kill?"

"I was never with Killian," I confess. Though, judging by everyone's expression, the only person who didn't know the truth was my best friend.

"Oh my god, Letty!" she screams. "Why would you lie about that?"

"I never lied," I point out. "I just didn't correct you. You should be mad at Cassie. She's the one who started the crazy rumor."

"Don't look at me," Cassie says, rubbing her belly. Robbie drapes an arm over her shoulder and steps in front of her. As if Tilly would hit anyone, let alone a pregnant woman. "I didn't lie either. You kissed Killian at my wedding, gave him your number, and then you left together."

"I only did that to make Jake jealous." I gasp at my own admission and cover my mouth. Cassie raises an eyebrow that says: *I told you so.* My hands drop in defeat. "I never had any interest in Killian." I turn and look at him. "Sorry, nothing personal."

He shrugs his shoulders, still smiling. Obviously, he wasn't pining over me either. This was nothing more than a chance for him to fuck with Jake, for whatever reason.

"If it was just sex," Tilly states, "then why did you want to make Jake jealous?" I don't answer her question. But I guess my expression reveals it all. "Oh, no, Letty... It wasn't, was it?"

An awkward silence falls over the party. No one is sure what to say. Cassie peeks up at Robbie. He nods. She turns back to the crowd and shouts, "It's a girl!" The conversation resumes as everyone circles the expecting couple to congratulate them.

I escape inside the house, grab a beer, and open it. Plopping down at the counter, I ponder. *I guess whatever illusion I had about things going back to the way they were is over.*

Maybe the timing is a blessing in disguise. The paperwork for the bar hasn't been signed yet. The check Ted gave me is sitting safely in my hotel. I could start over somewhere else. It's not like I have anything here anymore.

The sliding door opens and shuts. Seconds later, a body plops onto the stool next to mine. "Why didn't you tell me?" Tilly asks. She twirls her drink in her cup.

I shrug. "I don't know. I guess I knew you'd be angry."

"Of course, I'm angry!" she shrieks, further proving my point. She takes a deep breath and exhales. "I'm pissed that you didn't tell me." I tilt my head to look into her enormous amber eyes. "You're my best friend, Letty," she reminds me. "I thought we told each other everything."

"At first, it was all so new. I didn't know what it was between us. It wasn't worth the risk of ruining our friendship for some case of temporary insanity. Then everything was happening with Jax and you going to school. Things were over, and it just didn't seem worth mentioning."

"And now?"

"Still trying to figure that out."

Tilly looks off into the distance. "So, why'd you end it?"

"What makes you think I ended it?" I evade the question.

"Really?" Tilly quirks a brow at me. "I know my brother. More than I wish I did sometimes. He wouldn't fight a guy over a woman. Not just anyone. So, why'd *you* end it? And please don't lie to me, or give me some BS excuse."

"Because I can't be what he needs, what he deserves."

"And what is that, exactly?"

"You know." I shrug.

"No, please elaborate."

"This." I gesture to their picture-perfect home, filled with family photos and baby items. "I'm not going to bake cookies and have dinner ready when he gets home. I don't want children—ever."

"Ever?"

"No." I take a deep breath. If I told Jake, there's no reason I can't tell Tilly. "My mom, her cancer, it was genetic. Mix that with my dad and his history of alcoholism. I can't risk passing any of it down to a child. Or what if the kid's fine, but I'm not, and I leave them like she left me?" Then I share the realization I came to on my trip. "I love my life, Tilly. The drunks at the bar, the long nights. And now I can't wait to go off and explore the world. No part of me, besides thinking they are adorable and wanting occasional snuggles, desires a baby."

"You got the twins for that."

"Exactly," I agree. "That's enough for me."

"And Jake, he wants children?"

I nod my head up and down. "He didn't exactly *say* he wanted them."

"Oh, Letty..." Tilly rests her face in her palms.

"What?"

"Let me guess, because I know you both so well." She turns and gives me a half-cocked smile. "Jake probably alluded to the idea of having kids. More than likely because, when it comes to relationships, he has like zero experience and just assumes that's what every girl wants to hear. You panicked, told him you didn't want any. And instead of talking about it like grown adults, you decided for him. Because, in your mind, the only way you can have a happily ever after is by getting married and popping out babies."

Tilly takes my lack of a response as confirmation that she's right. Sadly, she is. And when I look at it that way, I feel like an even bigger idiot.

"Letty, I'm going to be real with you for a second."

Oh, this will be interesting. Brave and intoxicated, Tilly has shocked people with her drunken truths. Especially when compared to the quiet bookworm she usually is.

"I love you. Like a sister. Jake might be my twin, and Jax is the love of my life. But you, you're my soul mate. The yin to my yang. You're the Louise to my Thelma—obviously Jax is nothing like her husband but that's not important. Ride or die, or whatever other cliché you can come up with. So, when I say this, know it comes from a place of love. Letty..." She rests her hands on my shoulders and looks deep into my eyes. "You're being stupid."

"Stupid?" I sputter.

"Yes, you and Jake aren't exactly relationship gurus. Not that anyone really is. But the point is, neither of you has ever really been in a committed relationship. The closest thing to it is probably whatever cloak-and-dagger crap you guys have been trying to pull off. And that doesn't count."

"It wouldn't bother you if we were together?"

Tilly lets out a laugh and slaps her hand on the counter. "I'm married to Jax."

"That's different," I remind her.

"It's not—it's probably worse actually. Besides being my brother's best friend, he's also practically my foster brother. But that's another story." She shakes her head. "Letty, what I'm trying to say is: I love you both. And if you two being together makes you happy, who am I, or anyone else, to say a thing about it?"

I absorb her words for a second, but the concern still lingers. "What if he wants that white-picket fence family?"

Tilly shrugs. "On the off chance he does, then you're right. As much as it would suck, you aren't meant to be together. And that's okay. But you need to give him both the choice and the opportunity to *decide* what he wants."

"I don't know, Tilly." I shake my head, looking down the neck of my beer bottle. "I think I really fucked things up. I moved out while he was on shift, then dumped all that personal crap on him and flew off to Florida. Then today, with Killian... I doubt he'll ever want to see me again."

Tilly gives me a knowing grin. "I'm sure you'll think of something."

36

Jake

THAT WAS A FUCKING shit show. *What the hell was I thinking?*

Punching Killian like that. Starting a fight with him in the yard in front of our families, my friends. I'd been waiting for Letty to show up, but of course she had to be fashionably late. My plan to intercept her before she made it to the party got shot to hell when I left my post to take a piss. Then I got sidetracked by Eli on my way back. When I walked outside, my eyes were drawn to her immediately.

She was so gorgeous in that sundress. It reminded me of the first day we met at the sandbox. Different flowers and no ribbons in her hair. But it felt like we'd just come full circle. It was a sign telling me what I needed to do. I had to make her pick *me* this time. That was until that fucking asshole showed up, hugging and kissing on her like she was his.

She's mine. And that was the last thought I had before I practically flew down the steps and decked him. Letty's wide eyes said I made a huge mistake. I already had a lot of damage to repair. Convincing her that being an *us* was right. That none of the other crap mattered. I didn't care that my family found out, maybe the way they did wasn't the best, but fuck it. It was in the open.

Just sex... And all that doubt crept back in. I'd convinced myself that playing it down was her coping mechanism, a way to protect herself. Because this thing between us, it's more terrifying than any horror movie I've ever seen. I'm completely out of my depth.

But seeing Killian touch her evaporated whatever remaining doubt I had. The whispers that told me this was just fleeting...

I've never once felt an ounce of jealousy in my entire life, except when it comes to her. That distinct feeling I got today made me realize this wasn't the first time. I'm just finally able to name it. And again, not solely because of Killian and whatever rivalry we've started with each other. But over the years, seeing her laughing and touching other men had me clenching my fists. Or in high school, during prom, watching Keith's slimy paws all over her. And that was just the tip of the iceberg.

I know I can get to Letty. Make her realize we can be together. That it doesn't need to be all or nothing. I don't need children. I never even considered the possibility of having them until more recently. In reality, we don't live the right lifestyle. Just as much as I won't give up being a firefighter, I'd never ask her to quit the bar. It's who we are. Hell, Jax's suggestion about getting a cat seems like a great one. Or maybe a dog? The point is, not having children isn't an issue.

What I can't fix, though, is something I hadn't really taken into account. At the root of it all, she doesn't want me. Everything else was her excuse to avoid the reality. The truth. *I'm not what she wants.*

No, I refuse to believe it. There were moments. Ones where she looked at me and the world stopped. You can't fake that.

Pulling into my driveway, I shift the truck into park. I cleared my head driving around the country roads. Despite everything that happened today, I know I need to talk to her. Get past these barriers she insists on constructing. That being said, I don't know where the hell she is. She wasn't at the hotel, or at Harper's...

I stopped back at Tilly's, and after hitting me in the chest several times while calling me an *idiot*, my sister gave me a container with about half of our birthday cake jammed inside and told me Letty had left hours ago. Reluctantly, I came home to call it a night. I know she'll be at the bar tomorrow. I'll have to wait and talk to her then.

Once inside the house, I kick the door shut behind me. I stop by the kitchen and drop the container on the counter. Grabbing a beer from the fridge, I pop it open and make my way up to my room.

Worst birthday ever. Even worse than our eleventh when we went to some buffet in the Twin Cities. All of us ended up getting food poisoning, staying in a hotel, and fighting over a single toilet. Literally, the *shittiest* birthday ever. And this one beats that. To top it off, now I have a busted-up lip, a bruised jaw, and my ribs hurt like hell. I was lucky he held back. It's fucking terrifying to think how much damage he could inflict with a single punch. They don't exactly call the man KO just because of his initials.

Opening my bedroom door, I halt dead in my tracks. If I had a juice box in my hand instead of a bottle of beer, I think this scene would play out like the time Xander from *Buffy the Vampire Slayer* walked in to find Anya naked in the room.

Not wanting to risk breaking the bottle, I set it down on my dresser. "I was looking for you," I say, my eyes taking her in. Her hard nipples are poking through the thin fabric of my sheet.

"I've been here. Waiting for you." Letty sits up. The sheet drops and pools at her waist, her glorious tits on display. It takes all my strength not to jump into bed and suck one of those pink buds into my mouth.

"We should talk." My cock struggles against the zipper of my jeans. He thinks *less talking and more fucking* is a better idea.

"We could." She licks her index finger, trailing it down her chest to one of those pebbled beauties before circling it. Teasing me.

"You don't wanna talk," I point out. A victim of her spell, I reach behind me, grab the hem of my shirt, and quickly tug it off. Letty shakes her head no, as I crawl on the bed and hover over her on all fours. "As much as my cock is begging—pathetically, I might add—to sink into that sweet pussy *we've* missed dearly, I can't decide which one of us gets a taste first. Him or me. If it was physically possible, I'd do both."

"I've missed him too." The referenced appendage grows twice in size at the admission. "Perhaps while your tongue tastes me, I can taste him?"

"*Fuck*," I whisper, trying to grasp my fraying shred of sanity. "Spitfire, I want this. *Oh god*, how I do. But I want all of you. Much more than I want to just fuck you. So, if you're not all in, he's not going *all in*."

Letty cracks a smile, holding back a laugh. "Did you really just make a sexual innuendo while telling me you want to be my boyfriend?"

"Did you really think I'd do it any differently?"

Her smile grows, and her eyes light up. I want to burn this—every freckle and every line—into memory. "No, I didn't. Conventional really isn't our style, is it?"

"No, it's not," I agree, leaning down and nuzzling her neck. "But I need to know that this is more than just sex," I murmur against her skin. I stop breathing in anticipation.

Letty's nails lightly trace up and down my back. Her hot breath tickles my ear. "No more hiding," she whispers, before sucking my lobe between her teeth and nibbling.

"Thank fuck." I let out a relieved breath. I wasn't sure I could hold back any longer. Like a bolt of lightning, I spring from the bed and get naked. Hopping back onto the mattress, I lie flat on my back and pull her on top of me. Letty sits on my stomach, her bare pussy warm on my flesh. "Turn around," I order.

She does as I ask. Leaning down on her forearms, she sucks the head of my dick inside her hot, wet mouth and circles it with her skilled tongue. My eyes roll into the back of my head. Tauntingly, she shakes her ass at me. My hands grip her thighs and I squeeze before pulling her closer.

"You're going to sit on my face and suffocate me with that pussy." I bring her down and immediately delve my tongue deep inside her canal. Her muscles clench around me, and if I wasn't so lost in her euphoria, I'd erupt. Rotating her hips, she grinds down on my face. I can't breathe and I don't want to.

After a moment, she lets up and I take a deep breath before diving back in. I devour her as she sucks me down. It's almost like a challenge, who can make who come first. I suck her clit. She swallows me whole. Just like always, it's a game of push and pull between us. I wouldn't want it any other way.

"You know you're going to come first," she declares before taking me down her throat.

"Is that right?" I say through gritted teeth, holding on by a thread. "Wanna bet?" I smirk when she releases me to come up for air. Before she can reply, I fuck her furiously with my tongue while rubbing her clit. Her body quivers. She's so close to coming I can taste it. I let up so she can catch her breath.

"Deal," she rasps. "If I win, I pick our first date."

Before responding, I give her a long lick. "And if I win, I get to eat my birthday cake."

"That's kind of lame." She chuckles.

"Right..." I draw out as I look for the perfect spot. "Here," I say, before sucking her clit between my teeth.

"Holy fuck," she cries.

"Deal," we say in unison before resuming our mission. But because I want my cake and *to eat it too*, I play dirty. I insert two fingers into her throbbing pussy and apply pressure to her G-spot, then circle my tongue around her puckered hole.

"Oh god," she pants. Lost to the anticipation, all she can do is shakily jerk me off. Her movements mimic the rhythm of my fingers thrusting in and out of her.

"Do you want to come?" I tease.

"Please," she stutters.

"You know what I want to hear."

"Please, Jake," she pleads. "Make me come."

I slide one more finger into her tight cunt while I push the tip of my tongue past the ring of muscles. A rush of fluid leaves her as she climaxes around me. The room is filled with her sweet aroma. Once she's finished, Letty collapses on the bed next to me. With hungry eyes, she watches as I lick my fingers clean.

"Where are you going?" she asks when I stand from the bed.

Leaning down, I press a kiss to her lips. Letty sucks my tongue into her mouth, tasting herself on me. When we break apart, she collapses back on the mattress. "I want my cake," I remind her on my way to the door.

"Aren't you full?"

"Of you?" I look deep into her lust-glazed chocolate eyes. "Never."

Epilogue

Jake

PULLING INTO THE PARKING spot, I look up at the flickering neon sign of doom. I rest my head against the steering wheel and swallow hard. My heart flutters in my chest as dread washes over me. I don't know what sweet revenge the meathead has in store for me, but I have no doubt I'm in for some slow form of torture.

"Aw." Letty pats me on the back. Although she pretends to comfort me, I can hear the suppressed laughter in her voice. "It's just a little ink."

"Permanent," I remind her.

Over the past several weeks, the Irish son of a bitch has sent me several *inspirational* images he's found on the internet. A dick pointing into my mouth, looking like it was drawn on with a sharpie. There was an over-the-top one where the tattoo was positioned perfectly so that a woman's leg would go along one arm and down my side, leaving her hairy crotch in the crook of my armpit. Then the tramp stamps started.

On women, they're sexy as fuck. But on men? Unless it's a whole back piece, they're just a no. Especially when the asshole is sending me ghastly photographs of a permanently inked-on thong, which was designed to peek out above the waistline. I wouldn't be able to walk out in public shirtless ever again. Or play skins during basketball. The laughter and comments from the other guys would be endless. I know this, because if it was any of them, I sure as hell wouldn't let it go.

"It can't be that bad." She has to cover her mouth to hide her smile. I'm willing to bet a *tattoo on my cock* that she's been conspiring with Killian.

"You know what he's planning, don't you?" I accuse, pointing a finger at her.

Letty gasps, resting her hand on her chest. "Me," she says as though it's the most ridiculous notion.

"Yes, you." I grab her by the waist.

Letty follows my lead and hops over the center console and into my lap. I wish she would have worn one of those new summer dresses that she's been sporting for the last month whenever she's not working. Sadly, we came here straight from the bar, so she's in her usual attire. She hired two new bartenders, who double as waitstaff. After a few weeks of training, she's giving them a solo run tonight.

My fingers travel up her exposed thigh and measure if the crotch of her shorts can move over enough to allow me to fuck her quickly without too much chafing. Release some of my built-up tension inside her, with the added bonus of knowing she'll be sitting in the parlor with my mark on her.

Although I believe her when she says the whole Killian thing was a misunderstanding and the fucker was just messing with me, I like the security of knowing that she's mine for all the world to see. I glance up at the trail of love bites I put on her neck this morning. The foundation tones them down, but *I* can see them.

"Nuh-uh, mister," Letty scolds as she moves my wandering fingers away from her center.

"Please, I'll be quick." *Words I never thought I'd utter.*

Quickies are a new thing for me. Never been my style. Not until I found a woman I could remain buried balls-deep in for the rest of my life. And I'll take any opportunity I can to do it. Sometimes, between the bar and my shifts at the fire station, five minutes is all we get. But you can be damn sure those five minutes are used wisely.

"Jakey-poo." She teases me with the name she knows makes me hard. Though it's no longer slung at me as an insult, I've been conditioned over the years to respond to it. "We're late. The more you make him wait, the worse it's going to be."

I rest my face between her perfect tits and groan. "You're right," I say, muffled by the fabric of her shirt.

"Get your ass in there. The sooner this is over, the quicker we can get to dinner."

"Then dessert." I salivate at the thought.

"Yup, I even got a new flavor of ice cream to try tonight."

"What kind?" I lick my lips as I imagine the infinite possibilities.

Leaning forward, she whispers in my ear, "That's a surprise." She sucks my lobe into her mouth and bites down. I rock forward and squeeze her thighs in response.

Tonight, I remind myself. "Okay." I let out a defeated breath. "Let's get this over with."

Letty hops off my lap and we both exit the vehicle. As we step into the shop, the soft humming of tattoo guns can be heard all around us. Killian stands in the center of the room. Arms crossed over his chest, he glances down at the nonexistent watch on his wrist. "You're late," he says with an evil grin. "I was worried the brave firefighter was gonna chicken out like a little bitch."

"Nope, that'd be you," I toss out. Killian raises his scarred brow at me, as though he's asking me to prove it. I tuck my hands into my pockets and shrug. "I won the fight."

He laughs. Hard. Bending over, he slaps his thigh. "Only because I let you."

"So says you." I continue to dig my grave deeper. Stupid, considering he's about to have one of these guys put something atrocious on me. "I've got a yard of witnesses who saw me take the great KO Murphy to the ground."

"Care for a rematch?" he challenges.

"Nah, it feels wrong hitting an old man." Yup, there I go again...

Letty is no help. She's been snickering with her hand covering her mouth. *As if that hides her amusement.*

"If that's what you need to tell yourself." He straightens his back. "Okay, let's go." We follow him to a booth. Everything is laid out, waiting to be unwrapped so we can get started. "Take off the shirt," he orders. I let out a relieved breath. *At least it's not my face or my dick.* "Straddle the chair."

I glance around the space and realize someone is missing. "Where's the artist?" I question. Killian replies with a sinister smile that chills me to the bone. "No." I point at him. "That wasn't part of the deal."

"It wasn't *not* part of the deal either," he clarifies. Rather unhelpfully, I might add. And Letty's laughter is all the indication I need to know that she was aware of this the entire time.

"Dude, it's one thing to put whatever embarrassing thing you came up with on me. But I was hoping you'd at least give me the dignity of having it done properly."

"It will be," he assures me. He shows me his left arm and the ink that's plastered across his skin. It has no rhyme or reason, but it somehow works. And I guess it looks good. "That's all me. My buddy did the other arm and helped in some tough-to-reach spots." Killian undoes the button of his pants before pulling down his zipper. "I can show you more if you want. I have them in some very interesting places." That statement is directed towards Letty.

"No." I don't give her a chance to reply. I have a pretty good idea *where* he's referring to. Letty and I might be official, but that hasn't stopped her from fucking with me when the opportunity arises. Honestly, except for the fact that we live together now and have sex constantly, nothing's changed. It's perfect. "Let's just get this over with. Are you going to at least show me the design?"

His blue eyes sparkle with mischief. *I'll take that as another no.* Not wanting to drag this out any longer than I already have, I pull my shirt off and take my seat on the chair.

"Don't worry," Killian teases. "This will only hurt a *wee* bit."

Letty sits on a rolling stool and scoots forward.

"Did you decide on a name yet?" I ask her, in order to get my mind off what's about to transpire.

"I decided to keep it Harper's." For years, she's talked about buying the bar and renaming everything. I'm shocked by the sudden change of heart. Sensing my question, she continues. "Even though he moved, the bar is still his legacy. I want to keep it the same in his honor. There was a time I used to think that place was all I'd ever have."

"And now?"

"I realize I have so much more." She doesn't need to elaborate. I know exactly what she means. Taking her hands in mine, I rub my thumb over the small heart she got inked between her thumb and index finger while she was on vacation.

"We should go," I say. Letty bunches her eyes in confusion. "To Disney, soon."

She flashes me one of those bright smiles that still steals my breath away. "Great minds." Digging into her back pocket, she pulls out her phone and shows it to me. "I was already looking at going in October. Apparently, they do this whole Halloween theme. We could also go to Universal."

"You tell me when, and I'll get the time off." I stiffen as Killian preps his target area. Of course, it's on my lower back.

Letty continues to distract me from my misery by showing me all the different hotel options. Then she launches into images and information on the several Disney resorts around the world and what is special about each one.

"I love you," I blurt out in the middle of her presentation. She stops dead in her tracks and looks up at me with her big brown eyes. Doubt creeps in. The last time I tried to say it, she stopped me. But that was then, and this is now—*right?* Those golden flecks shimmer back at me with a warmth that melts my soul and makes everything, including Killian and his damn needle, fade away.

"I love you too," she says before pressing her lips to mine.

I almost forget about the tattoo until, and I swear it's on purpose because none of it has hurt much so far, the fucker starts scraping in color. Pulling back from her warmth, I count down the seconds until we can get home. I'm skipping dinner and going straight to my dessert.

"Okay, lovebirds, finished," Killian announces.

"Thank fuck." I spring up from the chair and rush to the mirror to see what he did. I was so distracted by Letty I paid little mind to what he was doing or how long it even took.

Please don't be a thong. Please.

"Here." Killian hands me a mirror so I can better see my reflection. Letty sports the most-killer poker face she's ever worn. Nothing is giving it away.

Glancing in the small hand-held mirror, I let out a relieved sigh before groaning. "You branded me," I point out. The tattoo is simple. A green shamrock that looks splattered on. It's the logo from his fighting days—the same one he uses for the bar. Letty can't hold back the laughter any longer and folds over to clutch her stomach.

"Come on, it's not that bad." He drapes an arm over my shoulder.

"No," I agree. It could have been a hundred times worse.

"This way, every time she looks at your ass, she'll think of me," he teases. Letty chokes from laughing so hard, and I elbow Killian in the gut. *Bastard.*

For a moment, it wasn't so bad. I'm sure there's a hint of Irish in my heritage somewhere I could use to rationalize the tattoo, or I could even say I'm a huge KO fan. But of course, he had to make it about my girl.

Killian snickers as he walks away to clean up the mess. Letty approaches and rests her arms around my shoulders. My hands fall to her slender waist. She glances in the mirror and chuckles again before looking back up at me. "If it'll make you feel better, I can get a matching one?" she offers.

"It would make me feel better," Killian adds, at the same time I say, "No."

The fucker cracks up. "Shame. Well, let's get you wrapped and ready to go, so you both can be on your merry way to frolic in the fields. Or whatever young lovers do in a small town."

Epilogue

Letty

"THIS IS RIDICULOUS," I murmur, walking blindly with Jake behind me. His hands cover my eyes, a silk scarf tied beneath them further blocking my vision.

"No, this is perfect," he assures me again.

"The blindfolded portion of the evening is great. But what's with the outfit and change of venue?" Not only did he prevent me from seeing where he's taking me, but he drove around for half an hour to confuse me as to where we were going. Did we leave town? Or did he just kill time on the back roads? *I don't have a clue.*

"Are you ready?" he asks.

"If I say no, can we go home?" My pulse races. I don't know why I'm nervous. Yes, Jake pushes my boundaries and forces me out of my reserved comfort zone. But, so far, I've loved everything we've done. Still, each time something new happens, old Letty—and her anxiety over the unknown—peeks her ugly head.

"Come on, spitfire, where's your birthday spirit?" he teases.

Maybe that's why I'm anxious. Things have been going well—*maybe too well?* Together, we survived the hottest summer we've had in decades. The bar is one-hundred percent mine, with practically all new staff, who I hand-picked and trained. Tral Lake Videos and Moore has been thriving. I still think his business concept is sweet. Except for checking on things and taking part in theme nights, he primarily lets the teens run it. Along with a shift manager. We just had the most insane Thanksgiving—*ever.* Now, here we are, at my very own birth milestone.

"Unlike you, I've never really been big on the whole thing. Staying home, drinking beer, and eating pizza is good enough for me."

I reminded him that in all the years he's known me I've never been one to celebrate. The dinner and cake Mrs. Moore used to bake me was always more than enough. I finally agreed when he said he wanted to do something with just us. Especially considering we just spent time with the whole family last week for the holiday. But I assumed it was going to be some ultra-kinky stuff. Not me getting dressed in this horrific pink tulle rejected bridesmaid dress he dug out of the back of the thrift store from hell. I'm praying he picked something this ugly because he didn't intend for the eyesore to survive the night, after he shreds it off me.

"I know, but I promise you're going to love this."

"And if I don't?" I challenge. Ridiculous, since he knows I will. Even so, bad habits are hard to break.

"You name it," he says eagerly.

"Anything?" I ask, full of suspicion. Last time he offered me a blank IOU, it was because he knew without a doubt I was soaked and ready for him. However, I have a feeling this particular wager is about more than the state of my panties.

"*Anything,*" he whispers, his breath hot on my ear.

"And if you're right?" He might be willing to give me carte blanche, but I can't say I'm as eager to give him the same liberties. His imagination seems to have no limits.

"Just say *yes.*" The word has my stomach clenching with a mixture of nerves and desire. That pulsing in my chest increases. My body tingles with anticipation, making my nipples hard.

"*Yes,*" I whisper. Instinct tells me that tonight that word will be used in a variety of manners, ranging from agreement to cries of ecstasy. Although my body's response to the situation hasn't changed, the root cause is no longer anxiety, but excitement.

"*Trust me?*" he asks the question softly.

"Always." Through all the ups and downs of the past six months, the one thing I've learned is to trust Jacob Moore. Sometimes, it's difficult, especially in situations like these. I spent years being let down by the one person who should have been there for me. I'll always be self-reliant. It's who I am. But just because I can do something on my own, it doesn't mean I *have to*. Not where Jake's concerned.

He lets out a sigh of relief before removing his hands. "Close your eyes," he instructs and unties the blindfold. And as requested, I squeeze them shut. Biting my bottom lip, I hold back my desire to bounce on my heels. "Open," he says.

Cracking one of my lids, I peek. Confusion settles in, and I open my eyes wide to take in the scene before me. We're at the video store. It's closed, and the curtains are shut, giving us privacy. Considering we've been together most of the day, he probably had Scott and the kids help set up. A table sits in the middle of the dimly lit room, only illuminated by the cake in the center with its burning candles. This level of corniness screams Scott. Turning around, I look at Jake. He's wearing a gray sweater and jeans.

Why does this all seem so familiar? I glance down at my horrendous outfit again. "*Noooo!*" I jump and clap my hands.

"Oh, yes," Jake replies with a big toothy grin. "Come on." He takes my hand and leads me to the table. Then he helps me climb on top before joining me.

And everything clicks into place. "*Sixteen Candles?*"

"It's great, isn't it?" He puffs out his chest, obviously proud of himself.

Although chick flicks were never my preference, they were better than the crap Jake and Tilly loved to torment everyone with. John Hughes movies became a guilty pleasure of mine. Once, and only once, did I make the mistake of mentioning to Tilly that I thought this was the most romantic thing I'd ever seen. And that if some guy ever did this, I'd...

No, there is no way he'd remember that? Those butterflies in my chest soar, and my palms sweat.

"Come on, blow out the candles. Make a wish." Jake's knee bounces from his position opposite me.

My eyes linger on the pink icing. I suck on my bottom lip as I contemplate my next move. In the movie, there is nothing left for her to wish for. Honestly, I'm in the same boat. But as I watch Jake fidget nervously, I know what I need to do. I take a large breath—because *somehow* he fit thirty candles on this thing—then I bend forward and blow. The room grows darker, but it's still partially illuminated by the rope lights he had installed around the place like a movie theater.

"Did you make a wish?"

I nod, though I quit wishing on stars and birthday candles years ago. It didn't take me long to realize they never come true. But for Jake, I take the risk of future disappointment because I have a feeling that's the last thing I will ever face again. Especially with him.

Jake smiles before submerging his hand in the cake and pulling it back out. "Want a taste?" he asks with his open palm covered in frosting and spongy goodness. He wiggles his fingers in front of me.

The tease that I am, I scoop some off with my finger before bringing it to my face. My tongue circles the tip before I suck the digit down. He shifts, his eyes trained on me as he eats the excess cake from his hand. His closed fist is holding onto something; then he opens his palm to reveal a small box. The cocky grin he's sporting says he remembers exactly what I confessed to Tilly all those years ago.

Back then, I regretted it. He teased me incessantly, saying it was nothing more than a fire hazard. Among other things. And now, here he is. Sometimes it feels as if he's trying to go back and right all the wrongs. Rewrite our history. Not that everything was bad. We still tease and push each other's buttons; it's who we are. Then there are moments like these. Moments where he takes my breath away.

"Letty." He clears his throat. "You once told me my tongue was only good for one thing." I wince at the reminder. Again, one of the wrongs. "And you were right."

"Jake—" He shakes his head, and I snap my mouth shut.

"It was made for loving you. Telling you I love you or showing you that I do when it's buried deep in that sweet pussy of yours." A smile tugs at my face. It wouldn't be Jake if he didn't make a sexual reference. "It might not know all the flowery shit a girl wants to hear. Sure, I could quote one of a hundred films, but those words wouldn't be mine. So I'll say this: Letty, I love you. All of you. Not just during those sweet times when you're crying out my name in ecstasy. But when you get pissed at me and stomp away mid-argument, purposely shaking that ass of yours. Letting me know exactly what I'll be missing that night. Or during the calm, when we just chill together, watch a movie, and eat popcorn. On the days when I only get to see you for five minutes, because that's all I can sneak in. The point is: good, bad, or occasionally ugly, I love you. Tee..." I stop breathing. "...will you—"

"Yes," I blurt out, not letting him finish the question.

"Really?" he asks with an eyebrow raised.

I nod vigorously. "Yes, more than anything."

He lets out a relieved breath. "I was worried you'd say no. I know we've dabbled with anal a little. But you tensed up a bit when I tried two fingers, so I got this." My jaw drops as he opens the box to reveal a small metal plug. Technically, it's jewelry. Just not the kind I thought. "I promise it will help."

"Okay." My shoulders deflate.

"What's the matter?" he prompts, noticing my disappointment. "If you're having second thoughts, it's fine. Believe me, I have a long list of things I can do with the rest of your—"

"No, no second thoughts," I interrupt.

He sighs. "You thought I was asking something else, didn't you?" My cheeks warm with embarrassment. *I feel so stupid.* "Let me guess." Jake leans to the side and reaches into his back pocket. "You were expecting something a little more... like this?"

Between his index finger and thumb is a simple white gold band. The tears well back up in my eyes. Again, he gives me that signature grin. *Asshole.* He knew exactly what he was doing.

"What do you say, spitfire? Wanna get hitched?" I punch his shoulder in response, and he laughs while rubbing the spot. "Okay, now I'm confused. Was the *yes* for butt sex? Because for a second, I thought you wanted to—"

Sitting up on my knees, which plunge into the cake and further ruin this horrific dress, I press my lips to his and effectively silence him. I pull back slightly and look into his eyes. My palms hold his face.

"Yes," I state again. A second passes before he flashes a smile that has my panties soaked. He slides the ring on my finger, then devours my mouth. "Jakey-poo," I get out between breaths.

"Spitfire?" he groans. My little pet name always seems to kick things up a notch.

"I'd like to eat my cake now." I scoop frosting from the table and suck it off my finger, demonstrating exactly what I want to do to him.

"This is why I fucking love you," he says as he stands to remove his pants.

Want moore Jake & Letty? Sign up for my newsletter to get access to bonus content.
Visit: https://bit.ly/WantYouMooreBonus
or scan

Moore By Frankie Page

The Moore Family Series:

Forever Moore (Tilly and Jax)

Expecting Moore (Robbie and Cassie)

Want You Moore (Jake and Letty)
Fighting for Love:

Flirty at Murphy's: A Murphy's Bar Novella

Last Round
Rose's Inferno Trilogy:

Retribution (Book 1)

Desolation (Book 2)

Pandemonium (Book 3)
Standalone Novella:

Learning to Love Again

New books are always coming visit

WWW.FRANKIEPAGEBOOKS.COM
to see the current list of titles available

Printed by BoD™in Norderstedt, Germany